10/05

MW01504766

A Dream Fulfilled

By Cynthia M. Hickey

PublishAmerica
Baltimore

First printing

ISBN: 1-4137-4775-2
PUBLISHED BY PUBLISHAMERICA, LLLP
www.publishamerica.com
Baltimore

Printed in the United States of America

This book is dedicated to my children and grandchildren, who were so excited when my first book was published.

Thank you all for your encouragement, and to God, who continues to allow my stories to come forth!

Acknowledgments

Thank you to all the brave pioneers, who forged the trail west and recorded it for history. Without the details of their journey, those of us who wish to experience this amazing time in our country's history would have to rely solely on our imaginations. Thank you again to all those pioneers who filled in the blanks for us. I relied on many Oregon Trail diaries while writing this novel. Ideas were used, but not actual people. Any character who may portray a person, living or dead, was accidental and unintentional.

And a special thanks to Danny Lee Ingram, author of *Pennies on the Tracks*, for his help in making this novel the best it can be.

Chapter 1

Lizzie had reached bottom. There was nowhere else for her to go. She looked across the small table at the faces of her younger brother and sister. She then glanced down at her father's Bible, which she held in her right hand, then at the guide book in her left. In the center of the table, between Lizzie and the two children, rested a small plain wooden box. The box was made of simple pine with no carvings or paintings to distinguish it from any other wooden box, except it held all the money that the three of them had to their name. Which was very little, considering how hard Lizzie and her brother had worked for it.

"Well, I've done it," she told them. "I've quit my job at the Whitmores'."

"Did old man Whitmore try messing with you again, Lizzie?" Zeke, her younger brother of twelve, sat up straighter in his chair. His young chin was set firmly in determination. "I'm the man of the house now that Pa's gone, and I've got to take care of you and Abby. Well, Lizzie, did he?"

She smiled sadly, and nodded. "This time Mrs. Whitmore caught him, and I was asked to resign—with no references of course." She sighed and looked towards the wooden box. "All we have to our name is in that little box there and the trunk under our bed." She looked around the small one-room shack they called home. During the day, sunlight showed through the cracks in the boards, and during the winter the cold wind whistled through. "I wanted to ask you two whether or not you want to stay and try scratching out a living here in New York, or if you want to follow Pa's dream West. I found his Bible and guidebook the other day, and I've spent a lot of time thinking about it. In the guidebook was his itemized list of expenses. It tells us everything we need to know, everything we need to purchase, and he has even listed several of the landmarks along the trail." She had, in fact, spent many nights lying awake weighing the pros and cons of such an undertaking. It was daunting, but to her young heart, it was accomplishable.

"How much money is in that box, Lizzie?" Zeke, the practical one, asked. "I've heard lots of people down at the paper talking and it takes money. Lots of it. We don't have a wagon or oxen. Heck, Lizzie, you don't even know *how* to drive a wagon. Plus, we have to take a train to Missouri. That alone will cost more than what is in that box, won't it?"

"We've got enough, I think. If we're frugal. We'll do it together. We can do this, Zeke. I know we can."

"Well, Abby can't help. She's only eight." He folded his arms across his chest.

"Do you want to spend the rest of your life hawking papers while Abby tries selling flowers on the street corner? Look at her, Zeke. Someone will pick her up and we'll never see her again. You've heard the stories. She'll disappear. She'll be sold to someone who will use her for evil. We can't let that happen. Ma and Pa would roll over in their graves."

Zeke looked over at his little sister. Abby stared back at him with her large blue eyes. Her pale hair, the color of corn silk, was tied back from her face with a red ribbon. Abby was small for her age, and Lizzie and Zeke had always been overly protective of her since their parents' death three years ago.

"I can *too* help," Abby stated, folding her small arms across her chest in imitation of her brother. "I can be the cook. I do most of the cooking now anyway."

"That's right, Abby. You're a fine cook." Lizzie dumped the money on the table and opened their father's guidebook. "Pa has everything written out right here, Zeke. He's written down everything we need, down to how much flour and salt. We'll need even less than he figured, since it's just the three of us. I've been saving every penny possible since I've been working, and Ma and Pa did leave us with something. We've got enough to get us to Missouri and get outfitted. Between the two of us, we'll manage. If we have to hire you out, we will. I can work too, if I have to. We've got very little. No furniture that we need to take. Just our provisions and the few clothes and blankets we have. We'll only need two oxen and a small wagon. We'll make do." The more she spoke, the more convinced she became that they could do it.

"Can we take Boomer and Buster?" Abby asked. "I won't go without them. They'll protect us from the Indians. I've heard scary stories about the wild Indians."

"Of course, we'll take them," Zeke told her. "We need those two mongrels. I'll dig out Pa's gun tonight and clean it. When are we leaving, Lizzie? It's already the end of February, and we'll have to move fast to get to Missouri. The wagons like to head out in April— May at the latest, to avoid hitting snow in the mountains. A lot of people heading West have already left for Missouri."

"Two days at the most, Zeke. We'll leave in two days." Two days and they would leave the miserable life they knew behind them.

"You two go on to bed, now. I've got to run out tonight."

"Where are you going, Lizzie?"

"I'm going out to sell a few more of our things. I can take them to the second-hand store. Go on to bed. I'll be back before you wake up." Zeke watched her seriously for a minute before nodding, and then led Abby to the single bed in the room that the three of them shared.

Lizzie sat back in her chair, holding their father's Bible and thought back to the time when they had been a happy family. Only three years ago, they still had their parents and had just left the country so their father could try making enough money working in the city to enable them to go West and begin a new life. A life of owning their own land. In the blink of an eye, they were left orphaned. Their parents had never made it home one night from the factory where they worked. On their way home, they had been run down by an out of control carriage.

Most of their finances had gone to pay off debts, although Lizzie had managed to stash a little away. She had found herself forced to seek employment as an upstairs maid with one of the elite and prominent families of New York. At the tender age of sixteen, she had begun back-breaking work and fighting off advances from dirty old men. She looked over at Zeke and Abby. It was all right for her, but they were too young for such a life. She held the Bible tighter to her bosom. Pa had dreamed of a better life for them in Oregon. They could follow his dream and make it a reality. She just knew they could.

Grandma Esther had sent them some vegetable seeds from her own garden last year before she died, and Lizzie had carefully stored them away in an empty gourd. They would be able to start right away with a vegetable garden. Zeke was strong. They would make it. She blew out the candle on the table and listened to the breathing of her brother and sister.

It was getting dark outside. She had better hurry with what she wanted to accomplish tonight. It was getting late. She rose, put the Bible back on the small table, and then parted the curtain that hid the alcove where she hung their clothes. She pulled out a few of their nicer things. Outfits their mother had made them for church and special occasions. They wouldn't need them on the trail. On a shelf overhead sat a couple of tattered carpet bags. She pulled these down and set them on the floor. Beneath the bed where Zeke and Abby were sleeping, was a small steamer trunk. She dragged it out into the center of the room and lifted the lid. A strong smell of cedar wafted upwards, causing her to sneeze.

The few precious material possessions they had left were stored in this box. A few books that their father had taught them to read on and some fabric pieces from a quilt their mother had never had time to finish. The quilt pieces waited for someone to take them up again and complete them. The quilts that their mother had managed to finish were being used on their bed now. The china that their mother had once cherished had been sold long ago. The trunk also included a silver-plated mirror and hair brush set and a small box of their mother's jewelry. The small box was what Lizzie was searching for. She put the box inside the pocket of her skirt, gathered up the dress clothes she had pulled from the closet, and glanced over to where her siblings still lay sleeping. She quietly pulled the door shut behind her as she left.

Lizzie kept to the shadows as she entered the alley behind their home. She knew the old woman who bought second-hand clothes would open up for her, no matter what time of the night it was. It was the man at the pawn shop who worried her. He was a grouchy old man, not given to politeness or to helping others. She needed to sell the things tonight in order for them to pack and catch the train on schedule. She didn't want the train to Missouri to be sold out of tickets and thus cause them to live longer in the city without employment or other means of earning money.

She peered into the gloom of the alley and listened to the snores of the people who were either sleeping or had passed out from too much liquor. She carefully skirted around the fallen drunks. She knew that the women who lounged in the alley doorways weren't going to bother her. Most of the people from this grungy corner of the city where they lived, watched out for her and the two children. Many of them had taken her, Zeke, and Abby under their wing when they were left orphaned, showing them how to survive in the unfriendly city. The ones who wanted to abuse them were kept in control by the other vagrants.

A couple of men reached out to grab at her skirt as she passed, but they were too drunk to be of much danger. She aimed a half-hearted kick in their direction and kept walking. Light poured from several of the open doorways, and tinny piano music serenaded the night of the alley. Lizzie wrinkled her nose and hitched up her skirts as a tenant tossed out a slop bucket, barely missing showering Lizzie with the filth. The tired old woman muttered a reluctant apology and slammed the door closed on the ramshackle shack she called home. Lizzie could see the back of the second-hand store she was headed to and quickened her pace.

Lizzie pounded on the door in front of her for several minutes before she caught a glimpse of a candle's gleam. The door opened an inch. Just enough for an eye to peer out. "Who is it?"

"It's Lizzie, ma'am. I'm sorry to bother you so late, but I was wondering if you could look at a few things I've brought and maybe buy some of them from me."

"Tonight? Now?" The old woman cracked the door open a little wider and scowled out at her.

"Please. We'd like to catch the train in a couple of days, and I've got to purchase the tickets first thing in the morning."

"All right, girl. But only because it's you." She opened the door and motioned for Lizzie to enter.

They were in a room at the back of the store. A small, dark room with only a slit for a window. The room held a small cot, one three-legged stool next to a rickety table, and a small fireplace. Lizzie tossed the clothes on the bed.

"My mother made these clothes," she informed the shopkeeper. Lizzie fingered them gently. "They're of very fine fabric. Could you look at them now, please? I'd like to get over to the pawn shop tonight, too."

"What do you want to go over there for, girl? That old man will only rob you blind. He doesn't have an honest bone in his skinny body." She pawed through the clothes, occasionally holding something up for a better look. Lizzie watched her, sadly. It was painful to see the last of their mother's things be sold. "Let me see what else you got."

Lizzie pulled the jewelry from her pocket. "It's only a bit of jewelry."

The old woman wiggled her fingers at her, motioning for Lizzie to hand her the box. "Let me see." She opened the box and rifled through the rings and necklaces. "What did you say you needed the money for?"

"We're heading west. I need this for the train tickets to get us to Missouri."

"West, huh? A fool's dream." The woman sniffed in derision.

"It was my parents' dream," Lizzie replied defensively.

"Didn't mean any harm. An old woman is entitled to her own opinion, isn't she?" She put the box into the pocket of the tattered robe she wore. "I'll take the lot from you. I can guarantee it'll be more than that old fool down the street."

12

"How much can you give me?" Lizzie asked. "I'd also like to look through the store, if I may. There are a few things we'll need that we don't have, and I'd rather buy them used if I can. I need to save money wherever I can."

"You're going to keep me up all night, girl. But—go ahead. I'm sure we can work out enough for the tickets and the what-not you'll be needing. Pick out what you need and we'll discuss the cost then."

Lizzie walked through the curtain separating the living quarters from the store, and stood still until the shop lady lit a lantern. She let her eyes adjust and slowly began walking the aisles, mentally running down the list of items her father had listed in the back of his book.

"Let me know what you'll be needing and we'll set it aside."

"I'll be needing the lantern you're holding."

"What? This one? There's another over there."

"I know *that* one works." She picked up a pink sun bonnet. *Abby would like this*, she thought. *And she'll need it for the sun*. She spied a blue one in a larger size and picked it up also. "We'll take these— and this man's floppy hat. We need a tin kettle, a cook stove, if you have one. Make it a small one. We have to conserve space. Oh, and a butter churn. I'm hoping to buy a milk cow in Missouri. A milk pail—no, not that one. It's too dented. I want three rain slickers, one in small. And some sturdy shoes. Do you have those?"

"Slow down. I'm not as young as you. I've got lots of shoes. Some in better shape than others." She tossed a black hat in Lizzie's direction.

"This is quite tattered, isn't it?"

"Can't be too picky, young lady. I'm practically giving you the stuff as it is. Let's see—" She browsed through the clothing racks. "Yes, I've got the slickers. Might not be small enough, but it's better than nothing. Over here is where we'll find the stove and kettle. Very good, here's a butter churn! Are you sure this is it? Got your bedding, needles, thread? Got any tonic? Taking two children into the wilderness won't be easy! There's all kinds of sickness to be had out there."

"No, I don't have any tonic. The apothecary shop will be closed now, and tomorrow is Sunday." Lizzie looked worried. "I hadn't thought of that."

"Probably a lot you haven't thought of. I've got a new bottle of tonic and one of cod-liver oil, too. I can get more. Here, take this too. Cholera runs rampant out there, I've heard." She added a bottle of bismuth to the pile. "My own sister went out to Californee five years ago. Kept a diary, she did. Here's a tip she wrote me about. Sew pockets on the inside of your skirts. Keep your valuables in there. Savages will rob you blind, if you let them. Some women even take to wearing men's britches on the trail. Imagine that! Buy some tobaccee when you hit Missouri. They love that, the savages do, and you can trade with it, too. Grab a handful of those cheap baubles over there. Savages love baubles. Got a gun? Good. Your brother know how to use it?" The old woman walked and grabbed things as she talked. Lizzie watched with dismay as the pile on the counter grew.

"Wait. This is too much. How will I ever get it shipped out? I don't think I have enough money." She counted through the change the woman gave her.

"Nonsense. You've got plenty. I told you I would help you out with what's left from your tickets, and I will. Run on over to the station, he'll still sell to you at this hour. He's a money hungry old fool, and I'll have you all finished when you get back. Pack it up in a box for you, too."

"Thank you. I don't know how I can repay you." She gave the woman a big hug.

"You can repay me by surviving, girl. That's all. I still think you're headed off on a fool's dream." The shopkeeper hugged her back, awkwardly patting her shoulder.

It was still dark when Lizzie made her way back to the little shack. She was pleased with the weight of the coins hanging heavy in her pocket. She slid under the blankets next to Abby and fell asleep smiling.

"Lizzie!" Zeke shook her shoulder. "Lizzie, wake up."

"What?" She sat up, rubbing the sleep from her eyes.

"Where's Ma's things, Lizzie? Tell me you didn't sell the last of her things!" Angry tears were welling in his eyes. "It's all we had left of her, Lizzie!"

Abby sat up in bed, confused and half asleep. "What's wrong, Zeke? Why are you yelling?" She turned, wide-eyed, to Lizzie. "Lizzie?"

"I had to sell them, Zeke. Please try to understand." Lizzie swung her legs over the side of the bed. "I kept a couple of her rings, her hairbrush set, and I sold the rest. I sold the last of our nice clothes, too. We need sturdier things to take us out West, and you said yourself it was going to take a lot of money."

"But Ma's things?" A sob caught in his throat. "Tell me we still have Pa's gun."

"Yes, we still have that." She stood up. "Today, we pack up what's left. Tomorrow, we dress in the last nice outfit we have and begin our journey. I bought us train tickets to Independence, Missouri, this morning."

"A train ride!" Abby bounced up and down in her excitement. "It'll be grand, Zeke. You'll see." She scampered from the bed. "I'll fix us some eggs for breakfast—right now. That way you two can start packing right away."

Lizzie smiled over at her. "It will be an adventure, won't it? Zeke?"

"All right," he conceded. The excitement over the upcoming train ride overshadowed his disappointment of his sister selling the last of their mother's things. "We'll make it the best adventure ever."

Lizzie drew the two children close to her and wrapped them in a hug. "It'll be the adventure of a lifetime."

Chapter 2

Lizzie held tight to Abby's hand as the locomotive screeched to a halt before the platform where they stood. Abby pulled free and clamped her hands over her ears against the noise. Lizzie glanced around her to locate Zeke. She relaxed when she saw him standing patiently by their trunks talking to the two dogs encased in the crate beside him. She waved to him and smoothed the fabric on the simple, navy wool skirt she wore. She double-checked the cleanliness of Abby's pinafore, regained her grip on the little girl's hand, and set off to find someone to load their trunks.

She sidestepped a heavyset man who was spitting tobacco. It narrowly missed her shoes, causing her to twirl to avoid his spittle. She swept her skirt aside in disgust. She bumped into another man in fancy dress, who reached out to grab her arm, and she was almost in tears by the time she spotted someone in uniform who looked as if he might be able to help them. He agreed to, for a small fee. Zeke followed him around, in order to keep the man honest, and the two girls boarded the train to find themselves a seat in coach.

Abby eyed the dirty leather seats in disgust. "We're going to get filthy," she exclaimed.

"Yes, Abby, we are." Lizzie removed a handkerchief from the sleeve of her jacket and wiped the dust and soot from the seat the best she could. "We're going to be dirty for a long time, I'm afraid."

"I don't like to get dirty." Abby looked down at her light blue calico dress with its spotless white pinafore. She fingered the lace around the cuffs of her sleeves. "This is the only good dress I have left."

Lizzie sighed and sat down. She motioned for Abby to sit across from her in order to save a space for their brother. She was terrified they might have to share their corner of the train with a stranger. She looked around her. The majority of the passengers were men dressed in all forms of dress style. There were men in long dusters and Stetson hats, men in woolen pants and flannel shirts, and fancy men in frock coats wearing a collar and tie. There were only a few women. They were mostly women in simple clothes such as herself. One woman wore a bright yellow dress with a bodice cut so low Lizzie was embarrassed for her. The woman's hair was dyed to an unnatural looking yellow color. One of the fancy men caught Lizzie looking and winked. She blushed and turned away.

"I can't find any kids our age, Lizzie," Zeke stated, sliding onto the seat next to Abby. "It's mostly foul talking men chewing tobacco and smoking. But I can tell you that everyone here is talking about heading west. It's exciting! I met one man who was talking about heading to California to look for gold. Gold, Lizzie." He bounced up in his seat, peering over the back. "Hey, Lizzie. That man over there is staring at you. Want me to tell him to stop?"

Lizzie grabbed the waistband of his pants and pulled him down. "Stop staring. Don't attract any attention. I don't want him coming over here," she whispered harshly.

"I saw this one man outside, and he was wearing a hat made from a raccoon. Remember my old raccoon hat, Lizzie?" Zeke sat back and folded his arms across his chest. "I'm getting me another one the first chance I get. I might even kill the coon myself. And I'm getting some moccasins, too. I'm going to trade something with the Indians for a pair."

"I want a pair, Zeke," Abby told him, joining in with his excitement. "And I want one of those Indian dresses and the boots that go up to here," she said, pointing to her knees. "I've been looking at pictures. And I want one of those feather headdresses. Can I have one of those, Lizzie?"

Lizzie smiled indulgently at the children's enthusiasm. She prayed it would last. *They would need every ounce of it in the next few months*, she feared. She removed the little hat she wore perched on her head, and set it on the seat next to her. Still smiling, she looked out the window. She saw a man tenderly kissing his sweetheart goodbye. She noticed a woman and two small children waving bravely towards a window at the front of the train. One of her favorite past times was making up stories of people she saw, imagining their life, their adventures. She looked away as the train began moving.

It didn't take them long to be covered with soot from the open windows. Zeke and Abby's faces were streaked black, and Lizzie was mortified to think she might look the same. Abby began to cough. "Close the window, Zeke, please?" she asked. "That smoke from the engine is foul."

"Sure, sis. Is it lunch time yet? I'm hungry."

"We can eat now." Lizzie dug into the small basket she had carried on the train with them. She had packed sandwiches and some fruit to last them the several day train ride, and had added a couple of canteens she had bought before they left. The sandwiches were wrapped in grease paper. "Save the paper," she told them. "We might need it for something." She bit into her sandwich, and grimaced. The soot had managed to get into everything.

"I'm stuffy, Lizzie," Abby whined. "Can't we open the window?"

"It's either endure the heat of the car or eat the soot. Which would you prefer?"

"We're already dirty," she said mournfully, "so let's open the window."

"It'll be cold," Lizzie warned her.

"I don't care. I hate being stuffy. I can't breathe, Lizzie."

Lizzie shrugged and Zeke stood up to release the window latch. "Here, son, let me help you with that." The man, whom Zeke had dubbed fancy man, approached them. He quickly popped the window open and sat down next to Lizzie.

"Excuse me, sir," she said, scooting away from him, "but you're sitting on my hat." He professed his apologies and stood, handing her the squashed square of navy wool.

"Edward T. Newton. At your service, ma'am."

"My sister ain't interested." Zeke told him, scowling. "Move on."

The man's dark eyes hardened, but his grin widened. "Why, you've got spunk, son. You'll need that out West."

"Who said we were going west?"

"Why, everyone's headed west. That's where the future is." He tipped his hat at Lizzie. "You need anything, ma'am. You just let me know. Always ready to help out a damsel in distress. Especially one as beautiful as yourself." Lizzie gave him a tight smile and watched him leave. She shook her head. She prayed she wouldn't have to endure much of that on their trip.

By nightfall, all three of them were tired, achy, and out of sorts. Zeke was bored and kept bouncing up in his seat to look around. Abby asked endless questions, and Lizzie tried to convince her to go to sleep. It was now too dark to stare at the passing landscape, and the oil lamps lighting the car were giving off another smelly smoke for them to deal with. "Oh, Zeke, please sit down. You're driving me crazy!"

"There's nothing to do on this old train. What am I going to do for three days? Why can't I go check out the other cars?"

"Because I said so."

"I should at least be allowed to go check on the dogs."

"I said no, Zeke." Lizzie began flipping through their guidebook.

"Well, you're not my mother. I'm going." Lizzie watched helplessly as Zeke stormed down the aisle and out the door to one of the other cars. She looked over at Abby who had fallen asleep. Her head bobbed from side to side with the movement of the car. She changed seats and laid the little girl's head in her lap. She laid her own head back against the seat and within minutes was asleep.

She opened her eyes and peered through the gloom. It took a few moments for her to realize what had awakened her. Then she realized the train had stopped. She noticed that Zeke had returned while she had been sleeping and was passed out full-length on the opposite bench. She gently removed Abby's head from her lap and stood up to look around. Several of the other passengers were doing the same. Across the aisle from her was a woman who looked to be in her early thirties. She must have come in from another car and was trying to reassure a small girl who seemed to be about Abby's age.

"Excuse me," Lizzie asked, quietly. "Do you know why we've stopped?"

The other woman looked up. "No, but my husband has gone to see." She held out her hand. "My name is Alice Johnson."

Lizzie smiled at the woman's friendly demeanor and extended her hand in return. "I'm Lizzie Springer. This is my sister, Abby, and my brother Zeke."

"You kids traveling alone?" Alice looked around the car.

"Yes. Our parents died a few years ago, and we're heading west to Oregon. My father had a dream about owning his own land out there."

Alice nodded. "My husband, too. There he is." Lizzie watched as the woman and her husband conversed quietly. Then the man left again.

"That's my husband, Ben. Dragging us across this God-forsaken country is his idea." She shrugged. "Anyway, he says there are some fallen trees across the tracks. They should have it cleared soon." She moved her daughter's skirt aside so she could sit down. She pulled the girl's head onto her shoulder. "This is Sarah, my youngest. I have three rowdy boys who, I imagine, are off getting into trouble—or helping their father. Their names are Joshua, Jacob, and Seth. Ben says the boys will be a big help to us on the trail. A big headache is more like it." She sighed, deeply. "I'm not taking being uprooted very well." She turned her head back to Lizzie. "I can't imagine you three young'uns taking this all on yourselves."

"We had nothing for us back there. Our Pa wanted a fresh new start for us, and well, here we are." Lizzie's voice trembled. "All our worldly possessions are packed into a couple of banged up trunks in the baggage car. We're hoping to get the rest of what we need in Independence."

"My husband will help you. It's a relief to me to know that there will be another young woman for me to gossip with. We'll make sure we get hitched up on the same wagon train west." Alice Johnson was a stout woman with a decisive demeanor. She wore a no nonsense brown skirt and a yellow cotton blouse. Her long, brown hair was pinned on top of her head. Her rough, calloused hands gently smoothed back the hair from her sleeping daughter's face.

Lizzie nodded. "I'd appreciate that." She sat back down and was asleep again before the train had begun moving. She woke the next morning to rain blowing through the open window. Abby complained about the wet and the cold and Lizzie jumped up to close the window. Her mouth dropped open with a gasp.

"What is that, Lizzie?" Zeke asked, standing beside her.

"It's a twister. A big one." A mile across the wheat filled prairie, a tornado roared parallel to the tracks. The rain showed the twister white against the dark sky. Bits of tree limbs and uprooted wheat stalks swirled in the funnel. Several of the other passengers had noticed the same view out of their windows, and the car was filled with gasps and murmurings.

"That'll tear up the track if it hits," Zeke told her, his voice quivering with fear. "What if it hits the train?"

"It's not headed in our direction," Lizzie reassured him. "Just enjoy the beauty and power of it, Zeke. It won't stay on the ground long." She was right. Within minutes it had lifted back up into the heavy clouds.

"Are we going to see twisters on our way west?" Abby wanted to know.

"I don't know, Abby. I hope not." Lizzie turned away from the window. "Anyone up for breakfast?" Lizzie passed out more sandwiches and fruit. "What did you do last night, Zeke? What time did you get to sleep?"

He shrugged and mumbled. "I don't know. I didn't do much. Nothing, really."

"Nothing?" She stared at him. "Zeke?"

"I took some of our money and gambled with it," he admitted, defiantly. "Fancy man over there, Mr. Newton, let me in on a poker game." He kept his head down and concentrated on his sandwich.

"Zeke Springer! Ma is probably rolling over in her grave right now! What gave you the right to gamble with our money? We need that. Every cent."

"It's no big deal. I won." He pulled some money out of his pocket. "Here's ten dollars. I won twelve, but I'm saving two dollars for tonight."

Lizzie set her sandwich in her lap. "I forbid you to go back tonight. Zeke, you know how Ma and Pa felt about gambling."

Zeke returned his sister's angry gaze with one of his own. "Well, they're not here right now, are they? I made us money, instead of losing it. We're ten dollars richer because I was willing to risk a little. The money I play with tonight is my own." He wadded up the sandwich paper and tossed it at her. "I'm going to visit the conductor."

"What's wrong with Zeke, Lizzie?" Abby looked up at her. "He's not usually this grouchy."

"I don't know, Abby." Lizzie picked up the tossed paper and put it back in the basket. "He's bored, I guess. We'll just have to pray for him, won't we?" She did know what was worrying Zeke. He had accepted the responsibilities of a grown man, instead of a twelve year old boy. He felt like he had to take care of Lizzie and Abby, rather than Lizzie, the oldest, taking care of him.

She looked out the window, tears welling up in her eyes. She was beginning to feel very inadequate at the job of raising Abby and Zeke, and the long train ride gave her too much time to think about it. She had overheard her father once, telling her mother how difficult the trip was going to be, and here she was thinking she could do it without them. Abby had gone across the aisle to get acquainted with Sarah Johnson so Lizzie tried to keep herself busy picking up after their breakfast and wiping the soot from the seats—again.

By the time they reached Independence, they were dusty, soot covered, and wrinkled. Not to mention ill-tempered and tired.

Chapter 3

They stepped off of a smoke spewing, soot-filled, very loud train into a city that was equally as dirty, loud, and teeming with life. The noise was overwhelming, and Lizzy was able to distinguish between several different languages being spoken. Independence, Missouri, was one of the most widely used "jumping off" cities for those heading west, and everywhere the three of them looked there was a sea of covered wagons, oxen, mules, screaming mothers, and running children. Storekeepers were standing outside their places of business, hawking their wares to everyone who passed by. Abby pressed close to Lizzie's side and clutched her hand. Zeke's eyes were wide with excitement.

Alice stepped up behind them. "Well, this—is a circus," she said matter-of-factly.

"It's frightening," Lizzie answered back. "I don't have a clue where to go from here."

"My Ben has gone to fetch our trunks. Suppose your brother ought to go, too. Then we'll be looking for us a wagon. Don't want to waste any time, or money, on a hotel room. You kids stay by me!" She reached over and grabbed the collar of her youngest son who had started to run off after Zeke. "You'll be killed dead by some horse! Run right over. Ben told me last night that we would have to find a group to hook up with. You are going to Oregon, right? Seems everyone is. You might as well stay by us. Now, Seth, I mean it! I swear these children have me frazzled." She pulled a handkerchief from the bosom of her blouse and wiped her brow with it.

"I'm obliged by the offer, and I'll take you up on it. I'll help you watch your children in return." Lizzie walked over and took Seth's hand in her free one. "Do you think Ben could get me a wagon, too? We don't need a big one."

"Sure. Sure." Alice looked around for her husband. "He's right over there. Come on, you little heathens. Let's begin this God-forsaken adventure." She led the way to where her husband was having a conversation with a small, wiry man who sported a floppy felt hat that kept falling forward over his eyes. The unkempt man had several days' stubble dotting his chin, and Lizzie wrinkled her nose at the body odor emanating from him. He spit tobacco juice constantly into the dirt around them. Alice interrupted them and let her husband know that Lizzie would need a wagon, also.

"Do you want mules or oxen?" the man asked Lizzie.

"I don't know." Lizzie looked to Alice. "Does it matter?"

"Oxen are stronger. Mules are faster," the man selling the wagons, spit and explained. Lizzie looked down in disgust to where his spittle had barely missed her shoe. "Who you got driving your wagon for you?"

"I'm driving."

"Well, now, that ain't possible." He shook his head. "Not many wagon trains will let a woman drive her own wagon. You need a man along. Women alone tend to slow things down." He spit again. "I'm sure you can find a man willing to go along with a purty thang like you." He grinned, revealing several missing teeth.

Lizzie squared her shoulders and stood taller. "My brother will help. We'll manage, thank you."

"Well, it's yore loss if you fail. I've got a couple of small farm wagons for sale. One of them oughta suit ya."

"We'll need a larger one than her. I'm thinking one of them Conestoga wagons I've heard of. I've got quite a brood of children," Ben interrupted.

"No, sir. Not a wise thing a'tall. Conestoga wagons are just too heavy. Ya'll won't never make it over them mountains. Might want to buy two small wagons just for yourself. If you've got a lot of things, you might want oxen. They survive really well out there, and if things get too tough—why you can always eat'em. The young lady here might want to think about mules, though. Might go in her favor when finding a train to hook up with. They're faster."

Lizzie sighed, audibly. "How many mules would I need?"

24

"'Bout six.

"Six? I haven't got that many things with me, and there are only three of us, and one is a small child." She turned to Alice and Ben. "Is this man honest?"

"He comes highly recommended," Ben answered. "With all these people, we're lucky he's got enough wagons and teams left to outfit us."

She turned back to the grizzly man. "Why six?"

"Four to pull the wagon, if you ain't got much, and two as extras. You need extras. The trip is hazardous. Most folks don't make it out there with all the animals they left with, and mules can purt near eat anything. You won't have to carry much feed for them, or the oxen."

"Fine." She sighed heavily and opened the small clutch purse she carried. "How much? Does the wagon have a cover, or do I need to buy one of those, too?"

"It's covered. Treated with oil, too. Left behind by some people who changed their minds about going. They was the smart ones. Independence is so bogged down by trains heading west you've got at least a two week wait," he explained. "Maybe more. Then you got to cross the river. That's dangerous. You'll probably have to live in that wagon for quite a while."

Lizzie rolled her eyes and began counting out the money required. Zeke ran up then and told his sister he had their trunks and asked her where did she want him to put them. She looked over at Ben and Alice for help.

"I'll get them," Ben said. "Put them over here with ours, and we'll load 'em in the wagons and find us a place to wait."

Zeke stood there and glared at the wagon seller when he heard how long they might have to camp. He stared at the man as if he were to blame for the two week wait they would have before crossing the river. He took off his hat and slapped it against his leg as he had seen the cowboys do. He looked at the wagon and mules that Lizzie had bought, running his hands down the mules' legs and then moved on to inspecting the wagon wheels. Lizzie looked over at Alice, and smiled. When Zeke felt he had been thorough enough, he straightened. "Guess they'll do." He turned to his sister. "What are we going to do for two weeks?"

"Well," Lizzie answered, fighting to keep the smile from her face. "I'm going to work. I'm going to that mercantile over there, buy us a wash tub, board, and soap and do laundry for money. I can see a lot of dirty people here. I figure I might be able to make money doing their laundry."

"And I'm going to help," Abby piped up. Not to be outdone by his sisters, Zeke announced he was going to work also and set out right then to find himself a job.

He wandered the crowded town, dodging racing horses and stumbling drunks, checking into every mercantile, saloon, and ironsmith he saw. Night was falling before he found a stable that was willing to hire him on as a stable boy, temporarily. He agreed to come back in the morning and turned to head back to his sisters.

He had only gone a couple of feet before he stopped and looked around. He had no idea where to go. The wooden sidewalks were shoulder to shoulder with people, and the street was teeming with horses and buggies. He stood on his toes and strained his neck, trying to peer over the mass of people. He could see the train off to his left but had no idea which way Lizzie and the Johnsons had gone.

"You lost, son?" A man walked up beside him. Zeke looked him over. He was a tall man, standing well over six feet, wearing a cotton, plaid, long sleeved shirt under a plain brown vest and worn tan trousers. A long brown duster flowed around his legs. Cowboy boots attributed to some of the man's height. Dark blue eyes peered out from a face that was shaded by the brim of a tan Stetson. The man smiled kindly as he waited patiently for Zeke to decide whether he would accept his help.

"I'm looking for my sisters." Zeke turned his attention back to the street.

"Where did you leave them?"

"By the tracks. We had bought a team and wagon, and I left looking for work. I doubt they're there now."

"I doubt it, too. They've probably found a place to camp. Not many places in the city left. Let's start on the outskirts." The man put his hand around Zeke's shoulders and successfully navigated him across the busy street. "My name is William Aiken. People call me Bill, or Aiken."

"Zeke Springer." He held out his hand. "We're heading west. Going to claim some land."

"Glad to meet you, Zeke Springer. I've been West. An amazing place. Rough trip, though." He swung Zeke around to avoid having him run over by a speeding buggy. "I'm going to lead a train out this spring, as a matter of fact."

"Really?" Zeke pestered the patient man with questions during their walk around the perimeter of town. Dark had fully set by the time Zeke spotted his sisters and the Johnsons. Lizzie was standing next to their wagon, casting glances in all directions.

"Great. Lizzie's worried."

"Trouble, huh?"

"Yes, sir."

Aiken shook Zeke's hand. "I'll leave you here, then. Good luck. It was nice to meet you, Zeke Springer."

Zeke nodded and sighed. He squared his shoulders and walked slowly to his sister. Instead of scolding him, she wrapped him in a tight hug. "I was so worried about you, Zeke. You got lost, didn't you?"

He nodded. "Yeah, but I did find a job. The pay's not too bad, and a train master helped me find ya'll. I reckon I can find my way back in the morning."

"Alice and I bought some paper today and put up fliers. Man who owns the mercantile said we'll probably have more business than we can handle. He'll even give us a discount if we do his laundry and buy all our supplies at his store. God is good, Zeke."

"Oh, Lizzie. The shopkeeper was only helpful 'cause you're so pretty." He punched her playfully in the arm and ran up to the pot that was hanging over their fire.

The mercantile owner and Zeke were both right. Alice and Lizzie did have more customers than they could handle, and some of their customers did come just to gawk. A few proposed marriage and Ben ran some off on the threat of death when their behavior crossed the line into being vulgar.

Lizzie scrubbed the last shirt in her tub that day and stood, arching her back to get the kinks out. "I've never worked so hard in my life," she told Alice. "Has Ben found a train for us to hook up with yet?"

"He said he was checking another one out today. Seems like they're all full." She hung a pair of trousers on a rope strung between two trees that served as their clothesline. "He went to check with the man who helped Zeke a couple of weeks ago. That must be him." She nodded her head towards Ben and a group of men who were approaching their camp. Seeing the tall silhouette of a man walking next to Ben, she whistled softly. "That is one tall drink of water."

Lizzie glanced at her in surprise before turning to greet the approaching group.

"Alice. Lizzie," Ben introduced. "This here is William Aiken, and the others are part of the deciding committee. Akin is the scout and leader of the train." Aiken tilted his hat in their direction. The others stared silently at the two women.

"Where's her man?" One of them asked.

Lizzie sat her jaw. "I haven't got a…man, as you so eloquently phrase it. It's just myself, my younger sister, and my brother."

"No disrespect, Miss, but we'll have to vote on whether or not you can go along with us. Right, Aiken?" He had to look up at the man beside him.

"Well, that's right, Martin. But let's not be too rash, here. I've met her brother, and he's a stout lad. They're with the Johnsons. Right, Miss?" She nodded, and he continued. "She has her own team and wagon. I don't see any harm in her coming along with us."

"She'll just slow us down!"

"Not with mules, she won't," Ben defended. "I've plenty of boys to help with driving her team and a couple of extras even to help with the extra stock."

"Well, we'll have to discuss this." The man Martin pulled the men over while Aiken stood off to the side. He studied the young woman standing beside him. He wore his hat pulled low over his eyes so she couldn't see him watching her. Her hair was light, the color of corn silk, and her pale skin was just beginning to show a light tan. A few freckles dotted her straight nose. Her eyes were a light blue, matching the bonnet on her head. Her lips were full. *Just begging to be kissed*, he thought to himself. Yep, she was going to be trouble. With her looks though, she was asking for it. Some of these men hadn't seen a nice, pretty girl like her in months. He noticed that she wrung her hands in her apron as she waited nervously for the committee to make up their minds.

Within minutes, they were back. "All right. We've agreed she can come, but she brings up the rear. We won't have any single woman slowing us down or causing havoc among the single men."

"Well, I—" Lizzie sputtered.

Aiken held up his hand. "Agreed. Ya'll go on back now." He watched silently as the group dispersed back to their own wagons. "I'm sorry about that," he said to Lizzie. "Some folks are just like that. It's our turn to cross the river in two days. Will you be ready by then?"

"Yes, and thank you." She held out her hand for him to shake. He stared at the small hand for a second before he took it. His hand engulfed her small one. The skin of her hands were rough from the washing, not a ladies hands at all, but a working woman's.

He noticed how the young woman's head barely reached his shoulder and how her blonde hair was damp and curly around her face. She frowned at his hesitation, her blue eyes darkening with anger at his scrutiny. "You might want to think about getting yourself and your brother some gloves. Driving a team of mules will tear up your hands." He tilted his hat again. "Let me know if I can be of any further help."

She nodded and turned to Alice and Ben, smiling. "Two days. Finally. Zeke will be so excited. Let's finish this as our last load of laundry and head down to the store to complete our supplies." Alice smiled in agreement and Ben tossed his hat in the air with a whoop. He grabbed Alice around the waist and swung her. Abby looked up from where she and Sara were folding the dry clothing, and laughed. The next morning, Lizzie and Alice were up before dark, sorting and packing their supplies. They laughed over coffee as they went over their lists. "Zeke is suppose to be picking up his last paycheck today," Lizzie told her friend. "With the money I've brought with us, and what we've made doing laundry, all together we should have enough for the trip and emergencies."

"No such thing as enough for emergencies," Alice told her, sipping the hot coffee. "I'll have Ben check out the brakes on all three wagons today. Need to fill up all the water barrels, too. Ben has a toolbox. One should be enough for this group, don't ya think?" Alice continued to talk in-between slurping the hot coffee. "I have to admit, Lizzie. I'm getting just a bit nervous. Rumor has it we'll be lining up to cross tomorrow."

Lizzie nodded. "I heard that, too. Then we'll probably sit in line for a day. Good morning, Zeke. Already been down to the blacksmith? It's barely light. What's that?" She pointed to the heavy wooden beam he was dragging behind him.

Zeke dropped the beam and plopped down on top of it. "It's an extra axle," he puffed. "I had the blacksmith pay me the last of my wages with it." He took off his hat and bowed his head, panting from the exertion of dragging it across town.

"And how are we going to carry that thing with us?" Lizzie demanded, pouring her brother a cup of the coffee.

"I'll have Mr. Johnson help me tie it up underneath the wagon." He stood and dusted off the seat of his pants. "People been saying that an extra axle, or wheel, could make all the difference in whether or not we make it West. If we haven't used it, we can always dump the weight before we head over the mountains. I brought over an extra wheel last night. It's propped up over on the other side of the wagon. Let's start loading this stuff. Where's Abby?"

"I'm here, Zeke." Abby crawled from the bed of the wagon, her hair mussed around her face. She yawned hugely and reached for a biscuit.

"You check off the items on this list while Zeke and I load."

Lizzie handed her the sheet of paper and a pencil stub. "Be careful. We can't have any mistakes."

"I'll be careful," she said, her mouth full of biscuit.

"I'll let you three be," Alice said, grabbing up her youngest. "I'd better get my brood up and to work ourselves."

"Four water barrels—full," Abby checked. "Two-hundred pounds of flour. Two-hundred pounds! How many biscuits am I going to have to make? Really, Lizzie!" She glared up at her sister.

Lizzie stood in the bed of the wagon and tied back the opening. "This is what we need, Abby. The guidebook is specific. Keep checking."

Abby sighed. "One hundred and fifty pounds of bacon, ten pounds of coffee, twenty pounds of sugar, ten pounds of salt, two bolts of fabric, box of bead necklaces..." The three continued packing and rearranging until the sun was well into the sky.

"Mornin'."

Lizzie poked her head out of the back of the wagon. "Good morning, Mr. Aiken."

"William, please. Or Aiken. No mister." Aiken stood looking up at her. "Everything ready?"

"I think so." She pulled the tarp aside. "We've room left. I've heard that's good. Is it?"

"Well, you don't want to be overloaded. You'll just end up dumping it out on the trail." He held up a hand to help her down. "Our train goes first tomorrow. I've got your wagon and the Johnsons' about mid-way through. Then you can fall back to the end of the line after we cross. Probably cross by early afternoon. Ever driven a mule team?"

"I have," Zeke said, climbing down from the wagon. "But Lizzie's going to tomorrow. I'm going to be swimming over with our extra mules."

Aiken squinted at Lizzie under the brim of his hat. "Think you can handle it?"

"Well," she said, looking towards the river. "I've been watching the other teams crossing this week, and as long as I can get the team on to the ferry and keep them still, it should go all right."

Aiken smiled. "Glad to see you've been thinking about it. See you tomorrow then." He tilted his hat and moved on to the Johnsons' wagon.

Lizzie gathered together her brother and sister. "Abby, I want you to stay in the wagon tomorrow. I'll be leading the mules, and Zeke will be herding the other animals. Zeke, you need to find the dogs by tonight. They're out roaming somewhere. We won't have time to hunt them down tomorrow." He nodded. "Abby, fix us some food today that will hold until tomorrow. We might not have time to cook. I'm going out to distribute the last of this laundry. We will *all* stay close to camp tonight, all right? All of us." She looked sternly at Zeke. He fidgeted and avoided his sister's eyes. She knew that he had been disappearing at night to run off with his friends or to gamble.

She continued to try and dissuade him from doing it, knowing how their parents felt about gambling, but it was hard to tell him to stop when he was winning. He did lose occasionally, but always seemed to make it up the next night.

After the children had gone to bed, Lizzie stood by the wagon, looking off toward the river. The crossings had ended for the day, and things were quieting down. Occasionally, she would hear a baby cry or a mother admonishing a wayward child. She could hear someone softly singing a lullaby and she smiled. A cow bellowed, and a dog barked. She looked back toward the town. Even the usually busy street was slowing down. She smiled as she thought of the busyness of the last two weeks and turned to join Abby and Zeke in the wagon.

Chapter 4

Lizzie was awakened the next morning by loud voices outside her wagon. She quickly grabbed her shawl from where it hung on a nail above some boxes, and peered surreptitiously out into the dawn. She parted the canvas covering just enough to allow her to see a man and a petite black woman standing in the shadows of the nearby trees. The man towered over the woman who stood quietly, head bowed, while he screamed at her. Lizzie strained to hear the woman's quiet replies.

"Where's your master, girl? We don't take to runaways here!"

"I'm a freed woman, sir." She flinched as the man raised his fist to strike her.

"Ain't no such thing. Ain't nobody here in Missouri gonna free the likes of you!"

"I have papers," she told him quietly.

"You ain't nothing but a lying..." He struck the woman, landing a blow alongside her head, and she fell to the ground with a small cry.

Anger welled up in Lizzie and before she knew what she was doing, she found herself standing before the huge man, her shawl wrapped tightly around her shoulders. She pulled her small frame as high as she could and stared him down. "Sir," she told him, in as stern a voice as she could muster up, "who gave you the right to strike my servant? You step back this instant, or I will have to call the sheriff!" Lizzie's knees shook beneath the calico dress she wore. If the morning light would have been bright enough, the man could have seen her fear in the wideness of her eyes and the paleness of her skin.

"Yours?" The man looked unbelievingly down on her. "If she's yours, why is she out here running around at night? She told me that she was freed."

"Sir, that business is ours, and as it is no longer night and my servant has returned, you have no grounds here." She nodded her head towards the rising sun. Lizzie turned from him and stooped to help the other woman up.

"What's going on here?" Aiken stepped quietly from behind the tree. He had happened upon the three shortly after the man had struck the woman and had stood aside, assessing the situation, his hand resting lightly on the gun he wore on his hip.

"Mr. Aiken, this man has struck this woman, knocking her to the ground." Lizzie's anger was still boiling. "Look. Her lip is bleeding."

"That right, sir?" Aiken walked up and stood before the man. Aiken stood a couple of inches taller, but the other man out weighed him by twenty pounds or more.

"This is one of them runaway slaves, and I aim to get myself one of them rewards!"

Aiken looked over at the two women, and Lizzie shook her head, silently pleading with him. Aiken sighed, and turned back to the man. "Seems like you are mistaken, mister. Seems to me like this woman belongs here. What train are you traveling with?"

"Ain't with no train. I live here. This is a respectable town. We don't hold to women wandering around at night. Especially ones of color. They're either a slave or a harlot."

"This woman seems to be neither. Make sure it doesn't happen again." Aiken removed his hat and offered his hand for a shake. "We're heading out today, and I'll watch over these two women myself. That all right with you?"

"Well…" The man looked over again at the women. "If you're sure she ain't no runaway." The man shook his hand and with one last glance over his shoulder, headed back into town.

"Thank you, Mr. Aiken."

"It's Aiken." He put his hat back on his head. "Lizzie, I don't ever want to see you facing down a drunken man alone again. You hear me?"

"Was he drunk? I was so angry I didn't notice." She smiled impishly up at him.

"You know darn right he was!" He smiled back at her before turning to the other woman. She *was* small. Smaller even than Lizzie, with skin the color of creamed coffee. A red scarf covered her hair, and the brown dress she wore was only a shade darker than her skin. She stood watching him warily, not moving, a small wrapped parcel at her feet. Aiken sighed again, and approached her. "*Are* you a runaway?"

"No sir, I'm not. I'm a freed woman. I've got my papers right here." She reached into her bodice and pulled out a small folded piece of paper. She handed it timidly to Aiken. "It says so right here. My name is Ida. My daddy was a poor white man, and right before he got sick and died, he freed my momma and me. She died just last week, trying to get here."

Aiken read the paper and handed it back to her. "Why didn't you show it to that man?"

"I tried to, sir. He can't read and said it was just some words on paper that I had made up. I can read, though, and I told him what it said. He said I was lying. I'm not a liar, sir," Ida said quietly, still standing with her head bowed.

"Look at me, Ida." She raised her head slowly. "You're a free woman with the papers to prove it. Don't walk around with your head down like a slave, anymore." She looked up at him in surprise. "Lizzie? Can she ride with you and the kids? I'm sure you could use her help."

"Sure she can. If she wants to." Lizzie looked questioningly at Ida.

"I'd be right proud to help you on this journey." Ida picked up her small parcel and tossed it into the wagon. She looked back at the other two.

"I'm going to be getting everyone in line to cross in another hour," Aiken told them. "Get the children up, tie down everything you can, and drive the team over there. It'll cost you two dollars to ride one of the ferries across. You can pay more for the animals or have Zeke swim them over like you said yesterday. Most people swim the extra teams across themselves. River's running high, but not too fast. Send Zeke to hunt me up before it's your turn to cross." Lizzie nodded at him, and he walked away, leaving the two women

35

alone. Lizzie watched him go, a soft smile on her lips. It had been a while since anyone, other than Zeke and Abby, had worried about what she did.

Three hours later, on April 20, 1853, more than two weeks since they arrived in Independence, Missouri, Lizzie found herself on the edge of the Missouri river, hands tightly clutching the reins, waiting to be ferried across. Ida sat quietly beside her. Abby held on to the back of the seat from inside the wagon, and Zeke was nowhere to be seen. She watched as the wagon in front of her lurched onto the ferry, causing the ferry to tilt and turn roughly. She glanced quickly over at Ida and saw that she looked just as frightened as Lizzie felt.

"Oh, my God!" Ida whispered in horror. Lizzie whipped her head back around to the river in time to see a small boy fall from the back of the ferry and land in the river. His mother began to scream hysterically as the boy's father held her back from falling over herself. The boy disappeared quickly under the muddy water. Ida began praying in earnest, her voice barely above a whisper. As the boy resurfaced, a man darted past their wagon and dove quickly into the rapidly moving river.

"It's Mr. Aiken," Ida said. They watched as he grabbed the boy underneath his arms and began pulling him to shore. Several times, the two disappeared under the river's murky water, but Aiken always managed to resurface with the boy in tow. Aiken pulled him to shore a few yards down river from Lizzie's wagon. She handed the reins to Ida and jumped down to help him. Aiken lay panting on the grass and looked up at her in gratitude.

"'Bout lost that one." He smiled weakly up at her. "Think you can take him across to his mother?" She smiled and, picking the boy up, deposited him in the wagon beside Abby.

"Hold on to him, Abby," she told her sister. She turned back to ask Aiken if he had seen Zeke, but he had already headed back to his horse. She started to climb back onto the wagon seat when she noticed that one of the ferries had returned. She grabbed the harness, and paying the ferryman his fee, led the wagon team onto the gently pitching ferry. Her eyes locked with Ida's who held tightly to the reins. She looked around again for Zeke and saw him struggling to lead their other mules and the Johnsons' oxen into the river. The older Johnson boys followed behind, whooping and hollering to encourage the animals to cross. As the ferryman pushed off from shore, she called to her brother. He wasn't able to hear her over the braying of the mules and the noise of the dogs.

The two dogs were running circles around the animals, barking and nipping at their heels, causing them to strain against their reins. Several times, Zeke landed in the mud on the bank of the river, pulled off his feet by the fighting animals. Minutes later, she watched in horror as he jumped astride one of the oxen and holding the other team's reins, headed them into the river. "Zeke!" He looked over at her and grinned hugely.

"I'll ride him across, sis!" he yelled back, waving his hat. A few times it looked as if he were going to lose his place on the animal's back, but he managed to hold on and even beat the ferry across the river.

Lizzie's feet slipped on the wet wood of the ferry deck, but she managed to hold on and they were able to safely deposit the little boy back into his crying mother's arms. Zeke had led the teams over to a large oak tree, and Lizzie was pleased to see that this side of the river had plenty of grass for grazing. Aiken had told them they would be camping there until the entire train had crossed over and had had a chance to rest the stock. Zeke unhitched the team and looked up at Ida.

"Who are you?"

"I'm Ida."

"Don't be rude, Zeke," Lizzie told him as she carried out the makings for their supper. "She's going to be riding with us."

"That's good." Zeke eyed her over the back of the mule. "You traveling alone?"

Ida nodded and hurried to help Lizzie. "Yes, sir. My momma and daddy are both gone to be with the Lord."

"Yeah? Ours, too." He waved to the Johnson boys, who were driving their wagons up close to theirs, and then he was gone.

Alice carried over her food to share their fire and looked over at Ida. She didn't speak to the young woman until supper was over, and the women were cleaning up. "I'm Alice. Lizzie told me you use to be a slave." Ida nodded, eyeing her warily. "Don't hold much to that myself. My people never were slave owners." Lizzie smiled as Ida sighed deeply. "You a Christian?"

"Yes, ma'am."

"Just Alice. Did your daddy own your momma?" Alice pulled up a small camping stool and set a basket of mending at her feet. "'Cause I was wondering how your daddy could have freed you, otherwise." Alice picked up a sock to mend. "I don't mean any harm by asking. You don't have to answer if you don't want to."

Lizzie and Ida sat themselves down with their basket of mending between them. Ida studied Alice silently for several minutes before deciding she really wasn't meaning any harm in her questioning. It was just a woman's curiosity.

"He inherited my momma when she was real young." Ida poked a needle through the hole in the sock she was darning. "Fell in love with her. He was quite a few years older than she was. When he found himself sick and dying, he freed us both. Momma died from consumption a few weeks back, and well, here I am." She bit off the extra thread. "Thought maybe I could escape the prejudice of the South by going west where there isn't any slavery. They won't give me any of that free land, 'cause I'm colored, but I figure I can always find me some kind of honest work. Work that isn't based on the color of my skin." She rolled up the darned sock and began another one.

Lizzie had sat quietly during the two women's exchange. She was trying to patch up a rip in one of Abby's dresses. "I'm glad for the company, Ida. I have to admit I was a little frightened about heading west with just the three of us. Abby's so little and Zeke...well, Zeke is Zeke. I'm sorry I told that man you were my servant."

Ida smiled at her. "Don't worry about it. It needed done at the time."

Lizzie nodded. "Well, most of our train knows you've been freed, but I'm sure there may be others who will make a fuss. You tell them what you need to. I'll back you up."

Ida looked up, pleased. "What about your folks? Your brother said they was gone, too."

"My mother and father died three years ago. In a carriage accident. I've managed to work and support us—but barely. My father had dreams of going west. We decided we would try to fulfill that dream for him and make a better life for ourselves." She stood up and stretched her back. "Anyone know how long we'll be camped here?"

Alice looked across the river. "Still a lot of wagons to cross. Heard a child drowned today too, and a woman. They both fell overboard. The woman was pulled under the ferry. Didn't have a chance, poor thing. I'm sure we'll give their families time to grieve before moving on. Ben says the grass is good here, and the stock can fatten up before we head on. He also says it's best to be one of the first trains out so as to have a good grass supply. Go too early, though, and there's snow. Go too late, and there's snow and no grass. Seems like after waiting weeks to cross, we'd be in a hurry." She shrugged her shoulders. "Let the men worry. I don't understand it all anyway." She picked up her mending. "I'll see you two in the morning. Good night."

For several days, Lizzie and others on the wagon train watched as the last of their fellow travelers were ferried across the river. Some people who didn't want to pay the ferry fee, tried rowing or swimming their goods across. Those waiting on the other side watched futilely as these endeavors usually ended in tragedy. Mr. Aiken tried coming by their campsite at least once a day to check on their well being, and Lizzie found herself looking forward to those times.

"Good morning, Lizzie," Aiken greeted, coming up behind her. "That's the last one to cross."

She smiled at him and continued to watch the last wagon being ferried across the river. "I'll be glad to see it done, Mr. Aiken."

"Aiken." He sighed. *Why wouldn't she drop the mister?* "We'll be pulling out day after tomorrow. May fifth. Are you and the children ready?"

She looked up at him. "As ready as we'll ever be, I imagine. It seems like we've been in this place for a long time."

He patted her shoulder. "Not so long, considering." He removed his hand from her shoulder and tipped his hat. "Send Zeke to hunt me up before evening, would ya? Need to fill him in on his turn to guard the stock at night." Lizzie smiled again before turning to Abby.

Abby was looking up at her with shining eyes and a wide smile. "Our adventure starts tomorrow, right, Lizzie?"

Lizzie put her arm around the little girl. "It sure does, Abby. Let's go see if we can't stuff some more of this dry wood in the wagon before starting dinner."

"Why are we gathering all this wood anyway, Lizzie?"

"Do you know what the guidebook says we have to burn if there's no wood available?"

Abby shook her head. "No, what?"

"Buffalo chips."

"Buffalo chips? What are…Oh!" Abby's eyes grew wide. "Are you serious?"

"Yep. I'd rather burn wood."

"Me, too." Lizzie helped her sister into the wagon. "I'll get the wood. You start gathering the makings of dinner."

Chapter 5

They rose early the next morning, ate a cold breakfast, and prepared their team to get in line. Lizzie put on her gloves and climbed up on the seat, Ida next to her and Abby behind them. She smiled brightly at Ida. "I can't believe we're on our way. I've got goose bumps just thinking about it." She started going over their supplies again in her mind to pass the time. Mr. Aiken had said he would come by and let them know their place in line. He was trying to convince the committee to move them closer to the middle of the train.

"Mornin', ladies," Aiken said as he tipped his hat. "Ready?"

"Yes, sir," Ida answered. "As ready as we'll ever be."

"Mr. Aiken, are we lining up now?" Lizzie draped the reins across her lap.

"There you are, Aiken!" Mr. Martin walked briskly towards them, his face red with exertion from his brisk walk. "You are going to put this wagon last in line, right? We haven't wavered in our decision. We don't want a team driven by *women* holding the rest of us up." He hooked his fingers in his suspenders. "And it ain't right that a nigra woman should ride ahead of my wife and son neither."

Aiken's lips tightened. "Mr. Martin, the wagons will all take a turn being last in line."

"Well, now that just ain't going to happen. The committee has already voted—you know that. I volunteered to come on down here and let you know of our decision, and we stand firm." He bobbed up and down on his heels. "You agreed when we hired you that the majority would rule."

Lizzie spoke up before Aiken could reply. "It's all right, Mr. Aiken. We don't mind following last."

"Well, that's settled then." Mr. Martin nodded in the general direction of the women's wagon before heading back to his own.

Aiken removed his hat and slapped it against his thigh. "It's not safe. Not for women and children to be placed last in the line." He turned to Lizzie. "You got a gun with you?"

"Yes, sir," Abby spoke up from where she was seated. "And Zeke has taught Lizzie how to use it, too."

"I couldn't help but overhear, Aiken," Ben said, pulling his wagon up alongside Lizzie's. "The wife and I will take the spot in line right after Lizzie and the young'uns. We'll help keep an eye on them. Between me and my boys they'll be all right."

"Appreciate it, Ben. I'll ride on back whenever I can." He shoved his hat roughly back on his head and stalked off to begin lining up the wagons.

Ben watched him go and whistled softly. "Wouldn't want to see that man mad. No sirree. I've got a feeling he's like a slow burning fire." He grinned back at Alice. "Ready, woman? Let's line up! Yippee!" He snapped the reins and pulled his team back to let Lizzie's wagon pass in front.

Lizzie laughed and held her reins tight. "Let's pray. Lord, we ask for your protection on our adventure. Keep your angels around this wagon train and help us find the easiest trail. Amen."

"Amen," Ida echoed.

Ten miles out of Independence they passed another train heading back. They all stopped their wagons to watch them pass. "Why are they going back?" Abby asked.

"Any number of reasons, I expect." Ida turned around, following the wagons with her eyes. "Better to turn back less than a day out than turn back a month out, right?"

"I guess so."

"I wonder what it could have been. Must have been something terrible to make them turn around," Lizzie wondered aloud. "Everyone seems so excited when they leave. Look, Abby. There's the Mormon graveyard we read about in Pa's guidebook."

"There sure are a lot of them. What do you think they all died of?" Abby watched the graves as the wagon began moving forward.

Lizzie shrugged. "I don't know. The guidebook didn't say."

The train traveled twenty miles that first day, and by the end of it, Lizzie and Ida didn't look much different in appearance. Both were covered with the dust of the trail being kicked up by the wagons in front of them. Lizzie shook off her apron and sneezed with the dirt that flew up. "I hope the whole trip isn't like this. Look at me!" She turned to Ida and began to laugh. "I guess I'm not the only one. Do you think we can use some water to at least wash our faces?"

"When does the guidebook say the next river is?" Ida swiped at the dirt on her own clothing. "If it's not far, I think we could spare some water to wash with. Abby, how did you fare in all this dust?"

"Fine." She poked her head up above the seat. "I kept the canvas closed as much as I could. You two look awful all covered with dirt." She brushed at a spot on her own dress. "I'm glad I wasn't sitting up front with you." She handed out a kettle and spoon. "Let me get some beans out, and I'll start cooking."

"Hey, Lizzie!" Zeke rode up on one of the extra mules. "What a day, huh? Aiken says if we keep going at this pace we'll be crossing the Elkhorn River day after tomorrow." He looked at the two women's faces. "Why don't ya'll wear a bandanna? You won't have to eat as much dust. The other men gave me one, and it works great." He shook his head as if they should have known better.

"Let me see it," Ida ordered. She looked at the triangle of fabric. "We could make us some of these out of scrap fabric." She handed it back to Zeke. "Thanks for the advice."

"Welcome." He hopped down from the mule. "When's dinner?"

"Golly, Zeke." Abby scolded. "We just pulled into the circle. I'm not a miracle worker!"

"Sorry, but most of the others have all ready started eating."

"We're last in line, Zeke." Lizzie told him wiping her face. "We'll be stopping last at night and starting out last in the morning. You'll have to be patient. Go take care of the stock, and we'll be ready when you get back." She peeled off her gloves and grimaced. "Mind if we take turns driving tomorrow, Ida? My poor hands aren't going to make it, gloves or not."

"I told you right off to let me take a turn. I don't plan on being a free ride, Lizzie."

Lizzie was shocked. "Ida! I never meant for you to feel like that. I'm grateful for your help in watching Abby and Zeke."

Ida folded her arms across her chest. "Well, that ain't enough. I want to help you drive." She smiled teasingly. "Besides, we can't have you messing up them pretty white hands."

Lizzie laughed. "The only thing true about them is that they're white. Underneath the dirt anyway." She turned her work worn hands over, noting the new calluses.

"Evening, ladies." Aiken walked up and removed his hat. "How was your first day?" He noticed Lizzie's raw hands. "Didn't you wear your gloves? I've some salve to help that." He reached into his vest pocket and handed her a small tin. "Doesn't smell very nice, but it does the trick."

"They got all dirty. That's how it was," Abby spoke up from where she was stirring the pot of beans. "Lizzie hates to be dirty."

Aiken laughed. "That so? I'm afraid you're going to be dirty most of this trip. Take advantage of the rivers as much as you can to wash up."

"Thank you, Mr. Aiken, I will. Would you like to sit by our fire tonight and share our beans?"

Ida looked at Lizzie in surprise.

Aiken smiled a slow, lazy smile. "I would like that very much, Miss Lizzie."

Zeke had returned by the time the beans were heated through, and the little group ate and talked until dark. Somewhere across the circle, they could hear a fiddle being tuned. The mournful sound drifted across the night air, beckoning everyone to the music. Zeke jumped up.

"Zeke," Lizzie scolded. "Put away your plate before taking off." He stared longingly across the circle before sighing and did as his sister had said.

"Do you dance, Miss Lizzie?" Aiken looked across the fire at her. "Folks tend to take the fun when they can on a wagon train."

"Yes, Mr. Aiken, I do dance." Lizzie answered quietly, not looking up from her plate of beans.

Aiken stood and walked over to her, holding out his hand. "Would you do me the honor of dancing with me?"

She glanced shyly up at him, and then over at Ida. Ida nodded for her to go on. "Abby and I will meet up with you in a few minutes."

Lizzie stood and tried to smooth out the wrinkles in the skirt of her dress. She nodded at Aiken and held out her hand. "I'd be pleased to dance with you, Mr. Aiken." He led her across the wagon circle and placed his arms around her waist as the fiddler began to play a waltz.

"What will it take for you to drop the *mister*?" he asked, looking down at her.

She smiled shyly. "For you to drop the *miss*."

"It's a deal." He swung her around the circle, causing her to laugh out loud in delight. Several of the older women watching from the side, frowned in disapproval. "I'm afraid I've damaged your reputation beyond repair," he told her.

Lizzie laughed again. "I don't care. I love to dance, and I've never seen anything wrong with it. King David danced in the Bible, did you know that?" Aiken's hand felt comfortable resting on her tiny waist and Lizzie looked up to where his large hand engulfed her small one. She smiled and looked up, her heart skipping a beat as she looked into his eyes. He stared down at her, a soft smile tugging at the corner of his mouth.

"Yes, I did." Aiken spun her in the other direction when another young man approached them to cut in.

"That wasn't very nice of you," she said. "He looked like a very nice young man."

Aiken shrugged. "One of the Miller boys. He can have his turn another night. There won't be very many nights that I'm not occupied with some conflict or tragedy."

"Are there many on these trips? Tragedies, I mean?"

"More than I'd like to admit to. A lot of it depends on the folks involved, I guess. Hot tempers and such." The music stopped, and he led her over to a log that had been dragged up to provide seating. "What are the three of you doing out here alone, if you don't mind my asking?"

Lizzie sighed. "Our parents died three years ago. My father wanted to head west. There was nothing to keep us in the East, so we decided to follow his dream."

"You've been asked this question a lot, haven't you? It's a big undertaking, Lizzie."

"I know it is. We've God on our side, though. The Good Book says nothing is impossible with Him."

"Well, now I've always found that to be true." They noticed Ida watching them from a few feet away.

"I thank you for the dance." She held out her hand for him to shake. "It was a wonderful ending to a rather demanding day, but it looks like my chaperone is here to fetch me."

He took her hand, and instead of shaking it, lifted it to his mouth and lightly brushed his lips across it.

"The pleasure was definitely *all* mine." He watched her walk back to her wagon and, picking up his hat from where he had tossed it earlier, walked back to take his turn watching the stock.

"Everything all right, Ida?" Lizzie asked, joining her.

"Yes. I'm just saving your reputation. You know that if you spend too much time with Mr. Aiken you're just giving Mr. Martin, and others like him, fuel to use against you." She handed a scrap of fabric to Lizzie. "I've made us some face rags for tomorrow."

"Thank you." Lizzie looked towards the corral where the extra stock were penned. "I don't care what people like Mr. Martin think, Ida. Mr. Aiken has always been nothing but a gentleman with me. I rather like him, I'm afraid."

"Maybe so, Lizzie, but be careful." Ida climbed up into the wagon. "We're not too far out of Independence for them to send us back."

Chapter 6

Now, why are we stopping?" Lizzie asked, turning to Ida. "Seems to me we just got started today. We'll never reach Laramie by June if we have to keep stopping." Lizzie handed the reins to Ida and leaned over the side of the wagon to yell at Zeke. "Zeke! Run up ahead and see what the hold up is, would you?" She wrapped her shawl tighter around her. "It's cold this morning, isn't it? I'm glad we had the foresight to stock up on wood. There wasn't any to be found this morning."

"I declare, Lizzie," Ida told her, holding the reins loosely in her hand. "You sure are out of sorts this morning."

"I'm sorry, Ida. I don't know what's wrong with me. I woke up cold this morning, and I've been grouchy ever since."

"It'll warm up."

Zeke ran back to them. "Lizzie, there's a narrow bridge up ahead that's owned by Indians. They're demanding a toll."

"A toll? How much?"

Abby's head popped out of the wagon. "Indians! I want to see the Indians, Lizzie. Can I?"

"Not now, Abby. You can see them when we cross the bridge. How much is the toll, Zeke?"

"Seventy-five cents." Zeke reached into his pocket. "I can pay out of my poker money, Lizzie."

Lizzie bit her bottom lip. "Seventy-five cents seems like an awful lot of money. Is there any other way across?"

"No. Mr. Aiken said it's best to just pay the toll. Tomorrow we hit another dangerous river that we'll have to ford. It's called the Elkhorn, and there's no bridge across it. Here's the money, Lizzie. I'll have to pay to cross the extra mules, too."

"Why, Zeke, that's crazy! Just tie them to the back of the wagon, and we'll lead them across. It's only two mules."

47

"I don't know…"

"Just do as I say, Zeke!" she snapped.

Zeke frowned and stormed off to get the mules. They had only moved a few feet by the time he had tied the mules to the back of the wagon. When they finally reached the bridge, Aiken was standing there ready to translate. Next to him were two Indian braves, dressed in buckskin britches and flannel shirts.

Abby was disappointed. "They don't look much like Indians to me." She withdrew back into the wagon.

"Mornin', ladies." Aiken tipped his hat. "Seventy-five cents for the wagon and another seventy-five cents for the mules."

"I'm afraid I won't pay that," Lizzie told him, but looking at the Indians. "They're attached to the wagon, and I'm only paying the toll once."

Aiken raised his eyebrows and translated. "They say seventy-five cents twice, Lizzie. They might think you're trying to rob them."

"That's silly. I wouldn't rob anyone. Anyway, I've said I won't pay that." She crossed her arms firmly across her chest. Ida sat looking from Lizzie, to Aiken, to the Indians, her brow creased with worry.

Aiken translated again, causing the Indians to laugh and talk between themselves. They pointed at Lizzie and guffawed, slapping each other's back. "They admire your stubbornness, it seems. One toll it is." Lizzie smiled and paid the toll, nodding her head at the Indians as they passed.

"I don't know how you stayed so calm, Lizzie," Ida told her, glancing behind them. "I thought for sure they were going to scalp us."

"They didn't look very dangerous to me."

Ida sat back. "Well, they did to me. How did you know that they would compromise?"

"Their toll was robbery and they knew it," Lizzie explained. "I'm going to have a fit if every time we cross a bridge, or a river, we have to pay somebody a toll. Nobody owns any of this out here. Anyway, they looked quite civilized to me. They were just trying to make a quick buck."

They rode into the early evening before stopping again. Lizzie looked around her in despair. It looked like Independence all over again. Everywhere she looked there were wagons waiting to cross the Elkhorn River. The wagons must have counted in the hundreds. "I don't believe it!" She handed the reins to Ida and climbed down. "Look at this. It's ridiculous. Abby, come on down here and help me get supper started." Lizzie stormed around the camp that night like a caged animal, grumbling about yet another delay.

"I'm driving tomorrow, Lizzie, and no arguing. You are as unpleasant to be around as a wet dog." Ida draped the reins loosely over the seat of the wagon. "Must be the strain of sitting on your bottom all day that has you all worked up." She cast a side glance at Lizzie before she climbed down and took the kettle from Abby. "Go on, girl. Fetch us some of them biscuits you made yesterday."

Lizzie stretched her back, and smiled. "You're right. I'm not being very pleasant. My whole body aches, but at least we're not covered with dirt today." She looked around them. "This might be a pretty place if there weren't so many wagons crowded around. But it's cold." She placed her hands on her hips and looked around them. "Ida, there's so many people here there's nowhere to go for any privacy."

Ida stopped what she was doing. "Well, looks like we'll have to be inventive. We'll walk off a ways with some of the other women and form a circle. One person gets in the middle to do her business, and the others stand around her, back facing inward and hold their skirts out--like this." She demonstrated by picking up her skirt and holding it out on both sides of her. "We'll take turns. I saw some women in Independence doing it."

Lizzie laughed. "I guess that'll work. It still doesn't give us much privacy, but at least no one will be able to see us while we do our business."

They were camped along the river bottom with the deep, wide river on one side of them and a huge bluff on the other. Trees lined this and the other side of the river, and wagons all around them were being dismantled and their goods set in piles.

Ben and Alice walked up to them. "We've got to dismantle the wagons and try floating them across," Ben told them. "According to Aiken, we'll be floating the women and children across and coming back for the supplies, if they won't fit on the rafts the first time. So--mark them somehow. Leave behind anything that isn't necessary." He glanced at the small pile of firewood they had put by.

Lizzie followed his glance. "The wood? But what if we can't get any more for a while, Ben?"

"There's other things to burn. Me and the boys will be by to take your wagon apart once we're done with ours. Alice will help you unload." Lizzie watched in dismay as he walked away.

Zeke came running up, his hat in hand. "You should see it, sis! It's sheer pandemonium. They're floating the wagons across like huge rafts and are using long poles to steer them. The poles keep falling in the water, and the wagons start floating down the river, running into each other. Those that don't have wagons are crossing on the backs of their horses, or trying to swim across. One man already drowned."

He stopped to take a breath and looked up at them, his eyes large in his face. "Mr. Aiken told me to come and help you guys and to take control of the mules. He's going to help me swim them across. He said we're going to cross differently than these other people. He's bound and determined to do this in an orderly way. He said he's never seen this much commotion crossing a river. He's studying the river to try and find us a safer way. He said our wagons are going to continue crossing through the night. He wants everyone across by morning."

By the end of the night, they had all their belongings piled next to the river with the wagon bed and canvas covering sitting next to the wheels. Lizzie and the others watched anxiously as Aiken swam his horse across, the end of a rope in one of his hands. Ben stood on this side of the river tying the other end of the rope to a tree. Aiken figured they could pull the wagon beds across using the rope. Ben had offered to go first, after Aiken. Alice and the youngest children were going across with Lizzie. Once Aiken reached the other side, he anchored the rope to a tree and whistled for Ben to start across. Mr.

Martin started arguing about the end of the line crossing first and waved his arms in the air as he paced the river bank.

Ben and his two older sons shoved their wagon bed into the river, and pulling themselves hand over hand on the rope, made it across the river with the wheels and supplies stacked neatly on the wagon bed.

Alice looked at Lizzie and smiled hugely. "He's some kind of man, my Ben." With the help of some of the others, the women shoved Lizzie's wagon into the river, causing the water to splash up and over, soaking Lizzie's precious stockpile of wood. She groaned and removed it from the raft. With Zeke holding tight to the rope, they piled on their other supplies. Alice's sons would bring over her supplies on another raft. Once Lizzie and Ida had grabbed hold of the rope, Zeke jumped off.

"What are you doing, Zeke? Get back on here," Lizzie ordered.

"Can't. I've got to swim the mules across. Aiken's coming back over to help me." Zeke slapped his hat firmly on his head and ran off.

The river was running swiftly, and Alice asked Abby to watch her younger ones while she helped Lizzie and Ida pull them across. Abby grabbed onto the shirt tails of Alice's children and found them a place to sit in the middle of their belongings. The three children sat huddled together. Sarah began whining right away about being wet, and Seth kept trying to stand up and see over the pile of supplies.

Ida yelped in pain as the wagon lurched, and the rope slid through her hands, burning them. "Pull harder!" she yelled. The women strained together, pulling against the fast moving river. The river roared over rocks and was causing the wagon bed to pitch and roll. Several times one of the three women would slip and almost lose her footing. Ida wrapped her skirt around her hands to cushion them. "We should have worn our gloves."

The women heaved in unison to pull the wagon slowly across the river. Alice's youngest child wailed with fear each time the wagon pitched to one side or the other and water splashed over them.

Lizzie and Alice watched with eyes wide as Ida's feet slipped on the wet wood. She flung her arms over the rope as she went into the water. She held on tightly until Lizzie could inch her way over and pull her back onto the raft. Lizzie's own feet threatened to slip several times before they were across, and her nerves were on edge by the time they reached the far bank.

All three of the women had raw hands and were soaking wet by the time the wagon was safely across. Ida's hands were bleeding, and Abby dug into their pile of supplies to find their medicine kit. Within the hour, Zeke and Aiken were across with the mules and had started to reassemble the wagon. "You women did real good," Aiken praised them. "Real good. Once these wagons are put back together, you need to rest. We start again early in the morning." With those encouraging words, he left them standing there, their shoulders slumping with fatigue. They watched as some of the other wagons followed their lead and began crossing, some of them swimming across their own rope so as to cross more than one wagon bed at a time.

The three women plopped to the ground, unmindful of their wet clothes. "I'm too tired to move," Alice told them. "You kids are going to have to come to me if you want something." Seth and Sarah threw themselves down next to her, and Sarah buried her face in her mother's lap.

"I was scared, Mommy," she whimpered.

Alice laughed softly as she smoothed back her daughter's hair. "Now, that was an adventure. One I hope not to repeat anytime soon."

"I'm with you, Miss Alice, but I've a feeling there are a lot more rivers to cross." Ida looked at her hands. "My momma would be horrified to see my hands. They look like a common field hand's."

Lizzie tossed her the salve Aiken had given her. "This works pretty well. It's greasy and doesn't smell good, but it takes the sting away." She lay back on the grass and idly watched as Abby tried putting a simple meal together. "I'm sorry, Abby. I just don't have the energy to help."

"That's all right." Abby put on some coffee. "Just biscuits and bacon tonight. Something fast and easy so you can get to sleep. If you tell me where you keep your food, Miss Alice, I can hurry and cook you up something."

"That's all right, honey. My oldest boy is a fair cook, and I can see from here that he's already burning our bacon." She sniffed. Smells of burning bacon wafted across the air. She got slowly to her feet. "You've helped enough today with staying by these two. You ain't much bigger than them." She reached out a hand to help her daughter up. "Sarah here is a bit spoiled I'm afraid, being the only girl and all."

Lizzie and Ida remained where they lay as Alice walked away with her two children. "That's the gospel's own truth," Ida stated. "That girl is the same age as Abby here and don't do a thing to help. Abby's only eight years old and does the work of a full grown woman." Ida winked at the little girl. "You keep it up, honey, cause your big sister and I are just weak babies compared to you."

"Oh, Ida, you're just teasing me." She handed them each a plate. "All I do is sit in the wagon all day and cook breakfast and supper." She took her own plate and sat next to them.

"That's enough," Lizzie told her. "We wouldn't be eating today if it weren't for you." She took a couple of bites of the bacon and pushed the plate away from her. "I'm too tired to eat. I declare, Ida. I'd better get toughened up fast. I thought working as a house maid was hard work."

Ida laughed. "You ain't seen nothing yet, Lizzie. Wait until you start setting up house."

Lizzie glanced lazily over at her. "How so?"

"There's land to be plowed and tilled for a garden. Meat to be butchered and smoked to eat through the winter, not to mention building a house. And that's all if you don't raise any farm animals." Ida took a bite of her biscuit and shook her head. "Yep. This is nothing compared to what's waiting for you."

"How do you know all this?"

"I told you my daddy was poor. He did everything himself. Him and my momma. I learned, cause I had to." She brushed the crumbs off her skirt. "Good night, Miss Lizzie. I'm turning in."

Lizzie nodded and lay back against the wagon wheel. Far off, she could hear the lonely sound of a cowboy on duty, singing softly to the stock. Crickets and bullfrogs joined in the serenade from the riverbank. The stars twinkled brightly from the evening sky and, off by the stock, Lizzie saw Aiken ride by. She yawned and got to her feet, ready to go to bed.

She smiled and thought of what Ida had told her. Yes, it would be hard setting up a home in Oregon, but at least it would be *their* home.

Chapter 7

Lizzie woke the next morning to the smell of coffee brewing. She lay still under the pile of quilts she was burrowed in and breathed deeply. She stuck her hand out of the covers and quickly pulled it back in. *It's freezing,* she thought. Swiftly, she tossed the blankets aside, pulled on her dress, and grabbed her shawl. She looked over to see Abby still sleeping and Ida's spot vacant.

"I thought I heard someone stirring around in here," Ida said, looking in the wagon. "Coffee's ready."

"It's freezing."

"I heard someone say earlier that we were down in the thirties. Someone thought to bring a thermometer. There's ice crust on the ground, too." Ida stood aside as Lizzie stepped down. "There wasn't much wood to be found this morning, but the grazing is all right, according to Zeke. Sure wish we hadn't had to leave that wood behind."

Lizzie looked around her at the camp that was just beginning to stir. She was always amazed at how muted the occupants of thirty wagons could sound in the cold morning air. Men murmured to the stock while women coaxed children from their warm beds and set around to getting breakfast. She saw Zeke over in the direction of the Johnsons' wagon. She waved good morning to him and sipped her coffee.

Ida handed her a bowl of corn mush with pieces of bacon and a drizzle of honey. "Eat. We leave in an hour."

"Yum! Where did you get the honey?"

"I did some mending for a woman who brought along a couple of bee hives to restart her colony when we get West. I don't sleep much, so I've been helping others in the mornings before you lazy people are up."

"This is heavenly."

"What's heavenly?" Abby asked, between yawns. The little girl was bundled up with her extra shawl around her head and had wrapped a thick blanket around her shoulders. Before Abby was finished, the whistle blew for them to load up and pull out. Ida pulled on her gloves and tossed Lizzie's pair over to her. Ida winked and climbed into the driver's seat before Lizzie could.

They spent the next few days in routine. Eating dust during the day and crashing exhausted and shivering into bed each night. Lizzie despaired of ever getting used to the physical hardness of the trail, or the monotony of each day. The train had been following the Platte River on the north side for the last few days. While the two women took turns driving, they watched the islands and sand bars near the river's edge. Firewood was still scarce, but grazing was good. On the fourth day, they stopped to cross another small river that Lizzie couldn't recall the name of, and then traveled on until nightfall.

By the time the wagons had pulled into their customary evening circle, the winds had picked up drastically. Ida crawled into the back of the wagon and rooted around until she emerged with their face rags, as she called them. She tied hers around the lower half of her face and crawled back out into the blowing dust.

Zeke had come over to help Lizzie who was struggling to undo the harnesses from the mules in the stinging wind. The mules balked, brayed, and pulled against her. She accepted the face rag from Ida gratefully. Abby huddled miserably in the back of the wagon, complaining that the dirt hurt her when she came outside the wagon. Finally, the mules were unhitched, and Zeke walked against the howling wind, back to their makeshift corral.

"Don't see how we can cook in this wind!" Ida yelled. Lizzie nodded and cringed as thunder boomed over their heads. The canvas on the wagon whipped and crackled behind them.

"Where *is* this wind coming from?" Lizzie struggled against it until the two of them gave up and joined Abby in the back of the wagon. They fed on hard biscuits and jerky for dinner that night, and Zeke stayed at the corral. He was kept busy with the animals who were also complaining against the strong wind and stinging particles of dirt.

It rained during the night, settling the dust, and the train set off early. Ida again took the reins that morning while Lizzie sat beside her mending their dresses, which were already beginning to show signs of wear. Abby ran alongside the wagons with Sarah Johnson, enjoying the cool day.

Traveling was slower because of the rain, and several of the heavier wagons kept getting bogged down in the now mushy trail. Lizzie got out to stretch her legs and waded through a muddy creek they were crossing, her feet making squishing sounds each time she lifted them from the bottom of the creek bed.

Wildflowers grew along the banks of the creek and she mentally checked off the names of the ones she knew. She heard Ida click her tongue at the mules who were beginning to falter and thanked God for the company of the young woman. Ida had told her the night before that she had just turned sixteen and her beau was meeting her out West where there was no slavery. Lizzie smiled at the romance of it and quickened her pace.

The air began getting heavy and muggy towards nightfall, and she lifted her hair from her neck, allowing the breeze to cool her. She had let her sunbonnet hang loose down her back earlier.

"Looks like a storm tonight, Lizzie." Aiken said, coming up behind her.

She looked up at the sky. "You think so? The winds are picking up, but there aren't very many clouds."

He reached over and ran his fingers through her hair. "You're hair looks like spun gold." He frowned as he realized the impropriety of what he just did and let it fall back into place. "I'm sure of the storm. It's going to be a hell-raiser. You women might want to have an early dinner."

"This is the strangest weather I've ever seen. It's cold in the mornings, hot during the day, and stormy at night." Lizzie twisted her hair up behind her and secured it again beneath her bonnet.

Aiken frowned as she hid her hair. "I'm taking Zeke off guard duty tonight. He'll be needed in your camp, just in case," he added, as she looked questioningly at him. "Storms out here can be brutal.

You might need an extra pair of hands. I'll see you in the morning." He tipped his hat at her and strode off to warn others of the coming storm.

Aiken's prediction rang true several hours later. Before the wagons were bedded down for the night, the winds had again begun to howl, and several minutes after that, the hail started. Lizzie sent Abby to the shelter of the wagon while Zeke ran off to calm the animals, and she and Ida hurried to put away the cooking stove and pots. Lizzie's arms were marked with red dots where the hail hit her exposed skin.

"I declare!" Ida yelped, as she narrowly missed being hit by a tumbleweed that threatened to knock her down.

Lightning flashed over their heads repeatedly and thunder boomed, causing Lizzie to jump and then slip on the hail that covered the ground. She landed heavily on her backside. She sat there stunned for a minute and then watched in horror as the strong wind caught the canvas of their wagon and rolled it over.

"Abby!" Lizzie fought desperately to get her feet underneath her and, failing because of the hail, began to crawl frantically towards the overturned wagon. "Zeke, help us!" Ida had already reached the wagon and was tossing things out the back in her fury to find the little girl. By the time Lizzie and Zeke reached them, she had pulled Abby out and was checking her over for injuries. Abby's face was streaked with tears.

Lizzie took her sister in her arms and hugged her fiercely to her chest. Abby had a few scratches on her face and a long rip in the sleeve of her dress but otherwise appeared unharmed.

"Everyone all right?" Aiken asked, running over. He took in the frightened women and the overturned wagon. The winds had settled some. They were still strong, but no longer dangerous, and he sent Zeke to find some strong men to help them. "You women unload this wagon, and we'll get her set back to rights." He laughed. "I never thought I'd see a woman's wagon that was light enough to tip over in the wind. Usually they're the ones having to leave things behind because they've got too much."

"It's not funny, William!" Lizzie let go of Abby and turned to face him, her blue eyes blazing. "Abby was in that wagon when it turned over. She could have been killed!" She broke down and began to cry, covering her face with her hands.

Aiken took her in his arms and laid his chin on top of her head. "She's all right, Lizzie. I'm sorry I laughed." He was still chuckling softly.

"You're still laughing," she told him, her voice muffled. By then, Ida and Abby were smiling, too. Lizzie lifted her head and joined in. "I'm sorry. I was just so frightened, and I tend to get mouthy when I'm scared."

Aiken kissed her forehead tenderly, startling her with his boldness. He placed a hand tenderly to her cheek and turned to gather together some men to help them right the wagon.

Lizzie watched him go, surprised at how safe and comforted she had felt with his arms around her. She saw Ida watching her, a smile on the other young woman's face and Lizzie smiled back.

Aiken soon arrived back at their wagon with the required help and the women quickly began to unload the wagon. With some pulling of ropes on one side and other men lifting the down side, using their combined strength, they were able to upright the wagon.

Twenty miles into the next day, they stopped to camp again. Another storm came suddenly upon them. This one worse than the night before. Instead of hail, the rain poured down in torrents, quickly leaving the ground around them ankle deep in mud.

Lizzie wouldn't let Abby, or any of them, in the wagon, so they huddled underneath it to try and stay dry. Within minutes they were soaked and shivering. The lightning cracked continuously, lighting up the sky, and Zeke crawled from underneath the wagon to go check on the animals. Lizzie jumped, and Ida screamed as lightning crashed down near them.

"Is that thunder?" Ida asked, peering out into the rain. "It's getting closer." Lizzie shrugged and pulled Abby tighter to her, trying to warm the little girl with her body. Ida crawled farther out into the rain and screamed. She dove back under the wagon as oxen and mules stampeded past them. "The stock is loose," she called above the noise. "It's a stampede!"

Abby buried her face in Lizzie's neck. Lizzie peered out through the downpour, searching frantically for a sign of Zeke. The wind and rain continued through the night with the three females huddled together in fear under their wagon. Aiken found them that way in the morning.

Lizzie sighed in relief and jumped up to greet him. "Have you seen, Zeke? He went out last night to check the mules and I haven't seen him since. Then the animals stampeded. William, I'm worried about him. What if he got trampled?"

"He's all right. He's a smart boy. He climbed a tree to avoid the stampede, and he's out right now with the other men trying to round up the stock. Lightning struck a tree close by the corral and frightened the stock." He glanced under the wagon to where Ida and Abby were, arms wrapped around each other, fast asleep. They sat in several inches of mud and water. "Did you stay under there all night?" He looked down at Lizzie, surprise across his face. "You stayed under there in the water and mud and cold?"

She set her face firmly and looked up at him. "I wasn't taking any more chances of the wagon tipping over with someone inside." She dared Aiken to laugh at her, hands on her hips. "I'd rather we were wet and cold—than dead."

He tried stifling his smile by biting his lip. "I guess I can see the sense in that." Aiken looked down at her covered with mud, her bonnet and hair hanging limp and wet around her face, and lost the battle. His shoulders shook silently at first, and then the laughter burst out of him, startling Ida and Abby awake. He held up a hand in apology and shook his head. He bent over, hands on his knees and continued to laugh, tears running down his tanned face.

"Go ahead and laugh, you big buffoon!" Lizzie whipped her wet skirts around her and stormed off through the ankle deep water to the wagon to change into clean, dry clothes. Aiken straightened up and wiped his eyes. He was still laughing as he watched her climb awkwardly into the wagon, her wet skirt weighing her down. He looked over at the shocked Ida and Abby sitting together in the mud and water under the wagon, and laughed harder. They continued to watch him as he walked on to the next wagon, his laughter now turning into snorts as he tried to stifle it.

The women and children spent the rest of the day waiting on the men to return with the scattered stock. Alice and her two youngest visited the Springer camp, and the women passed the time in mending and cooking. Wet clothing lay draped over every available bush and hung from nails in the wagon.

Alice sat there quietly, an undarned sock in her lap. "I've got news, gals." She took a deep breath and looked over to where the children were playing. "I'm having another baby."

"Why, Alice, that's wonderful." Lizzie set her own mending aside. "How exciting!"

"Not much to be excited about. It'll make number five. I'm a few months along now and I reckon this here baby will be born on the trail." She smoothed down her skirt. "I've been hiding it. Didn't want it to interfere with Ben's plans. I didn't want to hold him back, and I was afraid no train would let us sign on if they knew I was carrying." A tear slid down her cheek. "I reckon this baby will come around the middle of August. Ben got suspicious this morning, so I had to tell him. The swaying of the wagon has been making me sick since we started out."

"How did Ben take it?" Lizzie asked.

"Oh, pleased as punch, that man. Wouldn't bother him if we had ten kids." Alice picked up her darning. "Of course, he ain't the one doing the carrying—or the birthing."

"We'll help you, Miss Alice," Ida spoke up. "I've helped deliver lots of babies with my momma. Won't be nothing to it with this being your fifth."

"Lizzie," Zeke ran up, hat in hand. "Look over there. See the Indians? Aiken said they were Pawnee!" Zeke squatted down next to the women. "This is Sioux territory, but Aiken said they were Pawnee," he repeated in his excitement. "Pawnee, Lizzie!"

"They won't be coming over here, will they?" Ida sat up,

frightened. "I've heard the most awful stories of Indians."

"Nah. Aiken said they was peaceful, and as long as we leave them alone, they'll pass us on by."

They watched as off in the distance twenty mounted braves rode by at a slow gallop. They raised their lances in greeting, and otherwise it seemed as if the train didn't exist. The women breathed a sigh of relief when the Indians rode out of sight.

"I do hope that's all the interaction we have with savages," Alice said, rising. "I'd best get on back to my own camp and get supper started. Those boys of mine are always hungry."

The train set off again early the next morning and stopped at a creek named Dry Creek. The creek was dry most of the year, but this morning, because of the heavy rain the day before, it was swelling its banks. Aikin gave the order for everyone to camp until the creek went down. Two days later, they set off again and waited on the banks of yet another creek.

There was plenty of wood lying around this second creek, and while no one was looking, Lizzie piled some in the back of their wagon. She climbed out of the back of the wagon after depositing her final load and, turning around, bumped smack into a darkly tanned, naked chest. Her eyes followed the chest up into the painted face of an Indian. Quickly, she glanced around to see where Abby was and seeing her over by the Johnson's wagon, turned back to the stranger.

The Indian stood impassively for several seconds, staring. Lizzie swallowed hard and continued to return his stare, her hands hidden in her skirt pocket where she had stashed a small knife after they had seen the Indians a few days before. The brave reached out a hand and took hold of Lizzie's hair which had begun to fall free of her bonnet.

She whipped her hand from her pocket, knife in hand, and stepped back until she was against the wagon. "Don't come any closer," she warned. "I'll cut you!" The Indian looked down at the knife. His eyes hardened for a second as he looked from the knife to her. Lizzie stabbed at the air between them and was shocked to see the Indian begin to laugh. He reached up to touch her hair again.

"I see you've met Red Feather," Aiken said, coming from around the wagon. "He's harmless enough, Lizzie. You can put the knife away. I know him, Lizzie. He won't hurt you."

Lizzie was visibly relieved to see Aiken. "What does he want?"

Aiken said something in the man's native tongue and listened calmly to his reply. "He wants some of your hair. He said it shines like the sun." Aiken turned his attention back to Lizzie. "I have to agree with him."

"My hair!" Lizzie raised her hand to her head in shock.

"He's willing to trade for it." By this time, the three had been joined by Zeke, Abby, Ida, the Johnsons, and several other families. "The rest of his party is waiting right out there. They're waiting to see if we're willing to trade."

"My hair?" Lizzie looked over to where her brother and sister stood, both watching with wide eyes. She thought for a moment. "All right. I'll trade my hair for moccasins for Zeke and Abby."

"That all?" Aiken asked her. "He'll consider your hair worth more than that."

Lizzie took another minute to reconsider. "I'll take a pair for myself and Ida, too. Also, Abby has some ribbons she wants to trade. What else does he have to trade with?"

Aiken translated and the brave's face lit up with pleasure. He spoke rapidly and took off to where the rest of his party was waiting. Within minutes, five braves and two squaws had returned with blankets, trinkets, and wild honey. Lizzie took her small knife and, grasping her long hair which fell to her mid back, cut it off at her shoulders. She handed it to Red Feather with a smile. He in return, handed her the moccasins and a large gourd of honey. He held her hair above his head and whooped, causing Lizzie and the other women to jump and shrink back. Red Feather whooped again and ran for his horse, waving her hair around his head.

Without the weight of its length, Lizzie's hair curled. She fluffed it up with her hands and smiled with pleasure. It was so much cooler! She left her bonnet hanging around her shoulders.

"You didn't need to give him so much of it," Aiken told her, coming up behind her.

"I know. It's really freeing though," she said, giving her head a toss. She looked up at him, saucily. "Do you like it?"

He grinned. "Makes you look sassy with it all curled up around your face." He slapped his hat tighter on his head and turned. He was still grinning as he walked away, leaving Lizzie staring after him.

Chapter 8

Lizzie stared down at her feet the next morning which were comfortably encased in her new moccasins. They rose mid-calf and were hand sewn with tan leather. Intricate bead work decorated the sides and was stitched across the top of each foot. She stretched her legs out in front of her, and smiled. "These are amazingly comfortable, Ida. I can't imagine ever putting on another pair of shoes."

Ida wiggled her toes in her own pair. "My momma would faint right over if she could see me." She giggled. "But then she'd probably want to try them on herself."

"What day is it?"

"Well…I think it's Sunday."

"I thought so." Lizzie stood up. "I'm going to speak to Aiken about taking the day off. I miss church and seeing as it's Sunday, we should at least have a Bible reading. Don't you think? I don't want Abby and Zeke to let go too much of their faith out here."

Lizzie strode toward the other side of the wagon circle and searched for Aiken. He was standing with a group of men from the wagon train committee and he seemed to be in a heated argument with one of them. Lizzie stood uncertainly on the outskirts of their gathering.

Aiken noticed her standing there and excused himself. "Lizzie, is everything all right?"

"I can talk to you later. It looks like a bad time."

"No. It's fine. What's on your mind?"

She glanced around him at the group of men, and lowered her voice. "I was wondering if it would be possible to take Sundays off of traveling as a day of rest and Bible reading. There's not a preacher joined up with us, is there?"

"Afraid not." Aiken took her by the arm and led her over to the committee. "It's funny that you should walk up right now. We're discussing that very thing." Lizzie glanced up at him, confused.

"Gentlemen, this little lady would also like a day of rest and a time of Bible study."

Mr. Martin, the gentleman who had argued about having Lizzie along in the first place, stepped forward. "Well, sure she does, Aiken. All the women want a day of rest and catching up time so they can sit around and gossip. But the committee has voted to keep moving. We can't give in to the fanciful notions of a bunch of women."

"It would be easier on the children also, Mr. Martin," Lizzie spoke up. "The Lord has said that man needs a day of rest."

"Don't argue the good book with me, Miss Springer." Martin turned his back on her and started to walk away. "The world is run by men and should stay that way. That's the way the good Lord intended. If Aiken here wasn't spending so much time sniffing around your skirts, we wouldn't be having a problem."

Aiken swiftly stepped forward and, grabbing Martin's shoulder, spun him around. The forceful movement caused Martin to lose his footing and sit down hard in the dirt. "I will not have you insulting Miss Springer, Martin," he warned, his eyes flashing. He stared down at the astonished man, his fists clenched at his sides. "You mind your manners, or I'll mind them for you. I was hired to get this train through, and that's what I'll do. And I'll get it through on time. I give you my word." He nodded at Lizzie. "You'll have your day of rest, Lizzie. But mind you, if we hit obstacles that hold us back, we may have to continue traveling on Sundays in the future. At least some of them." He stared down at Martin, who remained seated on the ground, glaring up at Aiken and Lizzie.

Lizzie shot him a brilliant smile of gratitude. "You're welcome to join us, William, if you've a mind to. You too, Mr. Martin. I'll be reading from the book of Genesis in about thirty minutes." She nodded at the other gentlemen standing around and turning, walked back to her own wagon.

Martin stood up slowly and brushed the dirt from the seat of his pants. "You'll regret this, Aiken. Mark my words. Nothing good can come of us stopping. We can be overcome by Indians, disease, and the other trains will pass us up and beat us to the best grazing." He looked over at the rest of the men from the committee. "Don't force us to vote to hire another train master when we reach Fort Laramie." He glanced smugly around the group of men. "Right, gentlemen?" His scowl deepened as they drew away from him.

"My wife is pretty keen on stopping on Sundays too, Martin," one of them spoke up. "I'm not willing to fight with her over this. I've got no complaints about the job Aiken here has done for us."

Martin looked around the group. "Spence? Walter?" They shook their heads. "Fine. Suit yourselves. But mark my words. This train is asking for trouble." Martin picked his hat up from the dirt and slapped it against his thigh to rid it of dirt. "Giving in to the fancies of a bunch of women." He slapped his hat against his leg once more for emphasis and stalked away muttering, "I'm the head of my wagon, by God! I wouldn't dream of letting my wife rule the roost!"

Aiken watched him go, a frown creasing his forehead. "That man is trouble. Thank you, gentlemen, for standing by me. I think you made the right decision. Now, I think I'll go listen to a pretty girl read from the Good Book."

Lizzie sent Ida to fetch the children and was seated by the fire, Bible in hand, when they returned. "I think we'll start in the book of Genesis," she told them. "I think it's fitting since we all have a new beginning before us." She looked up with pleasure when Aiken approached them.

"Mind if I join you?" he asked, removing his hat.

"Are you a religious man, Mr. Aiken?" Ida asked in surprise.

"Well, no ma'am, I reckon I'm not. But I do enjoy a relationship with my Savior. Will that do?"

Lizzie smiled, and nodded for him to join them. "That'll do just fine." As she read, more people began to join them, and by the time she had read a few chapters into the book of Genesis, there were more than five families joined in to listen to her Bible reading. She closed the book and looked around at all their faces. "We'll do this each Sunday, right after the morning meal," she told them and then closed in prayer.

They all spent the rest of that Sunday catching up on each other's family news. One of the men, who had attended the reading, pulled out a harmonica and led the group in a small selection of hymns. Lizzie retired that night with her spirit renewed and a fresh outlook for the week ahead.

Ida took the first shift of driving the next day, so Lizzie took it as an opportunity to walk beside the wagon a bit. The morning was cool, so she left her bonnet dangling down her back. The two dogs bounded up, tongues hanging out, and trotted beside her to keep her company.

"Where have you two been? Haven't seen you for a few days. Abby will be so pleased that you're back." She bent down and gave them each a quick pat. "I thought you might've decided to stay back in civilization." Zeke rode past on one of the mules and excitedly called the dogs' names. He rode off with the dogs barking behind him.

"Morning, Lizzie." Aiken rode up beside her and slid off his horse. "Mind if I walk with you?"

She shook her head. "It's a beautiful day, William." She looked off toward where the Platte River flowed past. It was a ways away, but she could see a short line of wagons camped. They seemed to be headed back the way they had come.

"They're going back," she noted in surprise. "Why? That's the second train we've seen heading back since we started."

Aiken shrugged. "Sometimes things happen that cause a few wagons to turn around. It's usually death, or maybe they lost their guide."

"Couldn't they hook up with us?"

"They know we're here. If they want to hook up, they'll send someone over."

Lizzie watched silently for a few moments. "Thank you for standing up to Mr. Martin yesterday. I think the day helped everyone, don't you?"

He nodded. "I know it helped me." He draped his horse's reins over one shoulder and reached over to take her hand. He turned it over, noting the calluses. He lifted her hand and gently kissed the palm, causing Lizzie to blush. "You using the salve?" She nodded. They realized they were falling behind the train, and quickened their pace. "You want to ride?"

"What?"

"My horse. You want to ride him?"

"I don't know how."

"We'll ride double. I'll have you back in plenty of time to give Ida a break."

Lizzie smiled and nodded. Aiken helped her mount the horse and swung himself up behind her. Lizzie sat perched sideways with Aiken's arms on each side of her. He clicked to the horses, and they set off in the direction of the river.

Lizzie waved over her shoulder to Ida and settled back, watching the scenery pass by them. It was early enough in the spring that the grass was tall and green, waving gently in the breeze. It looked to Lizzie like an ocean of sparkling green. A sea of grass and wildflowers rippled across the plains between them and the river. The river sparkled off in the distance with blue rays bouncing off it. Across the river, a purple mountain range framed the horizon. Trees grew along the river's bank. The small train of wagons they had spotted earlier had camped on the shore, and Aiken turned to avoid them.

They rode in a comfortable, slow walk for about half an hour, making small talk, before Aiken spurred his horse into a gallop. Lizzie shrieked as she shrank back against his chest. Aiken's left arm tightened around her waist. Her fear was short lived, and Lizzie soon found herself laughing aloud. Her bonnet was blown from her head, and her hair blew around her face, whipping back into the face of the man seated close behind her. He smiled at her joy and urged the horse faster before turning back in the direction of Lizzie's wagon.

"This is glorious!" she closed her eyes, holding her arms straight out on each side of her. "I feel like I'm flying."

All too soon they were back, and he helped her down with one hand. He tipped his hat to Ida. "Thanks for letting me steal her away from you for a while." He smiled down at Lizzie, and kicking his heels into the horse's flanks, galloped off towards the front of the train. Lizzie helped herself onto the wagon seat and reached for her gloves, her smile still on her face.

"I'm thinking that man's smitten with you," Ida said smugly.

"He's a very nice man," Lizzie replied, pulling on her gloves. "I'm sure he treats all the girls the same."

"And I think *you're* smitten with him." Ida laughed and handed the reins over to her. "Oh, yes. I think you're smitten indeed." She jumped from the wagon and began walking to stretch her own legs.

Lizzie joined in with her laughter and told herself that Ida was correct. *I am definitely smitten.* She drove the wagon the rest of the day, dwelling on the way she had felt sitting before Aiken on his horse and how good it had felt to rest back against his hard chest.

She looked over at Ida who walked alongside the wagon and gave thanks to God for her. Having Ida along as chaperone allowed Lizzie to have the freedom to spend time with Aiken without raising too many eyebrows. She caught Ida's eye and smiled.

Chapter 9

The wagons pulled up next to the Platte River the following day around noon, and Aiken called a halt to enable the women to catch up on their washing and cooking. Abby and the two dogs ran in circles around the wagon, screaming and barking. When they knocked over a rack of freshly laundered clothes, Lizzie lost her temper. "Abby! Take those dogs somewhere else to play. Now I've got to wash these clothes all over again."

"Sorry!" Abby called to the dogs to follow her, and ran off closer to the water's edge. She began to amuse herself by skipping stones, and Lizzie noted that she was soon joined by Sarah and Seth Johnson. Lizzie gathered up the now muddy clothes, and walked upriver away from the children.

"Good morning, Miss." Lizzy looked up to see the gambling man she had met on the train to Missouri. He tipped his hat to her. "I do believe we've already met. Where's that feisty young brother of yours?"

"Mr. Newton." Lizzie nodded politely to him and turned back to her wash.

"Now, that's not a very warm welcome, Miss Lizzie." He sat down and leaned against a fallen log. "Not friendly at all."

"I wasn't aware that you were with our train, sir." Lizzie continued to scrub the clothes on the old washboard she had brought.

"I'm not. I usually travel alone." He lit up a cigar. "But I sometimes ride short distances with the wagon trains. I have to admit that with the pleasant surprise of finding you here, I might have to travel with you folks a little longer."

Lizzie tossed the last washed shirt into the tub. She straightened, and lifting the tub, propped it against her hip. "Now, why would you do that?" she asked, coldly. She started walking back to her wagon when Edward Newton took a hold of her arm causing her to drop the

71

wash tub. She sighed deeply as she saw the wash tumble once again into the dirt. She turned to face him. "Mr. Newton, I'm really not interested in your advances. You'd be wasting your time." She stared up into his sharp angled face. Dark brown eyes were shaded by the brim of a black hat. A thin moustache adorned the man's lips which were drawn back into a grin.

"It's *my* time," he grinned sardonically. "I could take you away from all this, Lizzie." He waved his arm towards the wagons. "I happen to be a man of rather comfortable means. A beautiful girl like you shouldn't be scrubbing clothes over a washboard." He reached up to finger her hair. "Pity you cut your hair, but it'll grow back." He took her hands in his, and frowned. "Your hands look like a scullery maid's."

She yanked her hands back and looked helplessly at the wagons which were several yards away. "I'm perfectly content where I am, thank you." She bent to retrieve her fallen wash. Newton once again took a hold of her and pulled her close to him, trying to steal a kiss. She placed her hands against the purple brocade vest he wore and pushed back.

"Step away from her, Newton, if you know what's good for you." Aiken stepped from around a tree, his pistol drawn. "Is he bothering you, Lizzie?"

"Yes, William, he is." Lizzie stepped back and went to stand by Aiken who placed his arm around her shoulder.

Newton smiled coldly, and held up his hands. "I see how it is, Aiken. It seems to me as if you've already won the prize."

Aiken leaned against the tree, crossing his legs at the ankles. "I wasn't aware we were in competition, Newton."

He winked at Lizzie, and tipping his hat, walked back to where he had tethered his horse. "I'm sure we'll meet again, young lady. You let me know when you get tired of slumming with cowboys and want the pleasure of a gentleman's company."

Lizzie felt Aiken's body tense up next to her. She placed up a hand to hold him in check. "He's not worth it, William." She stepped away and retrieved her laundry. Luckily, only one shirt had landed in the dirt this time, and with Aiken watching, she washed it and walked back to her wagon with Aiken keeping her company.

"How do you know him, Lizzie? I can't imagine that the two of you traveled in the same circles."

"We didn't. He tried sitting with us on the train." She laughed as she remembered. "Zeke ran him off that time."

"Good for Zeke." Aiken took the tub of laundry from her. "Don't go off alone anymore, Lizzie. We're in Indian Territory now, and with them, snakes, and lowlifes like Newton, it's not safe. Not even for your *necessary* time. Understand? You take a group with you—always." Lizzie blushed, embarrassed at how casually he talked about private things, and nodded. Aiken handed her back the laundry, and giving her a quick kiss on the cheek, strolled off to walk the line of wagons.

Lizzie watched him go, and remembering his warnings of Indians, glanced quickly around to locate her sister. She could see Zeke off with the rest of the men who were leading the pack animals in pairs to the river to drink, but it took her several minutes to locate Abby. She finally found her eating by the Johnsons' wagon. Abby waved when she saw Lizzie looking, and Lizzie hung the clothes to dry, using an extra rope she had brought along and had had Zeke extend from the wagon to a tree.

She placed her hands on each of her sides and leaned back, smiling in satisfaction as her back popped. She groaned and moved the tub over beneath the wagon. Wood was plentiful in this area, and she had to restrain herself from hoarding more of it. That silly guidebook of her father's had her in fear of not being able to find wood to cook their supper with. It mentioned several times how folks had had to use buffalo chips to cook with. She was absolutely certain she would never resort to that!

She realized that she hadn't seen Ida all morning and strolled around the camp looking for her. She found her several wagons over talking to a huge black man that Lizzie had never seen before. He was wearing patched overalls, and no shirt. His ebony skin glistened with sweat. He wore a pair of tattered boots on his feet, the toes showing through on one of them. Ida saw her watching and waved her over. "This here is Luke, Lizzie." Lizzie smiled and nodded. The man stared at the ground. "She's all right, Luke. You're safe with her. She's good people." The man looked up timidly, and Lizzie extended her hand.

"I'm pleased to meet you, Luke." She frowned over at Ida when Luke just stared at the hand she had offered him.

Ida took Lizzie by the arm and pulled her roughly behind the wagon. "He's gone and escaped from that wagon train we saw yesterday. He's a trained blacksmith, Lizzie. We can't send him back. I'll tell everyone that asks that he has met up with me. That he was following us."

"*Was* he following you, Ida?"

Ida didn't answer for a moment, then she nodded, her eyes wide in her face. "He's been following us, Lizzie. Waiting to catch up. He's my sweetheart."

Lizzie peered over Ida's shoulder to where Luke stood silently. "I don't know, Ida. Can we get in trouble over this?"

"This is Indian Territory. It's free land, Lizzie. At least I think it is anyway." Ida gripped her arm tighter. "You can't say anything. Promise me, Lizzie! You won't tell anyone?"

"All right, Ida. I can keep a secret, but what if William catches on? I know he was willing to let you come along, but what if the rest of the train makes a fuss? He'll have to do what they vote and I know that Mr. Martin won't take to having a runaway slave travel with us."

"They won't make him leave, Lizzie. We don't have another blacksmith. Look how strong he is. He'll come in handy and no one has to know he's a runaway. I'm freed. They'll think he is, too."

"Who's he going to travel with?" Lizzie took notice of the determined look on Ida's face. "Oh, no, Ida. He can't ride with us. It wouldn't be proper, and you know it."

"Not any more improper than you riding off alone with Mr. Aiken." Ida set her small jaw. "He'll sleep with Zeke." Ida nodded her head firmly and let go of Lizzie's arm. "Zeke always stays out by the smelly stock anyway. Luke will just eat with us." Lizzie looked over at the big man again. He was still, but the way his eyes kept darting in their direction, she knew he could hear them.

"Fine." Lizzie strode back over to where Luke stood. "You are welcome to share our fire, Luke, but you'll have to sleep out by the stock. No offense, but you can't sleep anywhere near the wagon or Ida."

Luke looked up and smiled timidly. "Yes'm. That's right fine with me."

"Call me Lizzie. I'm not your mistress, nor do I want to be. Just please, don't let me get into trouble over this." She shot Ida a look of warning. A splatter of rain fell on her head. "I can't believe this. My laundry!" She gathered up her skirts and sprinted for the hanging laundry. Ida smiled at Luke before running to help her.

The rain continued on into the evening, and as there was no wind, Ida and the two sisters sat in the back of the wagon. Lizzie worked on the quilt pieces of her mother's she had brought while Ida mended, and Abby practiced writing her letters. "I don't know why I have to do this all the way out here," Abby complained. "There's no books for thousands of miles."

Lizzie bit off the end of her thread. "You don't want to grow up stupid, do you?"

"No, but why can't I wait until we get to our new place and then study?"

"Because it's raining, and there's nothing else for you to do. This is a perfect time."

Abby pouted and turned back to her writing. "I hate rain."

Just about then, Zeke poked his head into the wagon. "What are ya'll doing?"

Lizzie smiled and motioned for him to come in. She handed him their father's Bible. "Here. Read."

"What?" He looked at her in astonishment.

"Read. We can't let your schooling totally stop until we reach Oregon, now can we?" Lizzie patted his shoulder and moved over so he could squeeze in.

"Where's Luke?" Ida wanted to know.

75

"I left him to watch the mules," Zeke muttered. "I should've stayed with him."

He set the Bible down on his legs. "If you want me to read, Lizzie, can't I at least read Pa's guidebook? That'll help us out here, at least."

"The Bible will help you anywhere."

"I know, but can't I please read the guidebook?"

Lizzie smiled and handed it to him. "Read about this river we're following."

Zeke scanned the pages. "Well...the Platte River runs all the way into Wyoming Territory, and in some places you can't hardly see across it cause it's so wide. There's lots of little streams and stuff that run into it." He flipped through some more pages. "Fort Laramie's less than two weeks travel from where we are."

"I sure hope we stop for a few days when we get there," Lizzie added.

"What for?" Zeke looked up from his book. "The more we travel, the quicker we get to Oregon."

"I want to take a hot bath."

"A bath! Women want the silliest things." He turned back to the book. "I'm going to climb up Chimney Rock and carve my name into it. We'll get there before we get to Laramie. Who cares about a bath?"

"I do," Abby spoke up. "It's hard staying clean on the trail."

"Well then, you're as silly as Lizzie. You're just going to get dirty again the next day."

"William doesn't go around dirty all the time," Lizzie pointed out.

"Sure he does!"

"No, Zeke, he doesn't. He keeps his face clean and washes his hands before he eats. He does his best to stay as clean as he can."

"Luke, too," Ida pointed out.

"Aw, man!" Zeke set the guide book down. "You're just saying that cause you two like them."

"Don't you?"

"Not the way you do. Your eyes get all shiny whenever Aiken comes around." He started crawling towards the canvas opening. "I never would've come in here, if I had known I was going to have to read and get a lecture on cleanliness."

Lizzie and Ida laughed as they watched him disappear over the back of the wagon.

Chapter 10

By morning, the clouds had disappeared revealing blue skies and little wind. Off in the distance, the group was able to point out Court House Rock and Chimney Rock. They were in Nebraska Territory now. Lizzie and Ida had tied on their face rags and were taking turns walking and riding. Abby ran back and forth between their wagon and the Johnsons'.

"Hey, Lizzie!" Abby ran alongside the wagon. "Look over there." She pointed to the east. Off in the distance they could see large animals grazing.

"What are they?" Ida and Lizzie looked at each other. They jumped in surprise as guns began going off near them, startling them. Several of the men from the wagon train ran for their horses and galloped off in the direction of the animals.

Zeke trotted by on one of the mules, his gun tied next to him. "It's buffalo, Lizzie." He grinned hugely and hurried to catch up with the others.

The two women watched in amazement as several more men raced off to join the hunt, guns in hand. The rest of the wagon train continued on, moving more slowly, while the men hunted the buffalo. Within minutes of the men's guns booming, the ground began to shake beneath them. Lizzie and Ida could feel the vibrations through the seat of the wagon. Lizzie glanced worriedly in the direction the men had raced off, and gasped. The horizon was dark and moving. Moving quickly towards them! Dust hung heavily in the air above the moving, thundering mass. Lizzie peered through the thick dust, trying to gauge exactly how far away the herd was.

"Abigail, get in the wagon!" Lizzie yelled over the noise to her sister. She grabbed the reins tighter and hollered for the mules to pick up their pace. They stopped and brayed, fighting against their restraints. To the east of them, the cloud of dust was growing larger by the second. As the dust cloud grew in size, the thunderous noise grew in volume.

Luke came running up, his breath short in the thick air, and ordered Lizzie to hold the mules still.

"I'm trying!"

The other wagons had moved on ahead of them, leaving their wagon alone. Luke planted his feet firmly, spread his legs apart and, holding a pan and a wooden ladle in his hands, stood his ground beside the wagon. "It's a stampede," he told them, his features grim. He watched what seemed inevitable, fully expecting to be run down.

"And what do you plan on doing with that pot and spoon?" Ida leaned across Lizzie. "Are you crazy? You can't possibly think you can head off a stampede all by yourself."

Lizzie quickly handed the reins over to Ida and crawled into the wagon. Within seconds she re-emerged with a loaded pistol in her hand. She stood on the wagon seat and watched the buffalo herd continue to stampede toward them. Her heart pounded with each thundering hoof and the dust was making it difficult to breathe, even through the rag she wore over her nose and mouth. She closed her eyes and began to pray. Abby was screaming from the back of the wagon, and Lizzie could hear Ida muttering prayers next to her.

Right before the herd reached their stopped wagon, Aiken came galloping up on his horse, rifle blazing. Lizzie opened her eyes and began shooting her pistol into the air while Luke pounded furiously on his pan. Just when it seemed that the buffalos would run straight into their wagon, overturning them, the herd split in two and thundered past the wagon in two seemingly unending lines. Abby watched in wide-eyed terror as the huge animals roared by, her screams lost in the din. It was several minutes before the last of the herd passed by and the dust settled.

Aiken replaced his rifle in its hoop. "Fools. Every one of them." He galloped off towards the returning men. The women could see that one man was returning slung over the back of his horse.

Aiken reined his horse sharply to a halt before the returning men and saw that it was Mr. Martin. "What happened?"

"He fell from his horse during the stampede," one of the other men explained. "The buffalo hunters started shooting to head the herd in our direction when they saw us coming. Guess they thought to scare us away from what they considered theirs. Martin's horse got startled and reared." The man shook his head. "There's not much left of him, Aiken."

Aiken lifted the horse blanket the others had flung over the body and grimaced. There was very little of the man left to recognize. The buffalos' hooves had caved in his skull and smashed his face, all but obliterating his features. There was no way to clean him up before his family saw him. The blood had dried quickly in the heat, blackening the blue shirt the man wore and flecks of brain matter clung to the lifted blanket and peppered Martin's hair.

Aiken looked back sadly at the line of wagons awaiting their return. "Guess I'll take him back to his family. I'll tell the rest of the wagon we'll be stopping here to bury him." He took the reins of the dead man's horse in his hand and headed towards the front of the line.

Mrs. Martin saw him returning with her husband's horse, the blanketed body hanging across its back, and began to wail. She grabbed her youngest son close to her. "I told him not to go. I told him."

Her older son whispered fiercely to her, "And you got smacked for your trouble." He stepped forward, and relieved Aiken of his father's horse. "Thank you, sir."

Aiken nodded and waited for one of them to ask what had happened. When the question didn't come, he said, "We'll stop here today to give you time to bury him." He set his lips firmly, and sighed. "I'm sorry, son. You let me know if I can help with anything. We'll get someone to drive your wagon for you if you need it."

"We'll bury him, sir...but thanks." The young man stared solemnly up at Aiken. "I can handle the wagon fine myself for the rest of our journey. We appreciate the time you give us to bury him." Aiken nodded again, and the young man turned away, leading his father's horse.

Aiken approached Lizzie's fire an hour later and slumped to the ground. She looked up from where she was adding beans to the pot. "Are you all right?" He nodded and placed his hat on the ground next to him. "Should I go see to Mrs. Martin?"

Aiken shook his head. "Her boys are seeing to her. Seems that's all the company they want right now. The widow's the only one who seems to be grieving. It doesn't appear as if old man Martin was much liked by his family." He lifted sad eyes up to her. "I hate it when we lose someone on this trip. Especially when it's to foolhardiness."

"The woman will grieve, William, even if her husband was cruel to her. It's all she knows. He was her husband," she told him matter-of-factly. She handed him a cup of coffee. "There was nothing you could do to stop it. Those men took off as soon as the buffalo were spotted, whooping it up. Did they get any?"

"What?"

"Buffalo? Did they get any?"

"A couple—before the buffalo hunters stampeded the herd. Zeke's over there now getting your share. You'll have meat to go with your beans tonight." Aiken looked up and noticed Ida talking to Luke. "I don't think I've met him." He smiled. "He's either a brave man, or a foolish one. I couldn't believe my eyes when I saw him facing down that stampeding herd with a pot and spoon, and where did you get that pistol?"

"Zeke won it in a poker game and showed me how to shoot and load it." Lizzie followed his gaze with one of her own. "Ida's taken up with him. I think they were trying to meet up when she ran across our train, or maybe he was following her. I think he's a runaway. She said he was a blacksmith."

Aiken sighed deeply. "Never took with slavery myself. I won't turn him in, but I won't stop his owners from taking him back either—if they find him. Thanks for the coffee."

"More?"

Aiken nodded. "You're doing really fine on this trail, Lizzie. I'm proud of you."

She blushed. "Some nights I'm so tired I can hardly get comfortable. Zeke's doing the work of a full grown man. I haven't heard one complaint from Abby, besides the grime. Don't think I could do it without Ida, though."

"She *has* been a blessing to you. I'm glad you've got another woman along on the trail."

"She'll come in handy when Alice Johnson's baby comes in August."

Aiken's head jerked up. "Baby? No one said anything to me about a baby."

"She didn't tell her husband either until we'd already started."

"Dang it! Sorry, Lizzie," he apologized. "A baby on a trail is not a good idea. So…Ida's a midwife?"

Lizzie nodded and stirred the beans, the odor from the pot causing her stomach to growl. "She said she's helped her mother deliver several babies." She spooned out some of the beans handed him a plate full. "When's the funeral?"

"Just before sundown today. They wanted a little extra time to say goodbye."

The widow Martin stood swaying slightly, a son standing rigidly on each side of her, as Aiken said a prayer over the grave of their husband and father. Martin had not been popular among the group of onlookers, but the entire train had turned out for his funeral. Weeks on the trail, and any diversion seemed to be welcome. The women had even set up tables laden with food that had been hastily prepared.

Lizzie looked around the group and noted Ida and Luke hanging on the outskirts of the gathering. She smiled at Aiken before heading in their direction. "William said he wouldn't turn Luke in," she whispered.

Ida smiled up at Luke, tenderly touching his face, and then turned back to Lizzie. "Thank you."

Chapter 11

Lizzie, come here." Zeke pointed the mules out to her several days later while he was hitching them to the wagon. He kept lifting the neck harnesses over their heads, and they would shy away. He let the harness fall to the ground in frustration. "They won't let me hitch them. I need you to hold them still."

Lizzie set the camp stove she had been using back in the wagon. "That's unusual. They've been really docile up till now." She walked around the mules, running her hands over them. "Zeke, look. They're covered with sores." She pointed out the raw spots along their necks. "It must be because of wearing the harnesses in the rain. You have been taking them off every night, right? Zeke?" She stood with her hands on her hips, waiting for his answer.

Zeke shuffled his feet in the dirt, looking at the ground. "Mostly."

"Mostly?"

He looked up at her. "Well, some nights I just let them go. We're last in line on this train, and the poker games have usually already started by the time I get the wagon unhitched." His look turned defiant. "All the guys play, Lizzie. I've been winning…mostly."

"I've asked you not to gamble." Lizzie's shoulders slumped as she remembered the extra gun and money. "But…you're not a child anymore, and you're going to do what you want." She sighed. "Just make sure you undo the harness on the mules—first. *Every* night." She turned back to the mules. "Pick out the sorest ones and replace them with the extra mules. I'll put salve on all the ones with sores."

"Gee, Lizzie. Thanks!" Zeke ran off to get the other mules.

"I can unhitch the mules each evening, Miss Lizzie."

"Oh, hello, Luke." Lizzie watched her brother run off. "That's kind of you, but Zeke won't learn any responsibility that way."

"Maybe I could just watch him. Make sure he does it right?"

Lizzie laughed. "You mean do it yourself and let him run off and play."

Luke smiled sheepishly. "He's just a boy, Miss Lizzie. A boy that does the work of a man. I have little enough work to do, and I do eat your food. I don't take turns on watch at night. Let Zeke do that. He enjoys the watch, and I'll care for the mules."

"It's a deal." She pulled the salve from her pocket and handed it to him. "The mules are yours."

The day grew hotter, and the timber less as the day wore on. Lizzie and Ida kept their faces covered with the face rags and fanned themselves with their bonnets. They could see Chimney Rock and Court House Rock off in the distance. Heat shimmers bouncing off the ground were making them appear wavy. Lizzie stood on the wagon bed and peered off in the distance.

"What's that?" she asked Ida. "More buffalo?" A mile or so ahead of them was a large dust cloud.

"Lord, I hope not." Keeping the reins firmly in her hand, Ida stood to look off in the direction Lizzie was staring. "Maybe. Looks like the train is stopping."

Aiken came riding back. "There's a drove of cattle ahead. We'll stop early today and let them get a day ahead of us. Otherwise, we'll be eating their dust until we reach Laramie." He tipped his hat at the two women. "Lizzie. Ida. Any idea of where I can find Luke?"

"He's back with the animals. Is something wrong, Mr. Aiken?" Ida asked, her brow creased with worry.

"Just a wagon wheel that needs tending to. Might even be a little money in it for him. I've been spreading the word that we have a blacksmith with us now." He smiled and headed off towards the spare animals where Luke was riding with Zeke.

Lizzie and Ida, along with several other women from the train, spent that wonderfully lazy afternoon, mending and gossiping. There was a lot of speculation about Luke and one of the younger women remarked about how romantic it was, Ida's sweetheart following her all the way out here. Alice rolled her eyes as the younger woman sighed, and then laughed when the girl's mother elbowed her to be quiet.

Lizzie found Zeke later that evening, sitting around a large fire, playing poker. There were several unfamiliar faces in the group, and she beckoned him over. "Where's your poker money?"

"What for? I'm playing. You interrupted the game."

"Are those cowboys from the cattle drive?"

"Yeah. They rode back and wanted to join in a couple of hands. They're harmless enough."

She held out her hand. "Give me the money."

"I said, what for?"

"I heard you the first time, Zeke. I want to see how much you have."

"A couple hundred dollars."

"A couple hundred dollars! How on earth—"

"I won it fair and square. Sometimes, I lose—but mainly I win. The men think I'm too young to play good. I use that to my advantage."

Lizzie bit her bottom lip and looked back towards the fire. "Wow, Zeke. We'll need that money when we reach Oregon." She was torn between what she thought was morally right, and their need of the money. "Let me hold most of it for you. Take just twenty dollars of it to play. I know the men from our train are fair, but what if those cowboys aren't? You could lose it all," she reasoned.

Zeke glanced back to the game. "All right." He counted out the money and handed it to her. "Put it somewhere safe," he warned. "I worked hard for it."

She nodded and stuffed it down the front of her waistcoat. "I'll hide it really good, Zeke. I promise. Good luck." She gave him a quick kiss on the forehead, which caused him to turn away in embarrassment, and she started to make her way back to their wagon.

"Hold on there, little missy." A man stepped out from behind one of the wagons. He had his hat pulled down low over his face, and the pants and shirt he wore were covered in dirt and stained with sweat. He stank, and Lizzie lifted a hand to her nose, trying to ward off his body odor. He spat tobacco out at her feet. "How about you hand over that money the little fella gave you?"

Lizzie stepped to the side to try and avoid him. "I'm sorry, sir.

You're mistaken. I don't have any money."

"Well now, you're not being truthful with me." He rushed forward and grabbed her arm. "I saw him hand it to you, and I also saw you stuff it down the front of your dress. Now hand it over nicely, or I'll just have to go fishing for it."

Lizzie looked back in the direction of the fire and realized they were too far away to see what was happening. She could yell, but they probably wouldn't hear her. She bit her lip and tried to decide what to do. Most of the wagon train had already gone to sleep.

The man grew impatient with her hesitation. "I said to give me the money!" He grabbed a fist full of her shirt and ripped it down the front, exposing the white undergarment she wore. The wad of money fell to the ground.

Lizzie screamed and struggled against his grip. "Let go of me!" She kicked at the man and missed as he tried to bend and grab the cash. Holding her shirt up against her front, she threw her body against him, causing him to sprawl in the dirt. The man cursed and lunged again towards the fallen money. Lizzie drew back her leg and landed him a heavy kick in the rib cage. With a roar, the man leaped to his feet and back handed her across the mouth. Lizzie gasped and fell roughly to the ground. He yanked her up again and drew his fist back for another hit.

"Mister, I suggest you take your hands off my sister." Zeke stood a few feet from them, his rifle aimed at the man's chest. "That's my money you're trying to steal. I don't take to people trying to take what I've worked so hard for."

The man looked at the young boy standing there and laughed. "You think you can take me on, son? Come on ahead." He turned his attention away from Lizzie, shoving her aside, and turned to Zeke. Zeke kept his rifle aimed at the man's chest and stepped back.

"I believe I can take you on," Aiken drawled. He walked out from the shadows, his pistol drawn. He reached over and helped Lizzie to her feet. "I suggest you step back and put your hands in the air."

The man glanced from Zeke to Aiken, and did as he was told. Aiken kept his pistol trained on him and motioned for Zeke to lower his gun. "Zeke, take your sister back to the wagon. You sir, go on back to your camp. You're not welcome here." Aiken bent down and retrieved Zeke's money. "Next time you show your face around here, I won't be so kind." He stood there until the man had walked out of sight in the direction of his camp, and then he turned to head towards the Springers' wagon.

He took hold of Lizzie's arm as she climbed down from the wagon. "What were you thinking, woman? Do you know what could have happened to you out there? Most of those cowhands haven't seen a decent girl in months. Much less a pretty and clean one. Where is your head?"

She jerked her arm away and tucked her torn dress front into the top of her undergarment, freeing her hands. "I've had enough manhandling tonight, thank you." She stalked over to the fire and poured herself a cup of coffee. "I was checking on my brother. I realized that there were strangers in camp and knew there would be a poker game."

"Speaking of Zeke, where is he?"

"I'm here." Zeke crawled out from beneath the wagon. "You should have seen Lizzie take on that guy, Aiken. She was like a cornered bobcat." His pride in his sister waned at the stern look on Aiken's face. "I gave her my winnings to hold for me. We didn't think anyone took notice of us."

"That's right. The two of you didn't think!" Aiken kicked the wagon wheel. He leaned one hand against it, and shook his head. "Zeke, leave us alone, would you?" The boy nodded and headed off to find Luke.

Aiken sighed deeply before turning back to Lizzie. "Woman, you're going to be the death of me." He took the cup of coffee from her and set it aside. Reaching out, he pulled her into his arms. "I got there just in time to see you fall to the ground, your dress torn. Do you know what went through my mind?" He tilted her face up to his and carefully wiped away the blood from her split lip. "I have grown quite fond of you, Elizabeth. The West is a dangerous place for a woman, especially one as beautiful as you are. You've got to realize it and be more careful." He kissed her tenderly. "Here's your money. Put it in a safer place than your blouse."

She smiled up at him. "My blouse would be perfectly safe with you, wouldn't it, William?"

"Don't tempt me, vixen." He kissed her harder. "I'm glad to know you're all right. Try to stay out of trouble. Laramie's only about a hundred miles from here. There's a whole new set of troubles for you to get into on the other side of it." He smiled down at her, his eyes tender, and gently brushed back a stray strand of her hair from her face.

Lizzie smiled and watched him walk away, her eyes shining over the top of her coffee mug as she took a sip.

Chapter 12

Another couple of days brought them to Court House and Chimney Rock. The train continued just past the two rocks and camped in the shadow of Chimney Rock. Zeke notified them right off that he was climbing the rock and carving his name. Lizzie smiled and watched him run off with a few of the other boys, the two dogs chasing after them. She gathered up their dirty laundry, and taking Abby and Sarah Johnson with her, set off toward the river. Ida remained behind to cook while Luke cared for the animals.

After Aiken's warnings, she was careful to keep the wagon train within yelling distance. A small rise hid the wagons from her view as she stepped to the bank of the river, but she could still hear the sounds of the mules and oxen. "Don't wander off, Abigail!" Lizzie called, as she set down the basket of laundry. Far off in the distance she could see the boys, just small specks now as they climbed the face of the rock. Occasionally, she could hear one of the dogs bark.

She made sure that the two little girls were within her sight before tying up her skirt around her waist and wading into the shallow water of the Platte River. She dragged the bound bundle of dirty laundry behind her. Using a large boulder set in the mud beside the bank, she began scrubbing one of Zeke's shirts. A few minutes later she looked up to once again check on the whereabouts of the girls. She couldn't see them where she had left them to play and straightened up to peer over the rise. She gasped and fell back into the water.

Six Sioux braves stood staring down at her. They were dressed in worn buckskin breech cloths, their chests and legs bare. Their faces were covered in war paint. Two of them had their hands over the mouths of Abby and Sarah. One of the braves held a finger to his lips and then made the hand cutting motion across his neck.

Lizzie nodded woodenly, letting them know that she understood. The lead brave then motioned for her to come out of the water. They laughed at the sight of her wet skirt bunched up around her waist and the soggy bloomers she wore underneath. She blushed and hurriedly untied her skirt, letting it fall heavily back into place.

Silently, the braves led the three captives into the brush where they had tethered their horses. Within seconds and with no sound but for the huffing of the horses, Lizzie found herself hoisted up behind one of the braves and the group galloped off. She looked silently over to where she could see the white tops of the wagons.

"Mr. Aiken," Ida said, coming up to him where he was grooming his horse. "Is Lizzie with you?"

"No, Ida. I haven't seen her since we pitched camp." He stopped brushing his horse's coat and turned to face her. "Isn't she down at the river?"

"She was." Ida began wringing her hands in her apron. "The clothes are still there, but Lizzie and the two little girls aren't. It's not like her to be gone this long without telling me. And she would never leave the laundry lying there."

Luke walked up next to Ida. "I found horse tracks, Aiken. Unshod ones. Down by the river." He put his arm around the stricken Ida, as she sagged against him..

"Aiken, Aiken!" Zeke ran up, out of breath. "Indians!"

Aiken put his hand on Zeke's shoulder. "Slow down, son. Where did you see the Indians?"

Zeke took a deep breath. "Indians took Lizzie. I saw them when I was up on the rock. They put Lizzie, Abby, and Sarah up on their horses and took off that way!" He pointed to the east.

"How long ago?"

Zeke shrugged. "I came right down off the rock when I saw, Aiken, but the rock's a long ways away."

Aiken and Luke's gazes met over the boy's head. Aiken grabbed a rifle and tossed it to Luke. He hurriedly shoved his pistol in its holster. "Come on, Luke. They don't have much of a head start. A couple of hours at the most. Grab the first horse you see, and Zeke, you go sound the alarm. Tell as many of the men to follow us as you can round up." Aiken tossed his saddle onto the horse and quickly tightened the girth. "I sure hope you can ride, Luke, because I'm not waiting around for you to learn."

Luke nodded. He gave Ida a quick kiss and ran for the nearest horse. The horse still wore the bit and reins, and Luke hopped up on its bare back. He didn't want to waste any more time by hunting down a saddle. Ida stepped to Zeke's side, putting her arm around him, and they watched as the two men galloped off in the direction that Zeke had pointed.

"They'll find them, Zeke. Now you go on and get those other men, ya hear?" She gave him a shove. Ida stood there, alone, and watched the two men until she could no longer see them.

Aiken and Luke began following the tracks from the river bed. They lost them a few times as the Indians rode through some small creeks but quickly found the tracks again on the other side. Luke looked behind them and saw the dust from the other men who followed them.

"Should we stop?"

Aiken shook his head and spurred his horse on faster. "Let them catch up. We don't stop for anything." He inwardly groaned as thunder began to roar overhead. The last thing they needed was rain, and now night was falling. Within the hour, the rain poured, washing out the remaining tracks.

"No!" Aiken stared up at the night sky. They couldn't afford to stop. They weren't sure of how far ahead the Indians and their captives were. He slowed his horse and turned to Luke. "Can you ride in this? I vote we go on."

"Yes, sir. I say we ride on. Hopefully them Indians will have to stop, too."

"Good man." They spurred their horses on through the rain.

Lizzie recoiled in horror as she put her arms around the sweaty chest in front of her. The horses were going too fast for her to stay on without holding on to something, and the Indian in front of her was the only thing available. She wrinkled her nose at the man's body odor.

He urged the horse forward suddenly, and for a moment, her face rested against his sweaty body as he leaned back. She shrank away from him and frantically wiped his sweat from her cheek. She tried turning to see how the little girls were faring and the brave said something harsh, pulling her hands tighter around him. She realized then they were riding in the opposite direction from their wagon train. She closed her eyes and prayed.

She could hear Sarah crying loudly and she watched as the brave who had her reached back and slapped the little girl to hush her up. Lizzie shook her head at Abby when her sister opened her mouth to say something.

Thunder boomed without warning and the rain came down in torrents. Within minutes, Lizzie and the girls were soaked. Lizzie reached up a hand to wipe her hair out of her face and almost fell from the back of the horse. The brave in front of her grunted something in anger and jerked her hands tight again. Lizzie looked over to where the two little girls sat miserable behind their own captors.

Night was falling before the group stopped. Lizzie's legs threatened to give way beneath her when she slid off the horse. Her thighs were rubbed raw from straddling the horse and she winced as she pulled the wet fabric of her skirt away from her body. There was nothing she could do about her wet bloomers, but wear them.

She looked around her with curiosity. They had stopped to make camp in a small ravine. A few mesquite bushes and thorn trees dotted the landscape. High, sloped walls rose on two sides of them.

The Indians tied the girls' hands behind their backs and loosely looped rope around their ankles, binding the three together. The rain was still falling, and Lizzie had them crawl under the meager shelter of one of the thorn trees. Soon the braves had coaxed a fire into starting beneath an overhang of rock and had begun passing around a bottle. Lizzie's eyes widened in alarm when she smelled the whiskey. When that bottle was finished, they started on another.

One of the braves came over and ran his fingers through her hair. His eyes traveled down her body, taking in the wet clothes which clung to her. It took all of her willpower not to shrink back. She stared defiantly into the dark brown eyes. The Indian laughed, patted her cheek sharply, and went back to the fire. Lizzie breathed a sigh of relief.

"What are we going to do?" Abby whispered.

Lizzie looked at the two girls. Sarah's face was bruising from where the Indian had slapped her. The ribbons were gone from Abby's hair, and it blew softly around her face.

"I don't know," she admitted. "Surely, someone is looking for us by now. We must have ridden for several hours. I'm sure Ida found the laundry I was washing."

Abby nodded, confident. "Yeah, Mr. Aiken is sure to be looking for us." She put her head in her sister's lap and shivered in the cold. Sarah looked up at Lizzie who smiled and told the little girl to lay her head down, too. Lizzie sat there carefully watching the Indians drink, trying to take note of their surroundings. She worked the rope which bound her hands against the small tree trunk behind her. She wasn't able to make much progress with shredding the rope but was doing a good job of tearing up her hands. She quit and leaned her head back against the trunk.

She was startled awake the next morning by the sound of a horse galloping into camp. The rain had stopped but not soon enough for her and the girls to dry out completely.

She sat up in alarm when she saw that the rider was Mr. Newton. He grinned over at her and tossed one of the braves the reins to his horse.

"Now, this is a welcome surprise, Miss Springer." He took off his hat and bowed to her. "I was only expecting them to bring you along and here I get the extra bonus of a couple of beautiful little girls."

"What is the meaning of this, Mr. Newton? I demand that you untie us at once."

"Still high and mighty, aren't you? Well, we'll see how long that lasts." His smile quickly faded.

"What do you plan to do with us?"

"Sell you, of course." Newton nodded over to the braves. "They'll take the two girls. Raise them up as their own or use them as slaves. It really makes no difference to me. Now, you—I have plans for you. There are a lot of gentlemen in the West who will pay good money for a white woman with your looks. One that is unmarked and without disease. Unless, of course—you could be persuaded to stick with me? I could use you in one of the gaming houses I own. Men would come for miles around to lay gold dust at your feet. Do you sing?"

Lizzie shook her head vehemently. "I'll never go with you willingly."

"Then I guess I'll have to sell you after all. Pity. You'd be better treated with me."

"You're really going to sell us?" Lizzie asked, as she struggled against her bonds.

"It's strictly business, my dear. Nothing personal—just business." He stood up. "I must go wake up our drunken friends now. They'd best be moving you along. They'll bring you to me in a couple of days. There's arrangements to be made, you know." Lizzie watched as he conversed with the drowsy braves and then, mounting his horse once again, rode off.

"Lizzie?" Abby woke up, her blue eyes wide in her face.

"Shhh. It'll be all right, Abby. I won't let him separate us."

"I don't want to live with the Indians," Abby began to cry quietly. "I don't want to be a slave."

"You're not going to be anyone's slave, Abby. I promise." Lizzie set her mouth firmly. "I promise."

Aiken and Luke found the ravine shortly after Newton rode out. They stopped just a few yards from it and belly crawled until they were able to look down into it. "There they are," Luke whispered. He pointed out Lizzie and the girls under the tree.

Aiken counted the braves and spotted the empty whiskey bottles. He smiled. "This will be easier than I thought. Here's what we do." He scooted back. "We're not going to wait for the others to get here. There's not that many braves down there and they'll be hung over after all that whiskey. I'll sneak around to the other side and, when I start firing, that's your signal to fire. Shoot as fast as you can. We want them to think there's more than just the two of us. They look like they were drinking pretty heavily last night and they will probably run, leaving Lizzie and the girls behind. Got it?"

Luke nodded and scooted back up to the edge, his rifle ready. Aiken hurried around to the other side of the ravine and pulled out a pistol in each hand. He hoped his plan worked. He didn't want to kill anyone unless it was absolutely necessary, and Lizzie and the girls looked unharmed.

His foot slipped on some loose rock as he made his way around the ravine and he stopped suddenly, listening for a cry of alarm. Not hearing one, he proceeded a little more cautiously until he judged that he was opposite of where he had left Luke. He took shelter behind a boulder, and aimed.

His first shot shattered one of the bottles and had the effect he had hoped for. The Indians yelped and scrambled for their horses. Luke began firing, and as predicted, the braves took off. Whooping and hollering they mounted in a running jump and galloped off, leaving Lizzie and the girls behind. Aiken stood and slid down the side of the ravine, sending a cascade of rocks before him.

"William!" Lizzie sat up in relief. "Thank God."

He fell to his knees beside her. "Are you all right? They didn't hurt you?"

She shook her head. "No, but Sarah's face is bruised where one of them hit her. Otherwise we're fine."

Aiken took a knife from his belt and began cutting at their ropes. "There's no end to the trouble you get into, is there?" He smiled at her. He laughed out loud when she lunged at him once her hands were free. He wrapped his own arms around her and kissed her. "You definitely keep life interesting."

"Did you come alone?"

"No. Luke is with me. Others are about half an hour behind us." He helped her up and held out another hand to the girls. Luke soon joined them and swept the girls up, one under each arm. Aiken swung Lizzie up behind him on his horse and Luke set one girl in front of him and one behind.

Lizzie let her head rest against his back. "You smell better than my other companion."

"Thanks," he said with a grin. He patted her hands which were wrapped around his waist.

"William—Newton was behind this."

"Newton?"

"He was going to sell Abby and Sarah to the Indians and said he had another buyer for me." She closed her eyes. "Thank you for coming after us."

"Wouldn't have had it any other way, Lizzie. Can't imagine reaching Oregon without you." He flicked the reins, sending his horse into a slow gallop.

They soon met up with the other men and Sarah's father jumped down from his horse. He ran up to them, tears coursing down his cheeks. He kissed the bruise on his daughter's face and wrapped her tightly in his arms.

Zeke and Ida cried too when they saw the others ride into camp. Ida quickly rushed Abby to the wagon to feed her and change her into clean clothes. Zeke handed Lizzie a cup of hot coffee. He watched her anxiously until he had satisfied himself that she was truly all right.

Aiken slapped Luke across the back and offered him a hand shake. "You can ride with me anytime."

Luke grinned hugely, his teeth flashing white against his dark skin. "Didn't know I could ride like that myself," he said. "Never had call to before. I'm going to feel it tomorrow though." He patted his backside. "Never rode anything but old farm horses before and then never faster than a trot."

Aiken laughed and slapped his back again. He then walked over and squatted next to Lizzie. "You should try and get some sleep, sweetheart. You've been through a lot."

She nodded. "I don't think my father really knew what this trip would entail when he planned it." She set down her cup and stood up. "It's one trial after another."

"Trials make us stronger," Ida added, joining them. "Aiken is right, Lizzie. You need to get your rest. Abby is already asleep, poor thing. Luke and I can clean this up." She smiled tenderly at the big man. "And my man also deserves a nice big dinner of his own."

"Well, I'm pretty hungry too, Ida," Aiken spoke up. "Think you could feed me before the two of you start getting all mushy?" He winked up at Lizzie.

Ida grinned back. "I think so, Mr. Aiken. I think so."

Chapter 13

They arrived at Fort Laramie around noon. The fort was rectangular in shape, made from bricks dried in the sun. The walls were fifteen feet high with a palisade in the center. At the top of the palisade, was a room that housed a cannon. The fort wasn't large enough to house the thirty wagons, so Aiken had them make their customary circle on the outside of it. The heat waves shimmered around the fort, causing it to look like a desert mirage. A few trees grew along the walls and Lizzie noticed that someone, in an attempt to make the place look homier, had planted a few wildflowers by the gate.

The excitement of those on the wagon train was contagious, and the children ran circles around their mothers who were trying desperately to clean them up. The parents were looking forward to the trading and purchasing of much needed supplies. The children were only interested in the soldiers and the few Indians they could see milling about inside the walls of the fort.

Aiken was greeted by the captain of Fort Laramie. Zeke lost no time in telling of the encounter his sister had had with the Indians. Lizzie blushed under the captain's sharp scrutiny and tried to make light of her situation.

"You're mighty lucky to be alive, Miss Springer," the captain told her. He removed his hat and ran his fingers along his handlebar moustache. "We've had some unpleasant encounters with the Sioux recently. Stupid, really. An incident over a cow got out of hand, but it did result in deaths on both sides, mostly whites. The Indians haven't been particularly friendly lately. They took over the Platte ferry not too long ago and killed the two men who ran it. We have to keep the cannon manned around the clock now."

Lizzie's eyes widened with the captain's report. "They didn't seem to be on the war path, Captain. They had captured us for a man named Edward Newton. He had plans on selling the children and myself."

"Newton? That man rides through here regularly. He does seem to bring trouble with him every time. We'll keep our eye out for him the next time he comes through. You enjoy your visit, and be careful on the rest of your journey. The Indians are beginning to resent the flood of white people moving across this land." The captain tipped his hat courteously and proceeded on his way.

Aiken slipped Lizzie's hand through the crook of his arm and led her to the small trading post inside the fort. It was crowded with bargaining men and women. He took her list from her and positioned her in a safe spot by the door. She was able to see the open field and saw that Zeke and Abby were watching the soldiers run through their daily drill. The soldiers marched in two straight lines, bayonets raised in front of their faces. One man, standing a few feet before them, called out orders which the soldiers followed in exact precision.

Soon, Aiken fought his way through the tide of people until he was back by her side, a huge grin splitting his face.

"What?" She could tell that he was up to something.

"I've got you that bath you wanted."

"Oh, William, really?" Lizzie's face lit up in anticipation. Aiken pulled her outside and around the corner of the building.

He took both of her hands in his, his face serious as he looked down at her. "I'd like to present it to you as a wedding present. Will you marry me, Elizabeth?" His eyes sparkled as he swept his hat from his head.

"Marry you?"

"I'd like to take care of you and your brother and sister. I've come to love you very much. I know it has only been a matter of a few weeks, but people get to know each other fast out here. I'll get down on my knee to ask, if you want me to."

Lizzie's breath caught. "It is sudden, but—yes, I'll marry you, William." She threw her arms around his neck and kissed him. "You just tell me when."

"Tonight? There just happens to be a lay preacher passing through. I'd like to arrive in Oregon as husband and wife and married by a preacher."

She smiled up at him through her tears. "I think that would be lovely."

Word passed around the fort quickly that there was going to be a wedding and the women rushed back to their wagons to start preparing a feast. Those who could play a musical instrument began tuning them. Soon, the atmosphere around the fort began to take on the feeling of a party.

Lizzie sat before Ida in a white organdy dress that Mrs. Johnson had loaned her. Alice had insisted on bringing her wedding gown with her when they started on this trip and was more than happy for Lizzie to be married in it. It was a bit large, but Ida expertly tacked it up in places and made it fit. She was busy sweeping Lizzie's hair up, leaving long tendrils falling on each side of her face. Abby ran in with wild flowers in her hand and handed them to Ida to place in Lizzie's hair.

Ida smiled softly over Lizzie's head. "Luke asked me to marry him, too."

Lizzie spun around. "That's wonderful, Ida. Let's get married together," she added impulsively. "You're the dearest friend I've ever had. You can stand up with me, and I'll stand up for you. I'm sure William won't mind."

"I'd like that, Lizzie. I really would." Ida's face shone with happiness.

"Good. I'll finish putting the flowers in my own hair and you go get dressed. I don't have a white dress for you to wear, but you're welcome to wear my yellow calico. We're close to the same size, although you are a bit shorter. It's not had to be patched yet and it will look so pretty against your skin." Lizzie talked fast with excitement and laughed out loud when Ida rushed to the chest to get the yellow dress.

Soldiers, travelers, and the civilians who lived at the fort, lined up in two lines on either side of the main street that ran through the center of the fort. The few wives who did live there had dressed in their best, smiling at the two wedding couples. Zeke walked his sister and Ida proudly to the men waiting for them at the end of the line. Abby walked before them, dropping wild flowers in the path of the two brides. It was a long walk. Lizzie's knees shook beneath the dress she wore. Zeke patted her hand, doing his best to stand in for their father. He walked straight and proud between Lizzie and Ida, his arms linked with theirs.

A small tear escaped Lizzie's eye and rolled down her cheek. She wished so much that her parents would have been able to meet William. They would have loved him, she knew. She took in a shuddering breath and allowed Zeke to place her hand in William's.

Aiken and Luke stood solemnly as they watched their brides approach, but Aiken couldn't resist the grin that spread suddenly across his face. He was a lucky man. Lizzie blushed as he took her hand in his.

The ceremony was simple, and the two couples couldn't have been happier. One lady even gave up some of her precious hoard of rice to toss a handful on the newlyweds. The men cheered and slapped the grooms on the back, making off-color jokes. Before they knew it, the brides were being led off in one direction, their husbands in the opposite.

Lizzie grabbed Ida's hand. "This is the happiest day of my life, Ida. Thank you for sharing it with me."

"I was honored, Lizzie. Now, I think I'm going to go claim my man back." She squeezed Lizzie's hand and headed off in the direction Luke had disappeared.

Aiken snuck up behind Lizzie and lifted her, spinning her around. "Hello, wife." He bent his head and kissed her, long and hard, then lifted her high in his arms. "The music's starting. Wanna dance?" She smiled down at him, and nodded.

The dancing and eating went on long into the night. Their friends from the other wagons had been placing small gifts at the feet of the two newlyweds all night. Finally, Aiken stood. "Enough is enough. Good night, folks, but I've got a new bride that I badly want to kiss until she swoons in my arms." Lizzie punched him playfully in the arm as she blushed furiously. Aiken led his bride away while the men cheered and whistled.

He stopped before a small building positioned at the back of the fort. "Luke and Ida are sleeping in the wagon tonight, the kids are being watched by the Johnsons, and I've managed to get us a room. The captain has graciously offered us his." He swung open the door and swooping her up in his arms, carried her inside. Kicking his leg behind him, he closed the door.

Lizzie sat on the edge of the bed and removed the crown of wilted flowers from her hair. She watched beneath lowered lashes as Aiken removed his boots. He smiled over at her and padded over in his bare feet. He lowered himself slowly down on the bed beside her.

"You all right?" he asked tenderly.

She nodded, and smiled. Aiken wrapped his arms around her and lowered them both until they were lying on their sides, facing each other. "I love you," he told her.

"I love you."

He reached over, cupping her face in his hand and drew her closer to him.

Lizzie woke the next morning and stretched her arms over her head. She opened her eyes to see Aiken looking down at her, his eyes sparkling. "Good morning, husband."

"Good morning, wife. You're beautiful, have I told you?"

She sat up. "I don't think you have. Not today at least."

"Then I'll say it again…you're beautiful." He leaned over and kissed her. "Ready for breakfast? We really should be heading back on the trail today."

She grabbed her dress from the foot of the bed and stood up. "It was wonderful to sleep in a bed again. I'm not excited about going back to sleeping in the hard wagon bed."

"We'll be sleeping in our own bed in a few months." He swung his legs over the bed and tugged on his boots. "Once we get there, I'll get to work building us a cabin and the biggest bed in the state of Oregon."

She laughed. "Come on. Let's go find Ida and Luke. She's probably already got breakfast started, if I know her."

He grabbed her arm as she turned away and pulled her back to the bed. "On second thought…"

She laughed again and pulled away. "Behave, William." She shrieked and ran for the door as he lunged towards her again.

She was right. Ida had already collected the children from the Johnsons' and was feeding them breakfast. Luke was bent over, working on the mules' hooves when they walked up. Lizzie hugged her brother and sister, and Aiken strode up to Luke. While the men conversed, the women ate and then started cleaning up.

"How are you, Mrs. Jones?" Lizzie asked, with a smile.

"Just fine, Mrs. Aiken. How about yourself?"

"I couldn't be better. I never dreamed that I would get married on this trip, Ida. I was figuring on finding me a job in one of the cities in Oregon. Maybe as a teacher." She giggled. "I don't think that marriage on the trail was in my father's plans."

"It never is." Ida folded up the cook stove and stowed it back in the wagon. "Now that we're getting ready to leave the fort, we'll have to think about the sleeping arrangements. We've got two families…and one wagon."

Lizzie stopped. "I hadn't thought that far ahead."

"I have." Aiken walked up behind her and kissed her on the neck. "Zeke will go back to taking his turn with the animals, and sleeping under the wagon when he's not at the corral. You and I will sleep in the wagon with Abby, and I managed to find a tent for Luke and Ida to pitch at night."

"You don't mind sharing with Abby?"

"Part of the package, honey. I'd feel bad if we banished her to the Johnsons every night." He winked down at her. "But once in a while might not be too bad." He stood back and looked at her. "And the package is definitely worth it." He winked at her again and got on his horse. "Time to get these wagons rolling."

Chapter 14

They were two days out of Ft. Laramie when they began passing the graves. Some of the graves had been dug up by passing animals, leaving bones scattered both in the grave and out. One of the graves, Lizzie noticed, had apparently belonged to a woman. The only thing left by the animals was her hair and the decorative comb that was in it. As the train proceeded, they came by discarded wagons and mattresses. On one of the mattresses were the remains of one of those who had died.

"William," Lizzie asked, tearfully. "What is it? What killed these people?"

"Cholera, I think. Keep moving." He spurred his horse on to let the wagons up front know to move quicker.

"Cholera," Ida exclaimed, hoarsely. They watched sadly as they passed by the graves. The dreaded word spread quickly up and down the line of wagons.

Later that evening, they came across a woman who was sitting by the grave of her dead husband. The train she had been on had left without her. She was thin to the point of starvation and didn't look up as they passed.

"Stop, Ida." Lizzie put her hand on the other woman's arm to stop her.

"Lizzie, what are you doing?" Ida exclaimed, as Lizzie hopped down from the wagon.

"I'm giving her some food. I'm going to try and persuade her to come with us."

"Get back in the wagon, Lizzie." Aiken ordered sternly, as he rode up on his horse. "You can't help her now."

Lizzie kept walking, a bucket of food in her hand. "I can try."

He jumped down from his horse and hurried to her side. "Please, Lizzie. I beg you. Don't go up to her. She's ill and you could put the entire train in jeopardy."

She stopped and looked up at him, her eyes glistening with unshed tears. She looked from him to the woman. Recognizing his reason and seeing the naked fear on his face, she nodded and set the food on the ground a few feet from the grieving widow. With a deep sigh, she turned and climbed back in the wagon, looking behind them until she could no longer see the woman.

Later that evening, Seth Johnson fell ill. He was the first. Alice ran up to them as fast as her expanding waistline would let her. "Ida. My baby, Seth. He's ill. He's vomiting and complaining of stomach cramps. I don't know what to do for him." She was frantic.

"I'll come, Mrs. Johnson." Ida shot a look over at Luke who was shaking his head at her. His eyes were wide with fright.

"I'm coming with you," Lizzie declared. She took the time to climb up in the wagon to grab her medicine box and then followed Ida to the Johnson wagon.

Word spread rapidly through the train as others fell ill to the mysterious disease. Several of the wagon owners panicked and set off on their own. Aiken tried in vain to stop them, even going so far as to stand in front of their wagons with his guns drawn. One of the others fired at his feet and threatened to run him over if he didn't move. Dejected, he turned and headed off to find Lizzie.

"She's not here, Mr. Aiken," Luke told him, sadly. "They went off to help the Johnson boy. Her and Ida both. I'm real scared, Mr. Aiken. I've seen what cholera can do."

"No!" Dread gripped his heart. "Watch Zeke and Abby, Luke. Keep them away from the infected wagons. Pull off a way if you have to." He took off on a run to the Johnson wagon. "Lizzie?"

She poked her head out of the canvas covering. "Yes, William?"

"Is it cholera?"

She shook her head. "I don't know. I've never dealt with cholera before. I've been giving Seth bismuth. I was told that it helps, but now he's getting delirious, and one of his brothers has fallen ill."

"Where's Mrs. Johnson?"

"Ben took her to another wagon. He didn't want to risk the baby."

He nodded. "I read in one of the Eastern newspapers that

dehydration is a major concern of cholera. Lizzie, you've got to try and get fluids into Seth. Do you hear me?"

"I hear you." She made to pull her head back in, and Ida stopped her.

Ida climbed slowly down from the wagon bed. "It won't matter none now, Lizzie. Little Seth just died. We can try the fluids on his brother." Ida hitched up her skirts and set off matter-of-factly to where the Johnsons were waiting.

Aiken stopped her with a hand on her shoulder. "Wait, Ida. Let me go. I'll tell them. There's little else I can do." She nodded and turned back to help Lizzie.

Two more people died before nightfall. A woman and another child. Lizzie sat by the fire, her shoulders shaking with her crying. That's where Aiken found her. He pulled her onto his lap and held her, not talking.

"It's so fast, William. Seth died within hours. Alice said he had started feeling poorly that morning, but she thought it was from drinking water from the river." She sniffed. "Do you think this is because I stopped to help that woman?"

"I don't think so. Cholera seems to hit with no reason. Besides, if what you're telling me is true, Seth fell ill before we ran across that woman."

"I'm not a doctor, William. I don't know what to do."

Aiken held her tighter. "How's the brother? Is he keeping the fluids down?"

She nodded. "For now."

"I want you to wash your hands, Lizzie. A lot. Every time you touch someone who is ill and before you move on to someone else, you wash your hands. Promise me?"

She looked up at him. "All right, I promise."

"I read in an Eastern newspaper that some doctors believe that the disease is carried from one person to the next. They don't know how yet. They say fluids and cleanliness seem to be the best things in battling it. No one knows why some die and others don't." He tilted her head and kissed her. "I want you and Ida to take shifts, Lizzie. I can't have you falling ill, and Luke is already beside himself with worry."

"How many more are ill, William?"

"About twenty, at the last count." He sighed heavily. "I've been spreading the word about the newspaper article, but some people are stuck in their ways." He helped her up and stood himself. "There will be a few more dead by morning."

She watched him walk away before going to relieve Ida. Her weariness showed in every line of her slight body.

Ida smiled at her as she climbed in. "He appears to be doing better, Lizzie. Look." John Johnson smiled weakly up at her.

Lizzie smiled back and felt his brow. "Are you thirsty, Johnny?" He nodded. "Just a sip, Ida, and then you go rest. I'll look after him for the next couple of hours."

Ida shook her awake several hours later. "Lizzie, its Abby. She's had the dysentery and vomiting. You'd better come."

"Oh, no." Lizzie bolted awake and jumped from the wagon. Lifting her skirts, she sprinted towards her own wagon and her little sister. Abby lay inside, thrashing in the throes of delirium. Aiken sat by her side, trying to spoon some broth down her.

He looked up at Lizzie, tears in his eyes. "I can't get her to take any of this, Lizzie. It just runs out of the corners of her mouth."

Lizzie fell to her knees beside her sister. "Abigail Springer, now you listen to me." Lizzie tried to keep her voice from shaking. "You need to drink this broth, you hear me?" Lizzie took the spoon from Aiken. "I don't want to get angry with you.

"William, you hold her still and I'll see if I can't get some down her." He placed a hand on each of the little girl's shoulders and held her. Lizzie managed to get a few spoonfuls down her sister and sat back. She grabbed a rag from a bowl nearby and began wiping Abby's brow. She squeezed some of the moisture from the rag between the little girl's lips. She prayed as she continued trying to squeeze water between Abby's clenched lips. Lizzie battled the disease through the night, shaking off her husband's hand when he tried to get her to get some rest. "Leave me be, William."

Aiken silently watched his wife, concern for her showing in every line of his face. He took in the dark circles under her eyes and the slump of her shoulders. The dress she wore was stained with perspiration and dirt. He lifted a hand to move her limp hair out of her face, she slapped his hand away, not wanting to be fretted over. Finally resigned, he climbed out of the wagon.

The next morning, Aiken parted the canvas covering and saw Lizzie lying beside her sister. "Lizzie!" His heart leapt into his throat and he bounded into the wagon. He gathered her up in his arms. "Lizzie?" He shook her gently. "Please, God. Not her. Not my Elizabeth."

"What?" she muttered, her voice muffled by his chest. "I was sleeping, William. Abby's better and I'm so tired."

Aiken laughed shakily. "I thought you had fallen ill, too."

She sat up. "I've been following the directions you gave me. I've made sure that I took the time to drink plenty of water, as well as getting as much down Abby as I could." She smoothed her hair back out of her face. "How many, William?"

"Two new cases and ten more dead." He looked at her sadly. "Alice was feeling poorly, but Ida took care of her, and she seems to be improving. I don't think it was cholera with her. Just exhaustion and worry."

"Thank God, William. But, ten!" She shook her head.

"I've been busy trying to get the bodies buried. Some people don't want to let go. One of the wagons that had taken off on their own came back last night. All fell ill and all dead this morning. An entire family." He stood up. "I guess we've been lucky— considering. Some trains lose much more than that." He peered outside into the sunshine. "We'll stay here until we find that no one else is getting sick. I'll go and fix you something to eat. Do you want more broth for Abby?"

She nodded and grabbed his hand. "I love you, William. I'm sorry I was cross with you yesterday."

He turned and smiled. "I love you." He kissed her before hopping down.

The wagon train camped there for a week. At the end of the week, the survivors stood over the graves of twenty-two of their friends and family. Most families had lost at least one member, others more. The dreaded cholera had swept through quickly, leaving sorrow and devastation behind it.

Lizzie looked down at her raw and cracked hands. She had washed them with lye soap as her husband had suggested. She clenched her fists to her sides, willing herself not to cry as dirt was heaped over little Seth's body. Crying wouldn't bring him back, or help her friend, Alice. Alice hadn't attended the funeral. Ben wouldn't allow it. He was afraid of her grief harming their unborn child.

Lizzie lifted her face heavenward and gave a prayer of thanksgiving. Her family had been spared. Her shoulders slumped with fatigue, and she leaned into her husband who put an arm around her. Luke and Ida stood nearby. Luke was holding Abby who was wrapped in a quilt. The little girl had wanted to come out and say goodbye to her friend. Seth's sister, Sarah, stood next to her father, silently crying. Her tears left tracks down her white face.

One woman stood wailing next to her husband's grave as they prepared to pull out the next morning. Lizzie stood and watched as Aiken begged her to come with them. The widow kept shaking her head repeatedly and threw herself prostrate across the grave. Aiken pulled her to her feet and tossed her, kicking and screaming, over his shoulder. Lizzie watched in amazement as he tossed her roughly in the back of her wagon and tied her in.

She had no other family so Aiken enlisted Luke as her driver, giving him instructions not to untie her until they were well away. The woman cursed and screamed her husband's name for several miles, before finally becoming silent. Lizzie's heart ached for her. Alice had not come out of her wagon, content to leave Ben to care for the other children himself.

Aiken led the group to the foot of the Black Hills. They had been without fresh water for the last few days. They had been drinking only what they had in their water barrels and they were looking forward to the fresh springs they knew they would be finding soon.

Lizzie looked around her at the pine and cedar trees. In the distance they could see the snow covered peak of Mt. Laramie. They passed through dark green valleys and lime covered ledges. The wagons bounced and jostled over rocks. Abby began complaining about the rough ride and Lizzie let her down to walk awhile.

They didn't come to fresh water until well into the afternoon, and the wagon train stopped only long enough to water the stock and fill the water barrels. Lizzie and Ida stretched their aching muscles, looking around them.

"Beautiful land," Lizzie noted.

Ida nodded. "There's not very much good wood for burning, though. Do you still have some of that wood stashed in the wagon?"

"A little. At least there's grass." She looked around for Aiken. "Have you seen William, or Zeke? I haven't seen them since this morning."

"Mr. Aiken took Zeke on ahead with him to scout out a place to stop," Ida told her.

They stayed for an hour and traveled another ten miles before stopping for the night. Aiken had gone on ahead of them earlier in the day and had found the train a beautiful place to camp with plenty of wood, water, and grass. He told Luke to untie the widow from the back of her wagon and then he had to chase her down as soon as she was free. She was determined to head back to her husband's grave. He fetched her back and deposited her back in the wagon, leaving her untied, but he sewed the covering closed.

"You can come out when you have your head on straight," Aiken told her. "I'm not going after you anymore."

"Show some compassion, William," Lizzie scolded. "She's grieving. He was all she had."

"I understand that, Lizzie. If she goes back, she'll die right alongside him. I can't have that on my conscience."

"What's she going to do when we reach Oregon? She can't build a homestead by herself."

"No, but she'll be alive. My responsibility is to get as many of these people there as I can—alive."

Lizzie watched his back as he retreated. She placed her hands on her hips and turned back to the sewn closed wagon. The widow sobbed inside, alone. Lizzie stretched out a hand toward the wagon cover then let it fall to her side. With a sob catching in her own throat, she turned to follow her husband.

Chapter 15

They continued traveling through the Black Hills for the next two days, bouncing over rocks. They worked at finding their way around the worst of the road, and traveled over the rocks and fallen trees when they couldn't go around them. Luke stayed busy in the evenings, repairing busted wheels and axles, and slowly he and Ida began to accumulate things of their own as those he helped paid him. Most of the people paid in goods, such as blankets, food or pots. Some paid in cash, and one family gave them a small pig, which Abby was glad to have in the back of the wagon with her.

Their last day in the hills, they stood looking out on the most desolate piece of land they had encountered yet. It was called, by some, the Devil's Crater. What a contrast to the hills they had just traveled over! There wasn't a tree or patch of grass to be seen, only dirt and rocks. The barren landscape stretched before them as far as the eyes could see.

"This must be what hell looks like," Luke muttered. He kicked his heels against the sides of the mule he was riding, heading him down the hill.

They didn't reach the banks of the winding Platte River again until night fall. The animals strained against their yokes and harnesses, crazy for a drink of water. Zeke and Luke had their hands full trying to keep the mules under control until they had them unhitched from the wagon.

Lizzie sat near the fire, blinking and trying to wipe the dust out of her eyes. "I swear supper tonight's going to taste like dirt," she told Ida. "I can't seem to get it out of my mouth, and my teeth are gritty with it."

Ida nodded. "I think it's settled into every crevice of my body. Let's gather up some of the women and head down to the river as a group to bathe. We can try to wash some of the grime off. Luke and Mr. Aiken can stand guard against Indians."

"I think that sounds wonderful." She headed off to gather up Abby, Sarah, Alice, and some of the others. Alice needed to be persuaded to leave the sanctuary of her wagon, but she did finally consent to follow the other women to the river.

Luke and Aiken stood guard, backs turned while the women stripped down to their undergarments and waded in. "Must be a mighty fine sight behind us," Aiken said, laughing.

"You are bad, Mr. Aiken." Luke smiled and tried to sneak a peek over his shoulder. "It's too dark. To see some of those ladies in their personals might just scare the tarnation right out of me anyway."

"And you say I'm bad." Aiken stepped over to a large boulder and sat down. The two men listened to the giggles and shrieks of the females. "Do you think they'd take watch while we bathed?" Luke shook his head. "Didn't think so. Guess we'll sneak on down here after they've gone to bed. I must admit I'd like to be out there with just Lizzie," he told Luke.

Luke laughed softly. "I was just thinking the same thing about Ida. There's not much privacy among thirty wagons."

Aiken looked back in time to see Lizzie's silhouette as she walked from the water. The wet camisole and bloomers clung close to her curves. The details were hidden in the dark, but seeing her shape against the moonlight was enough. He sighed deeply. "Sure isn't."

Lizzie shook as much of the dust from her dress as she could before putting it back on. The day had been unbearably hot, but the night was growing cool. She called for Abby to get out of the river and quickly wrapped her in an old quilt she had brought. Ida soon joined them, towing along a reluctant Sarah. Alice Johnson sat on the river bank, still dusty and hot, her clothes sticking to her back with perspiration. She had agreed to come with them but had sat on the bank while they bathed. The woman's grief showed in the slumped way she sat. She seemed not to hear the laughter and talk of the other women.

Lizzie glanced over at her, worried. "Alice has got to pull out of this slump she's in," she said to Ida. "The rest of her family is suffering, too."

"Just because I didn't go swimming doesn't mean I can't hear," Alice retorted. She watched as the other women from the train walked away, whispering and talking among themselves. "You let me grieve in my own way, Lizzie. My family is doing all right, and they are *my* family." She stood up and walked over to the others. "I just lost my baby boy. I'll grieve as long as I feel like it, and in any *way* I feel like it." With an indignant swish of her skirts, she headed back to her wagon, leaving Sarah behind with the others. Lizzie stood there, mouth hanging open, and watched her go.

"I didn't mean anything by it," she told Ida.

"I know you didn't, Lizzie. Mrs. Johnson didn't mean anything either. Come on, sweetie." Ida took Sarah's hand. "We'll get you fed. Then I'll take you back to your wagon."

The wagons pulled out the next morning, leaving the Platte River behind them. They were expected to hit the first of the poison water sometime the next day. The heat was up to ninety degrees in the shade, and even the women's sun bonnets weren't much comfort against the sun's blaze. The dust built up on them and turned to mud as their sweat washed it into the folds of their skin. The dirt became caked in their teeth, and they didn't even have the luxury of rinsing their mouths out with fresh water. Lizzie and Ida took turns plodding along beside the wagon, encouraging the mules to keep going. Abby did her best to fan whichever of them was driving, but she soon tired in the heat.

A dust storm hit them in the early evening. The wind flung the dirt into their faces, swirling and blowing away anything that wasn't under shelter or tied down. Abby took refuge in the wagon, against a worried Lizzie's orders. Despite the heat, she huddled under a pile of blankets. Still, the dust blew through the opening and covered everything. Lizzie and Ida struggled against the wind, the dirt stinging their faces and arms, while they strove to put together some sort of dinner. The men worked rapidly trying to put up a temporary corral for the animals and the dogs hid under the wagon, whining, their tails tucked beneath them.

Lizzie and Ida worked together, fighting to get a fire going in the wind.

A spark from the low burning fire blew up and set Lizzie's skirts on fire. She screamed and jumped back from the fire. The strong winds whipped her skirts around and fanned the flames. She tried ineffectively to beat them out herself. Her legs got tangled in the whipping skirts and she fell to the ground. Ida grabbed the nearest pot she could and tossed a pot full of dirt at her...and missed. Aiken heard Lizzie's screams from where he was tethering his horse and came running.

"Lizzie!" Aiken threw himself on top of her and rolled her on the ground, beating at the flames with his hands until the flames were out. "What were you thinking? You don't make a fire in this kind of storm? I swear, woman, you're going to give me gray hairs yet!"

She sat there quite still and stared at the large burned hole in her skirt. "I was trying to get food to feed *you*." She stood up and stared at him defiantly. "I'm sorry for thinking about you—after you worked so hard all day." She shook the embers out of her skirt and stalked away.

"Lizzie..." Aiken sighed, and turned to Ida. "She scared me—that's all."

"It'll be all right. She'll see your way in a bit." Ida kicked dirt onto the fire, putting it out. "It was my idea to start the fire, by the way. I just thought you should know before you get onto her too much." Ida left Aiken standing alone by the extinguished fire.

He turned and walked over to where Lizzie was standing in the shelter of the wagon, using the side of it to block as much of the wind as she could. He stood there and looked down at her. "Why didn't you tell me that Ida started the fire, Lizzie?"

"You didn't give me a chance. Besides, I was helping her."

He pulled her into his arms and rested his chin on top of her head. "I'm sorry. I worry so much about you being hurt on this trail. I can be pretty unreasonable at times."

"At times," she answered, smiling, content to stand with him sheltering the blowing dust. "I acted like a spoiled child, and I'm sorry. I know that you were just worried. I was, too. Are your hands burned?"

"A little, but they'll be all right."

She pulled back to look at them, turning them palm up. They weren't blistered, but were red from the fire. "Let me put some salve on them, William. They're going to hurt you tomorrow." She led him into the wagon. She retrieved the salve from the small trunk where she kept their medicines and gently began rubbing it into his rough hands.

Aiken drew in a deep breath and looked at her, his blue eyes darkening. "Where's Abby?" he asked, pulling Lizzie down onto the pile of quilts.

"Right here," Abby struggled to crawl out from under him. "But I can leave if you want me to."

Lizzie giggled at the astonished look on her husband's face. He started to stammer and she put her finger to his lips. Then she kissed him. "That's all right, Abby. We're just taking shelter from the storm. Right, William?"

He nodded and rolled over onto his back. "Yes, ma'am. We're just taking shelter." Abby began to giggle and tried to crawl past him. He grabbed her around the waist and flung her over his lap where he proceeded to tickle her. Lizzie laughed and sat up to watch the two of them play. She cried out in pain when they rolled onto her legs.

Aiken reached over and lifted up her skirts despite her protests. He grimaced as he saw the red, raw skin underneath. "Lizzie, you're burned. Why didn't you tell me?"

She shrugged. "It didn't really hurt until now. But now that the two of you have lain on them, they *really* hurt."

He picked up the salve from where she had placed it. "This is probably going to sting a bit. The skin is pretty raw looking." He rolled her burned skirt and bloomers up past her knees. Taking one leg in his hand, he gently rubbed in the salve, slowing when she drew in her breath against the pain and speeding back up when she let her breath out. "I don't think you'll scar. It doesn't look too bad."

"I'm not worried about scarring, William."

"Well, I would be. Couldn't stand to have those beautiful legs all scarred up. I might have to trade you in for someone who's undamaged." He winked over at Abby, who giggled.

They were interrupted by the sound of shouts and screams coming from outside. Lizzie started to rise, pulling down her skirt. Aiken pushed her back. "Stay here," he ordered. He jumped from the wagon bed and sprinted towards the far side of the wagon circle.

Another family had been foolhardy enough to try lighting a fire, and the strong winds had blown the embers around so that one landed on the canvas covering of the wagon. Days without rain had left everything dry as a tinder. Men were milling around the shooting flames, trying to approach the burning wagon. Frightened screams from inside the wagon rent the air. Luke doused himself with some of the precious water stash that stood nearby and, covering his face with his arm, climbed into the wagon bed.

"Who's in there?" Aiken wanted to know.

"The Miller's little girl," one of the men told him. "Mrs. Miller lit a fire, trying to use the wagon as a block against the wind, and—well, you can see what happened. The child was inside taking a nap. Didn't take it long to catch fire in this wind. It's a damn shame if you ask me. That fool colored boy has been fighting to get inside that wagon ever since he heard there was a child inside."

"I'd have done the same thing," Aiken told him. "Luke? Luke!" Aiken approached the tail of the wagon in time to see Luke emerging. He carried a small child in his arms, wrapped in a quilt. He was smiling.

"I got her, Mr. Aiken. Lucky little thing was sleeping near the front. The flames haven't burned through to the inside yet." Luke walked over and handed the girl to her mother. "She's coughing from the smoke, but she's alive and unburned. I'm afraid you're going to lose what's in that wagon, ma'am."

Mr. Miller took Luke's hand in a firm shake. "Bless you, Luke. Without you, my daughter would've died. You showed a lot of nerve, young man." He put his arm around his wife and they turned to watch their wagon burn.

Aiken slapped Luke on the back. "Well done! You all right? You're not burned are you?"

"A little singed, but I'll be all right. Don't tell Ida. She'll have my hide and start all that womanly fussing." He grinned hugely. "She'll find out soon enough from these folks, I reckon."

"We had our own little fire episode," Aiken explained. "Ida started a cooking fire and set Lizzie's skirts on fire. She's burned a little but not enough to worry about. Ida feels pretty bad. I don't think she'll let into you for saving that little girl, considering."

"Maybe not. What are the Millers going to do without a wagon? We're too far out to send them back to Laramie."

Aiken sighed. "They'll have to hitch up with anyone who has the room. I'll talk to everyone tomorrow about lending them what they can spare. The Millers still have their mules, so at least they won't have to walk to Oregon."

The generosity of the people Aiken was leading was overwhelming. With very little of their own to spare, they still gladly gave what they could. Spare blankets, an extra pot, water skins, and food all piled up at the Miller's feet. Mr. and Mrs. Miller stood there with their little girl and cried at the people's generosity. "May God bless you all," Mr. Miller said, his words catching in his throat. "May God bless you all."

Chapter 16

They continued on the next day through more high heat and desolate landscape. Lizzie glanced around her at the bare broken rock and dirt that stretched out before her as far as her eyes could see. There was no grass and very little shrubs. Ida walked beside the wagon, her skirts kicking up the dust. Both women had their face rags tied tight across their faces and the brims of their bonnets pulled as low as they could get them. They squinted and blinked continuously against the sun's glare and the dust. Abby tried sitting up beside her sister and finally gave up. They traveled well into the evening before Aiken finally called a halt.

The next morning, they woke to more of the same. Lizzie found herself dozing halfway through the day and was startled awake by the braying of the mules. She jerked tight on the reins and watched as a wagon ahead of them took off.

"Hold tight!" Aiken called, riding his mount full speed along the train of wagons. "Hold tight! It's alkali water! It's poison! Don't let the animals drink it!"

Lizzie was struggling to keep control of the mules and Ida hurriedly climbed up beside her to help. The mules strained and brayed as another wagon sped off. Lizzie could see Zeke and Luke fighting to restrain the two extra mules, and Zeke was dragged a short distance as his feet were yanked from underneath him.

"Thank God we didn't buy oxen," Lizzie stated. "Zeke would never have been able to handle them. And thank God William told us to buy gloves." The two women stood, planting their feet against the board in front of them and leaned back, using their combined weight to hold the mules in check.

"Look," Ida told her, jerking her head to the side. The herd of loose animals had bolted and was stampeding towards the alkali water. Aiken galloped his horse until he was between the herd and the water and began firing his pistol in the air. The majority turned aside but several plunged head long into the water.

"The dogs." Lizzie whipped her head around at the frenzied barking. "Abby, call the dogs. You've got to keep them away from the water."

"No, Lizzie, look at them." Abby peered over their shoulders. "They're helping herd the animals away. See." Buster and Boomer were indeed dodging in and out of the herd, barking and nipping at the heels of the mules and oxen until the men were able to surround the livestock and stop them.

The women smiled in relief and watched as the men formed a line in front of the animals, turning them back toward the wagons. Soon, the wagons were moving forward again. The animals that had drunk from the alkali water were dead by nightfall, causing several of the families to begin discarding items that weren't needed. Some of them did not have a full team left to pull their wagon.

Again, the train set off the next morning at daybreak, wanting to get in as many miles through the barren landscape as they could in order to get the wagons to the Sweetwater River as soon as possible. They reached the river a few hours before nightfall. Aiken rode down the train informing everyone that it would cost them three dollars a wagon to cross and the stock would have to be swum across. Lizzie sighed and handed the reins to Ida so she could get their fee from inside the wagon. She was too tired to argue the fee with anyone this time.

The river was high and running very swift. Lizzie watched as Luke and Zeke each climbed onto the back of one of the mules and proceeded to follow the other swimmers into the quick running water.

Halfway across, Zeke lost his hold and slipped into the water. Zeke yelled out as the swift current caught hold of him. Lizzie screamed out for Luke to grab him. Luke looked up, and realizing there was no way for Zeke to swim against the strong current, reached out and grabbed a hold of the boy's shirt, keeping him from being swept downriver. Zeke's mule struggled to swim and rejoin the mule that Luke was riding. The whites of its eyes showed with fear. A panicking cow was swept into the mule and Lizzie and the others watched as both of the animals were lost down the river.

Luke managed to hold onto Zeke until the two of them safely reached the opposite bank. Lizzie turned her attention to the bridge ahead of them. It was rickety and missing planks from several places in the middle. She looked apprehensively down at the raging river as Ida handed the Indian their fee. Resigned, she flicked the reins and set off over the bridge. The bridge swayed and creaked as they made their way little by little across it. Ida's eyes were wide in her frightened face and she continuously muttered a prayer as they inched their way across. When they were halfway across, the bridge lurched violently to one side.

"Lizzie!" Aiken shouted from the other side. "Hurry. One of the posts is giving way!"

She looked back to see the Johnson wagon approaching close behind her. Beneath them, the bridge was sagging and slowly giving way. Abby screamed from her position in the back of the wagon and Lizzie stood. "Giddup!" She flicked the reins violently. The mules brayed and fought against the swaying bridge. They pulled against the reins, the whites of their eyes showing. Then, they refused to take another step. Lizzie handed the reins to Ida and jumped from the wagon.

Her skirt got caught on the seat of the wagon and she tumbled over the side, landing hard on the deck of the bridge. Holding on to the wagon, she managed to get her feet back under her. She fell to her knees, banging them hard, as the bridge gave another violent jerk. She could see Ben Johnson also struggling to move his team across the bridge. With both of the wagons sitting on the teetering bridge, Lizzie could see that it wouldn't hold much longer. She grabbed the front of the mule's harness and pulled.

"Come on," she screamed, and almost fell again as the bridge shuddered under her feet. The Indian toll keeper had already run onto the bridge and was trying to help Ben move his team back.

"Go, Lizzie!" Aiken pushed her to the side. "I'll get the team. You

121

go!" He tugged on the animals as Ida began whipping them harshly with the reins. Abby sat screaming in the back of the wagon and Lizzie moved to get her. "I said go!" Aiken shoved her roughly in the direction of the bank.

"You need my help!" She saw that the mules were still balking. She left Abby and hurried back to his side and pulled along with him. Tugging together, they managed to get the team and wagon across the bridge, the Johnsons' wagon close behind them. The bridge collapsed as Ben Johnson moved his wagon onto the bank of the river. They watched as the bridge was washed downriver, its boards shattering apart as it struck the rocks.

Lizzie collapsed to the ground, shivering. Her husband put his arms around her and pulled her close to his chest. Abby and Ida rushed to their side. Luke ran up and swept his wife off her feet, raining kisses on her upturned face.

"We lost one of the mules, Lizzie. I'm sorry." Zeke stood before her, his hat in his hand.

"Oh, Zeke. I'm not worried about that mule." She pulled herself away from Aiken and put her arms around her brother. "I'm just thankful you're here. Mules can be replaced. You can't." She turned to Luke. "I owe you my gratitude, Luke. You saved Zeke's life."

Luke grinned back at her. "He's a tough boy, Miss Lizzie."

They camped on the banks of the Sweetwater that evening. Aiken was shocked when he saw his wife the next morning. "What are you wearing?" he demanded.

"A pair of Zeke's britches." She climbed out of the wagon wearing a pair of tan canvas pants, rolled up at the ankles, and a flowered calico shirt waist. Her face rag was tied around her neck.

"Well...take them off. You're not running around in a pair of Zeke's pants."

Lizzie stood firm before him. "Yesterday, my legs got tangled up in my skirt and I was almost washed down the river. These are more practical and a lot more comfortable. I'm either wearing these, or my bloomers. The leg is burned through on my bloomers, but I'll wear them if I have to. I'm going to sew Abby a pair of pants—the first chance I get."

"Over my dead body!" Aiken's eyes flashed under his hat. "As your husband, I demand that you change back into a skirt."

"William, you're being unreasonable." Lizzie put her hands on her hips. "I know that I promised to love and obey, but this is one area I'm not going to give in." She walked over and poured herself a cup of coffee. Blowing on it to cool it, she sat down, avoiding her husband's eyes.

He watched her incredulously. The pants were baggy on her and when she sat down, they rose up a couple of inches, exposing the moccasins she wore. The feminine shirt, the boy britches, and the moccasins together made a comical picture. And to top it off, she had her flowered bonnet hanging down her back and her face rag tied on the front.

"You beat all, woman. You really do." He shook his head and walked off, laughing.

Lizzie smiled at her victory and motioned Ida over. Ida was also dressed out in britches and an assortment of women's clothing. "How did Luke take it?"

"Well...he didn't walk off laughing. Took one look at me and stormed off without saying a word." The two women looked at each and burst into laughter. "He knows better," she added.

They laughed harder when Abby joined them. She had hitched her skirt up between her legs and had tucked the end into her waistband. She had left her bloomers in the wagon, leaving her thin pale legs sticking out like white sticks.

"What?" she demanded. "You two are wearing britches, so I made my own."

Lizzie held her side, laughing until tears streamed down her face. Ida choked on her coffee, spewing it out in front of her. Zeke walked by, glanced at the hysterical women in their new getups and walked on, shaking his head. He had heard his father mention before that there was just no understanding women and Zeke didn't even want to try.

They heard the cry to move out, and the women got shakily to their feet. Lizzie offered to drive when Ida said she was going to get started on a pair of decent pants for Abby.

They traveled up the Sweetwater Valley that day, the weather turning colder. One of the mountains to the side of them was already topped with snow. There was no wood or grass on their side of the river, but the water was clear and slow flowing. They stopped to camp that night beside it and swam the stock across it to graze on the other side where the grass was plentiful. Aiken told everyone they would camp here an extra day to enable the women to catch up on washing while the animals had grass to feed on.

"I don't know what's worse," Lizzie complained, slapping at her neck, "the dust, or these dang mosquitoes."

Ida set down the shirt she was scrubbing. "At least the dust doesn't eat you." She slapped her arm, leaving a blood smear from the squashed bug. "We eat the dust."

"Mind if I join you?" Alice Johnson stood before them, her arms loaded with a basket of laundry.

Lizzie smiled, relieved to see the woman out of her wagon and apparently not harboring any grudges. "We'd be pleased if you joined us, Alice." She rose and took the basket from her. "How have you been feeling?"

Alice stretched her back, her stomach protruding in front of her. "Little Junior here is pretty active." She patted her stomach. "I was worried a little over the excitement of crossing the river, but everything seems to be fine. I'm mighty glad you'll be here to help me, Ida."

Ida smiled in return and tossed a wet shirt in the basket. "Is your milk cow still giving milk?"

"Some. I'm taking care to drink a little each day, like you told me. It's hard for me to drink it when I've got little ones who need it."

Ida tossed the last shirt in the basket and stood up. "You've got a little one growing inside you that needs that milk more. You drink it, Miss Alice. You're looking a little peaked." Ida picked up the basket and carried it back to the wagon.

Alice watched her go. "She's a bossy little thing, ain't she?"

Lizzie nodded. "She can be. But…I've found that Ida is usually right." She stayed and helped Alice do her laundry. "I don't know what I'd do without her. She's been a big help to me on this trail."

"And now you've got Mr. Aiken," Alice added. "Could be you'll have your own little one shortly after we reach Oregon."

Lizzie blushed. "I've got my hands full enough with Abby and Zeke."

"My boy said he sees Zeke gambling a lot," she said, changing the subject. "It's not fittin' for a boy his age to be gambling."

"Nothing I can do about it," Lizzie answered. "I've tried. He's making money at it, at least. We'll need it when we get to where we're going."

"Yes, well..." Alice folded her last item of clothing. Lizzie picked up the basket before she could.

"I'll carry it for you."

Alice nodded and continued, "My Ben has also said he's seen you and your colored friend wearing britches—and little Abby, too," She pursed her lips. "It ain't ladylike, Lizzie. People will talk."

"Let them talk." She looked down at her skirt. "It's more comfortable than this."

"What does your husband think?"

"We've agreed that when we're not traveling, I'll wear a dress." Lizzie stopped at Alice's wagon and set the basket down. "I'm not worried what other people think, Alice. This trail is hard enough and has enough trials without worrying over every little thing that might set someone off." She gave the woman a quick hug and turned to leave.

"But, Abby is wearing them all the time, too, and now Sarah wants a pair."

"It's not a big deal, Alice." Lizzie sighed. "It's easier and safer to wear pants when climbing in and out of the wagon. Abby can be a girl again when we get to Oregon. I'd rather she looked a little unfitting than fall and get run over. All because of propriety."

Chapter 17

The occupants of the train settled down once again into their daily routine of battling the heat and the dirt. In some places they found themselves walking through sand that was ankle deep. After the first day of walking with moccasins full of sand, Lizzie tied her pant legs tight around her ankles, using some of her sister's hair ribbons. Abby whined and scolded when she saw what they were being used for. Lizzie shushed her and trudged on. Good water was becoming scarce, but small pools of poisoned alkali water could be seen all around them.

Lizzie glanced across the river when they camped that night. The side they were on had very little grass for the mules to graze on. They had left the good grazing behind a couple of days ago. The other side of the river showed plenty of grass and wood to burn. Unfortunately, there was no way to cross the wagons. Either the water ran too swiftly, or the bluffs were too high and steep.

The air began cooling down more as the emigrants entered the Black Hill Mountains and a slight drizzle of rain fell constantly through the day, making them miserable. By nightfall, they were grumbling and complaining. Fatigue showed in every line of their bodies and Ida and Lizzie stared crossly at each other over their cooking fire.

"We haven't even begun to climb the mountains yet," Lizzie stated. "I'm too tired to eat."

Ida nodded. "Well, one of us needs to get dinner for the men. They'll be hungry when they've finished tending to the stock."

"I'll do it." Abby joined them at the fire. "I can cook up what bacon is left and some beans. It isn't much, but it'll fill their bellies."

"You're a jewel, Abby. Have I told you that? You cook most of the time. It doesn't seem right." Lizzie stood up and groaned. Placing her hands on her lower back, she leaned backwards until she heard the popping of her vertebrae. "Ahh!"

Aiken walked up softly behind her and kissed her behind her ear. "Want a back rub?"

She turned into his arms. "I should be giving you one."

"I didn't drive a wagon today." He tucked a stray curl behind her ear. "I just ride a horse up and down the train. Piece of cake compared to what you and Ida do. Sit down." He pulled up a log and patted the ground in front of him. Lizzie smiled and sat down, relaxing as his firm hands kneaded the flesh of her shoulders.

"That feels wonderful." She closed her eyes and leaned back.

Aiken laughed and edged her forward. "I can't do it if you're leaning back against me."

"Sorry." She let her head loll forward. "William?"

"Yes?"

"Will it be difficult crossing the mountains tomorrow?"

"Not these. These are nothing more than hills. It'll be a few more days before we hit the Rockies. You *will* be able to see snow sometime tomorrow, though."

She spun around to face him. "Snow? It's only June."

"The snow will only get worse as winter approaches. It'll be getting colder, too, so you might want to round up some of your warmer clothing." He kissed her. "I'll go fetch Luke and Zeke. Tell them supper's ready."

"Snow," Lizzie said in disbelief. She shook her head. She pulled the collar of her shirt tighter around her neck against the chill of the evening. "And cold."

"I've never seen snow," Ida told her. "Not where I can touch it anyway. It'll be nice."

"It'll be nice and wet and cold." Lizzie took the plate of bacon and beans that Abby handed her. "Abby? Do you know where I put our coats?"

"They're in the little black trunk. I saw them the other day when I was putting my boots away. The scarves are in there, too." Abby sat down beside her and began to eat. "I'm looking forward to playing in the snow," she stated. "It'll be like Christmas, only in June, and with no presents."

True to his word, Aiken pointed out the patches of snow along the road after they had driven for a few miles. He rode up with a fistful of wild flowers for Lizzie.

"Flowers!"

"They're growing close to the snow patches. I figure one of the snow drifts ahead must be six feet deep. The road is pretty clear, though. We shouldn't have any trouble getting the wagons through."

Lizzie handed the reins to Ida and took the flowers. "They're beautiful, William. Thank you."

Luke strode up to them, a bucket in one of his hands. A huge grin split his face. He tilted the bucket and tossed the snow it contained over Ida's head. She shrieked from the icy wetness and jumped up. Luke winked at her, backing up quickly. "You said you wanted to see snow," he teased.

"Not down my neck!" She brushed at the snow and turned so Lizzie could get it out of her collar. Luke laughed as she grumbled, then he followed Aiken back to the front of the train.

"Can we make some snow ice cream, Lizzie?" Abby asked. "We've got a little honey left back here."

"If there's snow tonight where we camp, we'll have ice cream."

"Yippee!" Abby jumped from the wagon and ran back to tell Sarah.

"I was cold before—now I'm freezing," Ida griped.

"I never knew Luke had such a mischievous streak," Lizzie said.

"You have no idea, Lizzie. I swear that man never grew up."

"Maybe it's just that he was never free enough before to act like a child."

Ida looked at her. "You're right. I never thought of it like that, Lizzie, but the farther we get from the southeast, the happier Luke gets." She got a determined gleam in her eye. "And I intend to make sure he stays that way."

"How?"

"I'm not sure, but Oregon is far enough away from where we came from. If we don't go into town too often, no one will be the wiser about Luke." She glanced down at her lap, smiling. "It's kind of early, but I think I might be with child."

"Ida, that's wonderful! A new family *and* a new life." Lizzie looked ahead to where she could see her husband. "We have both been very blessed."

Not wanting to wait, Abby and Sarah ran up, grabbed a bucket, and set off in the direction of the snow bank Luke had told them about. They returned as the wagons were stopping for the night, cold, shivering, and happily looking forward to their snow ice cream. Lizzie got the honey from the back of the wagon and poured it in a thin stream over the snow. She smiled as she watched the children enjoy the rare treat.

They woke the next morning to freezing temperatures. Aiken broke the ice on the water bucket in order to make a pot of coffee. Lizzie peered out the wagon to see light snow drifting down and her husband stomping his feet and blowing on his hands to warm them. He saw her watching and smiled. "Come on. Join me."

"I'd rather not. I'm warm in here." She pulled the quilt tighter around her. "Ida and Luke must have been freezing last night."

"I'm sure they managed to stay warm enough," he laughed. "Come on, Lizzie." He motioned one hand toward the mountains. "Look how beautiful they are all covered with snow." He reached up a hand to help her down.

"It is romantic," she agreed, leaning into him. "But it is so cold for June."

"It'll be hot again when we leave the mountains," he assured her. "Enjoy it while you can."

"How much longer, William, till we get to Oregon?"

"A couple more months, Lizzie. I know it seems like forever, but we'll get there." He leaned his chin on the top of her head. "Did I mention that I already have a stake on some land? I bought it the last time I was out. It's the prettiest little valley you ever saw. Nestled snug between some mountains, with a little creek running through it and lots of grass for grazing cattle. You'll love it there."

"I'll love it, William, because you'll be there with me." She tilted her head up for a kiss.

A small band of Indians rode by the wagon train that morning, wrapped in skins against the cold. They glanced expressionless in the direction of the white people and continued riding past them. The ten braves were accompanied by two squaws and were pulling a litter, piled high with furs, behind them. Lizzie and Aiken stood still and watched them ride past.

"I didn't see or hear them," Aiken said in surprise. "It's a good thing they were peaceable enough."

"Do you think they want to trade?"

He shook his head. "Doesn't appear so. They rode on by, almost as if we weren't even here." He frowned as he thought. "I think maybe we should start pulling out. They didn't seem aggressive, but they weren't overly friendly either."

"Do you think there'll be trouble?" Lizzie looked worried as she watched the Indians ride out of sight.

"Anyone can be trouble if they're hungry enough." Aiken lifted his saddle and hoisted it on his horse's back. "Get Abby up and make a quick breakfast. I'll ride on and let everyone else know."

They drove on about eighteen miles and camped a short distance from Pacific Springs. It was a good place to water the stock and refill their water barrels. Lizzie looked up from where she was unpacking the things for dinner and was startled by the sight of several Indian braves watching her from the bushes. She stepped back to the wagon and carefully removed the rifle from under the seat.

"Put it down, Lizzie." Her husband came up behind her. "Don't show any signs of aggression."

She put the rifle back where she found it. "William…"

Three of the braves came forward, one walking ahead of the other two. He held up his hand, palm out. "Hungry." He motioned towards the food. He said something else they didn't understand and one of the squaws emerged from the trees with her arms loaded down with furs. "Trade," he said. The woman laid the furs at Aiken's feet.

"Lizzie, pack them up some food. They're only hungry." Luke emerged from around the wagon and the braves stepped back. They looked at him with wide eyes. "I don't think they've ever seen a black man before, Luke."

Luke nodded and stopped. "I'll just stay back here," he said. "I don't want to startle them too much. Ida, come over here by me." At the sight of Ida, the Indians began speaking rapidly to each other. The leader walked up to Luke and touched him then turned and said something else to his comrades. The rest came forward and began studying Luke and Ida. They touched the skin of their faces and grabbed at their hair.

"Ouch!" One of the squaws had tried taking some of Ida's hair with her. The bun which Ida had put her hair up in was falling down. Ida slapped her hand away and glared. "Luke, do something. They're going to tear us apart."

Luke pushed Ida behind him. "Stop."

Aiken picked back up the rifle Lizzie had set down and went to stand between Luke, Ida and the Indians. "Go now," he told them. "Take the food and go."

The Indians stopped and looked at him. They looked from the gun up to his face and back towards Luke. Then the leader smiled and motioned for the others to follow him. Like ghosts, they picked up the supplies Lizzie had packed and disappeared back into the trees, leaving behind a small pile of furs.

Ben Johnson ran up, his own rifle in his hands. "Ya'll all right? I stood over there," he pointed, "and watched. Waited to see if you needed me. Some of the other men noticed what was happening, too. We stood by."

"I appreciate that, Ben." Aiken lowered his rifle. "They were just hungry and curious."

"Hungry and curious my foot!" Ida said loudly. "That one woman just about *ripped* my hair out."

Aiken laughed. "They were just curious, Ida. They didn't mean you any harm." He looked in the directions they had disappeared. "I was going to send men out to hunt, but I'm thinking we'll wait until tomorrow." Although the Indians had appeared harmless, Aiken was left feeling uneasy. Hunger does strange things to people and these Indians had definitely appeared hungry and downtrodden.

Chapter 18

William," Lizzie said the next morning, "some of the stock is missing. Zeke told me this morning. One of our mules is gone, too. We've only got the four left now." She stood with her hands on her hips and peered around. "Do you think those Indians stole them?"

Aiken was saddling his horse. "I think so. Luke and I and some of the others are going out looking for them." He pulled the cinch tight. "Keep the rifle close by. I've told Zeke to stay with you. They can't have gotten very far with the stock. Don't worry. We'll find them, Lizzie." He swung his leg over the saddle.

She put her hand on his knee. "Be careful, William."

He winked at her. "Be back before you miss me." He trotted off to join the others and the women watched as their husbands rode off in search of the missing animals.

Lizzie turned to Abby and Ida. "Well, there's no water for washing, but we can catch up on our mending. Zeke, why don't you spend this time going over the harnesses? Make sure they're all in good shape." She looked back in the direction Aiken and the others had ridden. "If we stay busy, the time will go faster." She looked around her. "Where are the dogs?"

Zeke shrugged. "I haven't seen them since early this morning."

Lizzie picked up the rifle and pulled her shawl tighter around her shoulders. "Come on, Zeke. We're going to find them. I bet those Indians lured them off so they could steal our mule."

"Lizzie, are you sure?" Ida asked, worried. "I don't think Mr. Aiken would want you wandering off."

"I won't be alone, Ida. Zeke has his rifle and I have this one. We're going out after the dogs. We'll be back before the men return." Ida watched as Zeke followed his sister.

The trees and underbrush were thick where they entered the

woods. Lizzie stopped to look around her. The sun barely cut through the branches overhead, leaving them in deep shade. "Will you be able to find our way back, Zeke? We could easily get lost in here."

The boy nodded. "Sure." He whistled and called the dogs by name. They stood and listened, waiting for an answering bark. "Do you think they could have headed back, Lizzie? Back to water?"

She shook her head. "I don't see why. There's snow around if they were thirsty." They continued walking for another hour with no sight of the dogs. The damp leaves under their feet let them trudge on with virtually no sound. Lizzie sat on a fallen log to rest, looking around her. They hadn't brought food or water with them. She hadn't expected to be gone this long. The forest was silent, except for the occasional bird, and she breathed deeply of the cold air. Zeke sat on a stump a few feet in front of her and sighed. He leaned his elbows on his knees, resting his chin in his hands. Lizzie looked up at him, freezing in fear.

"What?" Zeke's eyes opened wide at the look on his sister's face. He moved to stand up.

"Don't move, Zeke," she whispered. "Stay perfectly still." She slowly lifted her rifle off the ground. "There's a bear behind you."

"A bear!" he yelped and jumped up, disregarding his sister's warning. The bear, in reaction to Zeke's yell, rose on its hind legs and roared. Zeke flinched at the sound and rushed forward to stand next to his sister.

"I told you to stay still!" Lizzie's arms shook as she struggled to hold the rifle steady. They watched as the bear fell back onto all four of its paws. It huffed and slapped its front paws against the ground.

"Back up slowly, Zeke." She ordered him, quietly. "Don't startle it or make it mad."

"I'm scared, sis." Zeke lifted his own rifle, aiming it in the bear's direction.

"I know," her voice quavered. "I am, too." Holding their rifles in front of them, they began to slowly walk back the way they had come. Zeke stepped on a dry twig which snapped loudly in the crisp air, and they froze. Suddenly, the bear roared and charged. Lizzie shoved

Zeke out of the way and dove to the ground. She began to crawl frantically toward the thick underbrush, stifling her screams. A sob escaped her throat and she glanced over her shoulders to see that the bear had turned its attention toward her. She leaped up and began to run.

The bear quickly followed and swiped at her, raking her shoulder with its claws which caused her to drop the gun. Zeke picked himself up off the ground and scrambled for his own gun. He had dropped it when Lizzie had shoved him down.

He watched helplessly as the bear snuffed and pawed at his sister. As she lay still, not moving, he was spurred into action. He quickly brushed the damp leaves from the barrel of his gun and took aim.

Lizzie had fallen to the ground and lay still, curled into a ball, her arms protectively covering her head. She tried to slow her breathing and not whimper with fear and pain. Her shoulder was on fire where the bear's claws had swiped her and she could feel the blood running from the wound, soaking into the ground beneath her. The bear's hot breath blew across her face. It smelled rancid and sour, and she could feel the bile rise into her throat. The bear continued to rake at her, trying to roll her over.

Zeke aimed his gun and yelled, "Hey! Hey!" The bear turned swiftly in his direction, its back paws catching in Lizzie's skirt and leaving a deep rake across her thigh. Zeke aimed and fired, his bullet taking the bear in the shoulder. The bear roared and once again rose to its hind legs. Zeke aimed and fired again. This time his shot took the animal in the throat, dropping it to the ground with a moan. He stood still to see if it was going to move. It lay still, and after several seconds of the bear not moving, he rushed to his sister's side. "Lizzie. Lizzie." He shook her shoulder.

"Don't touch me," she said weakly. "It really hurts, Zeke."

Zeke looked down her body and noticed the bleeding wounds on her shoulder and thigh. "I'm sorry, Lizzie," he said, the tears running down his face. "I'm sorry I moved. I know you said not to."

"It's all right, Zeke." Lizzie patted his arm softly.

"Can you get up?" he sobbed.

She shook her head. "I don't think so. You'll have to go and get help."

"I won't leave you here."

"Zeke, you have to. Give me your coat. I'm freezing here on the ground. Please, just go get help." She closed her eyes against the pain.

Zeke hurriedly took off his coat and draped it across her. He placed her rifle close to her hand and sprinted off in the direction of the wagon train. The tears flowing down his face, kept pace with his legs as he ran. He swiped low hanging branches out of his way, not bothering to duck or go around. He yelped in fear as he startled a pheasant from a bush and it rose squawking into the air. Every snap of a twig, or rustle in the brush caused him to run faster, his breath catching in his throat with fear.

Soon, he heard voices calling their names. "Here! I'm over here! Hurry!" Aiken and Luke burst through the underbrush, followed close behind by several of the other men.

Aiken grabbed Zeke by the shoulders and shook him roughly. "Where's Lizzie?"

Zeke panted. "Over...there..." he pointed. "She's...hurt, Aiken. Really bad. A bear."

Aiken's face paled. "Show me."

Zeke led them quickly back to where he had left his sister. No one spoke as they ran. Luke laid a hand on the boy's shoulder and squeezed, reassuring him. Zeke looked up at him gratefully. "She told me not to move, but I did. It's all my fault, Luke." Zeke broke into sobs. "I've never been good at listening to her and now she's hurt really bad. She was bleeding something awful." Luke pulled the boy close to his chest, his eyes meeting Aiken's.

Aiken heard Zeke's words to Luke and turned to run, calling his wife's name. He paused for only a moment when he saw the dead bear. He fell to his knees by Lizzie's side. Blood stained the snow beneath her to a dark red. Her pale face blended in with the white of the snow. He placed a finger against her neck. She was unconscious, but alive. He wrapped Zeke's coat more snugly around her and lifted her into his arms.

"You men take care of the bear," he ordered. "There's steak and skin there that can be used. Zeke, you come with me. You can carry the guns." Zeke nodded and moved to follow his brother-in-law. They didn't speak and Zeke had to run to keep up with Aiken's quick pace. Lizzie moaned occasionally from the pain, causing Aiken to walk faster.

Ida was watching for them and put a hand to her mouth when she saw Aiken carrying the unconscious Lizzie. "What happened?"

"A bear." Aiken laid her gently in the back of the wagon. "She was attacked by a bear." He climbed in after her and rummaged through their things until he found the little chest that held their medical supplies. He noticed Abby peering fearfully through the canvas opening. "Abby, go boil some water. Ida, I need help." He began to cut away Lizzie's clothing from her wounds. Where the blood had dried, the fabric stuck to the wound, causing it to bleed freely again when he pealed it away. Tears ran down his face at the sight of her ripped flesh. The wound across her thigh was much deeper than the one on her shoulder. The weight of the bear had torn some of the flesh away from her thigh, leaving a deep, wide gash, rather than the scrapes that were on her shoulder. Hurriedly, Aiken ripped one of his wife's petticoats into bandages. "Hurry with that water!"

Ida climbed into the wagon, a pot of water in her hand. "Here you go. We had already started boiling it for coffee. What do you want me to do?" She kneeled across Lizzie's body from him.

"Hold her down. All I have to disinfect it with is whiskey. It's going to hurt like hell." He gritted his own teeth and poured it into the wound. Lizzie woke up and screamed, fighting against Ida's hands. The sound of her pain rang through the campground and Zeke grabbed tightly to Abby's hand.

Aiken poured some more whiskey on the wound, and grabbing one of the bandages, tied it tightly around her leg. He reached over and caressed her cheek. "I'm sorry, sweetheart. I'm almost finished." He repeated the procedure with her shoulder and sat back. Lizzie, mercifully, had already passed out from the pain. He rubbed his hands across his face and looked at Ida. Her mouth was firm and her eyes wide in her face. "We have to watch for infection now. I couldn't stitch her up, Ida. I can't stitch up gouges. She'll have a nasty scar, and maybe a limp." His shoulders shook as he broke into sobs. "She's in God's hands now."

Ida moved over and put her arms around him. "That's the best place to be, Mr. Aiken. The *best* place. You go on out. I'll watch her for a while."

"I'm not leaving her."

"You need to go talk to Zeke. That boy is out there crying his heart out 'cause he thinks this is his fault." She took a deep breath. "You go help him. Come back later. I'll watch her real close. I promise."

He nodded. "You're right, but come and get me if she wakes up." He looked down at Lizzie's white face and pulled another quilt up over her. He nodded again and disappeared.

Zeke and Abby were standing right outside, waiting for someone to let them know how their sister was. Aiken stood for a minute, looking down at them. He took a deep breath. "She's...fine. For now. Zeke, it wasn't your fault."

"But she told me to be still. When she saw the bear, she said don't move." The boy's tears started fresh. "I didn't listen, Aiken. I didn't listen to her. I got scared and I jumped up and yelled. She pushed me out of the way and took up the rifle. She put herself in front of me, Aiken." Zeke launched himself at Aiken, throwing his arms around him.

Aiken patted his back. "That's how she is, Zeke. She probably didn't even think twice about it." He sat the boy back away from him and looked him in the eyes. "That's what she would do no matter who it was, Zeke, but especially for someone she cares about. It's not your fault." He pulled him close again and reached for Abby. He held the two children tight. "Now, we pray. That's all that's left for us to do."

"We went looking for the dogs," Zeke said, his voice muffled against Aiken's chest. "She wanted to."

He nodded. "Yeah, Ida told me. The Indians had them. We got all the animals back, but for one ox that they had already butchered."

"Mr. Aiken?" Ida called from the wagon. "She's awake. She's asking for you."

William jumped quickly into the bed of the wagon and kneeled beside Lizzie. He brushed her hair back from her face. She smiled weakly up at him. "You hurt me," she said teasing, her voice barely above a whisper.

"I'm sorry." He leaned down and kissed her forehead.

"We went looking for the dogs," she told him. "Abby loves those dogs."

"Shh. I know. Ida told me. You should sleep now."

"I can't sleep, William. It hurts too much." She closed her eyes against the pain. He jumped up and shoved his head through the canvas opening.

"Zeke! Go see if anyone on this wagon train has any blasted laudanum!"

Ida spoke up from outside. "Lizzie should have some in her chest, Mr. Aiken."

"I let Alice use it. She needed it to help her sleep after Seth died," Lizzie spoke up quietly. "She should have it."

"I'll go right now," Zeke told them. He reappeared a few minutes later with the small blue bottle of laudanum. Aiken sent him a smile of thanks.

"Here, sweetheart. Take a swallow of this." He propped her up against his arm and tilted the bottle into her mouth. She swallowed and smiled at him before closing her eyes.

Aiken sat there and watched her sleep over the next couple of hours, his anxiety for her growing as she tossed to and fro beneath the covers. Her temperature had been steadily rising through the night. "Ida!" he yelled.

She emerged quickly from the tent she shared with her husband. Luke and the others had skinned the bear and had returned shortly before nightfall. "Mr. Aiken?"

"I need some snow," he told her. "Her temperature is rising. I need to bathe her in it. We need to bring her temperature down."

Luke stopped Ida. "I'll get it, honey. It's too cold out here for you." He took the bucket from her and ran half a mile up the road to where the cleanest snow drifts were. The cold air rose in steam off his body as he ran. His fear and exertion had him sweating, despite the cold. Aiken was waiting impatiently for him when he returned. Luke handed him the bucket and stood outside the wagon in case his friend should need him again. Ida walked over and draped a quilt around his shoulders.

He smiled down at her. "I thought I told you it was too cold out here."

"We'll keep each other warm," she told him, moving under the quilt with him. "I can't sleep for fear of Lizzie. I'll wait out here with you."

For two days they camped there, Lizzie battling with the fever and infection. Occasionally, one of the others on the wagon train would come by to quietly check on her progress, and a couple of wagons becoming impatient, headed on without them. Luke did the best he could to hold the train together, leading the men on hunts and searches for wild roots and berries. Ida and Alice cared for the children, being especially careful to act optimistic around Zeke and Abby.

On the third day, Lizzie awoke, alone, and sat up. She looked around her and stretched, wincing at the pain in her shoulder and leg. She crawled painfully to the wagon opening, dragging her injured leg behind her, and peered out. She could see Aiken sitting alone by the fire.

"William?"

He spun around and ran to her. "Praise God!" He pulled her into his arms, bringing her outside. "She's awake! Zeke! Abby! Lizzie's back with us!" He spun her around and kissed her. "I sure have missed you, Elizabeth Aiken."

"I've missed you, too, William. How long have I been ill?"

"A little more than two days," Ida answered, walking towards them with a smile on her face. "And we were mighty worried about you."

Zeke and Abby came running when they heard and Zeke burst into tears, wiping his nose on his sleeve. "I'm so sorry, Lizzie."

"Put me down, William."

"Lizzie…"

"Please." She looked up at him imploringly. "I need to stand."

He nodded, understanding, and placed her on her feet, keeping his arm around her for support.

"I'm going to be fine, Zeke. Really. See." She tried taking a step, and Aiken caught her before she fell. "It looks like it'll be a while before I'm walking, but I'm going to be just fine." She held out her arms to hug her brother and sister.

Luke came walking up with a crutch he had carved from a small tree. "Miss Lizzie, this will help you walk in no time." He showed her how to place it under her arm.

"Thank you, Luke. That's very thoughtful of you."

"She won't be using it for a few days, Luke. She's going back in the wagon right now." He scooped her up again and turned to see the rest of the train watching them, smiles on all their faces. "We're pulling out tomorrow, folks," he told them. A loud cheer echoed through the woods, sending the woodland birds into flight.

Chapter 19

They pulled out the next morning with Lizzie bundled up in the back of the wagon and Abby sitting beside her— chattering non-stop. She was full of curiosity about Lizzie's encounter with the bear, and since her brother-in-law had kept her away from Lizzie during her recovery, she was bursting to ask questions.

"Were you scared, Lizzie?" she asked, her eyes wide. "'Cause Zeke said he was scared."

Lizzie smiled. "I didn't really think about being scared until I was on the ground with the bear leaning over me. Then I was really scared. I thought I was going to meet Jesus right then and there."

"More like the devil according to Zeke." Abby sidled up closer to her, being careful of Lizzie's injured leg. "He said that old bear roared and huffed, slapping at the ground with its big old feet." She shivered. "I think I would have just sat down and cried. Did you cry, Lizzie?"

"No, Abby I didn't cry." She tucked the quilt tighter around them against the cold of the morning.

"Did it smell bad? The bear's breath, I mean. Like rotten meat? 'Cause I heard once that bear's breath smells really bad."

Lizzie closed her eyes and leaned her head back against the few crates they had in the back of the wagon. She remembered the rancid smell of the bear's breath as it breathed on her, and she relived the terror as it stood over her and roared. She sighed. "Yes, Abby, it smelled very bad."

Abby nodded grimly. "You're lucky to be alive, Lizzie."

"Yes, I am."

The road had begun angling steeply upwards as they talked and Lizzie felt herself sliding slowly along the bed of the wagon. One sharp lurch slid her abruptly against the tail of the wagon bed. She yelled out in pain. Abby stood to help her and pitched head first out the back.

"Abby!" Lizzie peered out to see her younger sister lying on her back in the dirt of the road. "Ida, stop the wagon!"

"I can't Lizzie." Ida turned to her. "Mr. Aiken said we had to keep the team moving forward, or we would start to slide down this hill. Once we start sliding, we won't be able to stop and would slide right into the wagon behind us."

Lizzie watched in horror as the Johnson's wagon turned the bend behind them. She pulled herself painfully to her feet and climbed slowly out of the wagon, crying when she jumped down to the road and jarred her leg. She fell to her knees and crawled quickly to her younger sister who was just beginning to stir. Lizzie looked her over for signs of broken bones and sighed with relief when she didn't find any. "Abigail. We've got to get off this road. Can you walk?"

Abby sat up. "I think so, Lizzie." She reached up and touched her head. "I think I hit my head when I fell."

Lizzie glanced up as the Johnsons' team came closer. Ben shouted at them to move, knowing he couldn't stop or go around them. "Come on, Abby. We'll crawl together. I won't be able to stand up again."

Abby watched in terror as the Johnsons' oxen bellowed just a few feet from them and she hurriedly scurried to the edge of the road, pressing her small body against the rock face. Lizzie made her way more slowly, wincing as the rocks dug into her knees. She joined Abby against the rock and watched as the Johnsons passed them.

"You're bleeding again, Lizzie." Blood was soaking through Lizzie's bandages and skirt.

Perspiration beaded Lizzie's brow and she drew in her breath shakily. "I'll be fine, Abby. Run on ahead and get William for me, will you? I'll rest here until you get back." She noticed the bump forming on Abby's forehead. "We need to put something on that," she said. "Tell Ida—after you get William."

Abby nodded, and lifting her skirts, ran past the wagons, yelling Aiken's name. She found him several wagon lengths ahead.

"Aiken!" Her sharp tone caused him to pull up on his horse's reins. "I fell out of the wagon and Lizzie came to get me. She hurt her leg again, and she's bleeding!" Abby stood there out of breath as Aiken galloped his horse to where his wife sat. He jumped off before his mount had come to a complete stop.

"Elizabeth?" Her eyes were closed and he tenderly smoothed her hair back from her face, his eyes traveling down her body. "Lizzie?"

"I'm fine, William. I hurt my leg again getting out of the wagon."

He looked down the hill and could hear the braying of mules and bellowing of oxen. "I'm going to help you on my horse, Lizzie. The stock is coming up this hill, and we're in the way."

She nodded.

"I'm afraid it's going to hurt, honey, but I'll be as gentle as I can." The stock was in sight now and moving quickly in their direction. They could hear the gunshots from the men driving the animals forward. Luke saw Lizzie and Aiken sitting in the road and quickly assessed the situation. He ran in front of the animals waving his huge arms. He shouted, trying to slow the herd down. The animals didn't stop and he had to dive off the road and into the bushes in order to not be run over himself. Aiken swiftly scooped Lizzie up in his arms and ran for his horse. "Quickly, Lizzie. Put your foot in the stirrup."

"I can't, William. I don't have enough strength in my leg." She looked over his shoulder in terror. "They're coming right at us!"

William slapped his horse on the rump, causing it to jerk and run ahead of the stampeding stock. He looked around them quickly and rushed back to the rock face. He set Lizzie on her feet against the rock and shielded her body with his as the animals lumbered past. One of the oxen's horns ripped through his shirt, getting caught, and pulled him a few feet down the road with them.

"William!"

He fought his way back along the rock wall and pressed himself tighter against her. "I'm here. I'm all right." They stood that way for several minutes while the stock passed. Zeke and Luke ran up to them.

"Lizzie?" Zeke looked up at her.

"She's fine." Aiken scooped her up again in his arms.

"You're bleeding, Mr. Aiken," Luke told him. One of the oxen's horns had left a shallow gash along his right ribcage.

"It's just a graze, Luke."

They made their way slowly to the wagons that were waiting for them at the top of the steep hill. Zeke ran ahead and retrieved Aiken's horse. The way down the hill was slightly less steep, and with Abby securely in the wagon behind Ida and Lizzie sitting before her husband on his horse, the wagons slowly made their way to the bottom. They traveled on that day until they came to the Green River where Aiken called them to stop and pitch camp. They would rest and ride the ferry across the river in the morning.

The weather was still cold when they awoke, and the winds were picking up. Lizzie pitched a fit when she heard the price for crossing on the ferry. Eight dollars a wagon! It seemed the farther west they got, the more expensive the tolls. She pulled herself up until she was looking out the front of the wagon, past Ida. A white man stood on the ferry with his Indian wife beside him. Lizzie ached to be able to get down and walk over to them, demanding to know the reason for such a high price. She watched as Zeke and Luke braved the icy water of the river to swim the stock across. She crossed her arms over her chest and sat back.

"What day is it, Ida? Do you know?"

"Close to the end of June, I think." Ida flicked the reins to move the mules forward onto the ferry.

"Halfway there," Lizzie said to herself. "Or close to it. Only…halfway." She shook her head, wondering whether she could do more of what they had already gone through. According to her father's guidebook, they've passed the easy part. The hard traveling was still ahead of them.

She looked out the wagon again. As far as she could see there was nothing but the desert with more dirt and sand. A ridge of mountains lay a day or so travel ahead of them. She shivered against the cold wind and drew back into the wagon.

The ferry carried them across without incident and they began to travel across the desert toward the mountains ahead of them. They wrinkled their noses against the stench and Ida pulled her face rag up over her nose. The road they were traveling on was strewn with dead cattle that hadn't been able to make it any farther.

Lizzie noted that the occupants of previous wagons had abandoned some of their household items in order to lighten their loads. Chests and armoires, bed springs and mattresses, along with books and tools, lay strewn amongst the animal carcasses. She watched sadly out the back of the wagon, breathing shallowly against the stench, as they drove by the discarded items. She was thankful they had so little when they had begun this trip. There was little for them to have to pick through if the time came for them to lighten their wagon.

They traveled into the evening and on into the next. That second evening they camped at a small spring at the foot of the mountains. Ida started a fire while Aiken gathered up Lizzie and brought her out to join them. The night was cold and the small group sat huddled under blankets while they ate the simple fare that Ida and Abby had prepared.

"I've instructed everyone to leave behind anything that's not essential," Aiken told them. "The mountains we'll be traveling through are bad, but there are worse than these farther down the trail."

"We didn't have much to begin with, William," Lizzie told him. "I guess that was a blessing."

He looked over at Abby. "And you young lady, will walk alongside the wagon, not standing up in it, you hear?"

She nodded and smiled.

They traveled twenty miles the next day and camped near a cold, clear mountain stream. There was plenty of grass for the stock and sage brush to burn. The night was cold and promised a magnificent sunset from the top of the mountain. Aiken parted the canvas covering of the wagon and went inside. Lizzie sat there, hair unbound, with a brush in her hand.

"Have I told you you're beautiful?" he asked her, kissing the nape of her neck.

"Not today," she smiled.

"Well, you are. Bundle up, beautiful. We're going for a walk."

"A walk, but William…"

"I'll carry you. Come on." He held out his hand. Lizzie took his hand, and he helped her from the wagon.

"Should I carry you like a baby, or would you like a piggyback ride?"

Lizzie giggled. "Which is easiest for you?"

"Piggyback." He grinned mischievously. "Are you wearing your bloomers? We don't want anyone ogling your legs."

"William, really." She looked around her. "Is everyone going?"

"Well, mostly the children and the other hopeless romantics." He hoisted her up on his back. "You let me know if this pains you too much." He led the way with the children scampering around them, the dogs running and barking ahead of them, and other couples walking alongside. They were in the lower mountains, so the walk wasn't too strenuous. Small trees and bushes lined the path to the top of the hill. Aiken set his wife on her feet and turned her to look.

The view spread out before them was breathtaking. They overlooked the barren land they had traveled over. The river, a silver ribbon, wound lazily through the prairie, cutting a path through the desolate landscape. The crowning touch was the sunset. Brilliant reds, oranges, and yellows streaked across the sky as if applied by an artist's paintbrush. Lizzie drew in her breath with the beauty of it and slipped her hand into her husband's.

"Oh, William. I've never seen anything like it. There's nothing to obstruct our view. Nothing at all. It's like a dark ocean spread out before us. It's magnificent!"

He squeezed her hand. "I stop here every time I travel through. I never tire of looking at it. It is truly one of God's masterpieces."

"It's amazing," she said, dreamily, "that something so dreary and brown during the day, can be so alive and bursting with color once the sunset strikes it."

Luke stood next to them, his arm heavy across Ida's thin shoulders. Lizzie noticed tears shimmering in his dark eyes.

"Luke?" she asked.

"I've seen so much ugliness in my life, Miss Lizzie, that something this beautiful truly does restore my soul."

Ida leaned her head into his shoulder. "Soak it up, my husband. Draw on this beauty when times in your life turn ugly. God sends us these gifts when we truly need them."

The four of them stood silently reflecting on the glory of the scene before them. The sounds of the children playing, and the dogs barking, provided a soothing background noise. Aiken pulled up a small boulder for his wife to sit on.

"I've asked Luke and Ida to homestead with us," he told her. "There's a small parcel of land that runs the border of our property. I'm going to buy it for them and they can pay us back. That way they'll be close—but not too close."

She looked up at him. "Thank you, William. I've grown quite fond of our friends." She reached up and took Ida's hand.

"The Johnsons will be homesteading less than a day's ride away," he added. "You'll have your company you crave so much." He kneeled down beside her and whispered, "And when our own young ones come along, you'll have Ida to help you through your labor and there will be friends for our children to play with."

Lizzie blushed and lay her head on his shoulder.

Chapter 20

Several days later it rained during the night, again, and the travelers woke to more freezing temperatures and frozen water barrels. Aiken told Lizzie and Abby to walk beside the wagon since they had mountains to cross, and Lizzie soon found herself falling behind. Even with Abby's help her crutch would get stuck in the mud of the road. She grew irritable and sat on the side of the road as the Johnsons' wagon passed by them.

"I'm sorry, Abby, but I've just got to rest." She propped her crutch against a tree and leaned back, closing her eyes. "I'm cold, I'm wet, and my leg hurts."

"I'm sorry to hear that, Elizabeth Springer."

Lizzie's eyes flew open. Edward Newton stood before her, a smirk on his handsome face. He wore black pants, a long black duster, and a purple brocade vest over a sparkling white shirt. Not a speck of dust marred the perfection of his clothes. Lizzie looked down at her own mud stained dress and ragged wool coat. She sighed and grabbed Abby by the arm, pulling her closer.

"You're a fool for coming around here, Mr. Newton," Lizzie told him. "Especially after the stunt you pulled the last time. My husband would like nothing more than to shoot you."

"I've been called many things, Elizabeth, but never a fool." The smile left his face and his eyes grew hard. He looked at her crutch. "Seems you've been injured." He smoothed his moustache with his finger. "Pity, really. I had such plans for you, my dear. Oh, well. With your looks I'm sure the men would look past a little limp. And your sister will still fetch me quite a price." He reached over and softly touched Abby's smooth cheek.

Abby whimpered and pressed herself closer to Lizzie. "Please leave, Mr. Newton. My husband will be coming to get us soon." She looked up the road in hopes of seeing him.

"Husband? Well, I am surprised. I thought maybe that was just a ploy to send me on my way. There's no stopping the surprises with you, is there?" He let his eyes follow in the direction hers had taken. They could see Aiken astride his horse, riding down the road in their direction. Newton tipped his hat. "Until the next time, ladies." He stepped back and disappeared into the trees lining the road.

"Lizzie, was that Newton?" Aiken held down his hand to help her up.

"Yes." She allowed herself to be pulled up behind him. "I think he's following us. He gets bolder, William. It's not just me he wants now, but Abby, too."

Aiken positioned Abby in front of him and turned back. He peered into the trees where Newton had disappeared. "I'll shoot him if I see him again, Lizzie. If he comes anywhere near you again, I'll kill him."

She sighed. "That doesn't seem to be much of a deterrent."

They camped that night halfway up the next mountain. Above them they could see snow covered mountains, and below them, in a small green valley, they could see a small Indian village. Aiken ordered the wagons to stay close together, not wanting a repeat of what they had a few evenings before. Some of them were getting drastically low on extra stock. The trail was beginning to take its toll on the poor beasts.

The women struggled to light their cooking fires with fingers that were stiff with cold. Their breaths showed in the air. The people grumbled to Aiken as he rode past.

"Mr. Aiken," one man said, standing before his horse. "We waited to leave with you in May because you told us that we would cross these mountains before the bad weather. My children are crying because they're cold."

"This isn't bad, Mr. Robbins. Bad is what would be waiting for us if we had left a month later." Aiken tried to move his horse past the man.

"My children are hungry. My wife has no energy left in her, and our rations are running low."

"I am sorry, sir. You should still have plenty of rations to last you, if you followed the guidelines I handed out in Missouri. These woods are full of animals for the hunting. Feel free to hunt them when we stop in the evenings."

Others approached them and crowded close, voicing their own concerns and complaints. Aiken stilled his nervous horse and looked around at their faces. "We will be out of these mountains within the next day or two. Then it will be the heat and lack of water you'll be complaining about. We're all tired and cold, folks. We just need to make the best of things and keep moving."

"The Israelites complained against Moses when he was leading them to the Promised Land." They all turned to see Luke standing, arms folded across his chest, leaning against one of the wagons. He walked towards them. "And the Lord led them through, just as He promised to. Just as He will use *this* man to lead *you* through." He stood close to Aiken's horse. "This man is willing to go forward with an injured wife and the added responsibility of children. None of you have an injured one in your party. Mr. Aiken isn't asking anyone to do what he himself isn't also doing. We all left behind our pasts in the hope of a better future. Anything worthwhile requires work and some hardship. Go on back to your wagons and let Mr. Aiken be. Look around you and see what you have." Luke parted the way through the crowd, allowing Aiken to follow on his horse.

"Quite a speech there, my friend." Aiken dismounted.

Luke smiled. "It is human nature to grumble when things are hard, Mr. Aiken. Just as it is our nature to forget the bad when we come to finally see what it is we've been striving for. They'll come around."

"Are you a learned man, Luke?"

"No, sir. Can't read or write. Not even my own name." Luke slid the saddle from Aiken's horse and handed it to him. "But my daddy knew the Bible from his daddy, and my momma could read some. They wanted to raise me right, even under the bondage of slavery."

Aiken clapped him on the shoulder. "Well, they did, Luke. They surely did."

The next day took the wagon train over another steep mountain, pebbled with rocks. It was the worst road they had traveled over yet and at the end of it, Luke was kept busy repairing broken wheels and axles. They had completed the worst of their first set of mountains. It was Sunday and they camped for the day next to a clear stream with plenty of wood and grass. The temperature reached up into the hundreds as the women washed and mended, and the men hunted and cared for the stock.

Lizzie read from the Bible as had become their Sunday morning ritual—when they could afford to stop. The group around her was small that morning. The few that were there mopped at their faces with soggy bits of fabric and swatted at mosquitoes. The children raced to the creek after the reading to cool off and gain a reprieve from the biting insects. Abby started running a fever later in the day from the mosquito bites, along with several of the other children, and fell asleep on a quilt while Lizzie read.

The next morning they started up another mountain, much smaller than the others, and camped near the top of it. The weather was still warm, but a breeze blew over them, cooling them a little. Some of the younger children still suffered from fevers. When evening came, and the weather cooled, they set off again, crossing several small creeks. Luke kept a close eye on the wagon wheels, noting with satisfaction how the water from the creeks swelled the wood of the wheels, causing them to tighten against their frames.

They came across another Indian village early the next day and Aiken halted the wagons. He rode alone into the village and returned some time later with the news that the Indians were friendly and willing to trade. This raised the spirits of the travelers and they chattered happily as they spent a while going through their meager belongings for items to trade.

Lizzie and Ida gathered up a few yards of spare fabric and ribbon. They were hoping to trade for roots and vegetables. Zeke took along his shoes as he had taken to wearing either his boots or moccasins. He wanted to trade them for a pair of the buckskin breeches that the Indians wore. His wool pants were rapidly thinning and were covered with patches. Lizzie handed the fabric and ribbon to Ida to carry and grabbed her crutch.

The Indians had laid out brightly woven blankets to display the beaded jewelry and leather clothing they had made, along with pemmican and several varieties of vegetables. Several of the women exclaimed over the jewelry, while Lizzie and Ida made their way directly to the food.

"Potatoes!" Lizzie exclaimed. "They'll be wonderful in a stew. And look, Ida, carrots!"

Ida held up an onion. "Let's get as many of these vegetables as we can get with our fabric, Lizzie. They'll keep for a while in the bed of the wagon." She studied the pemmican critically. She held a piece to her nose and sniffed, before putting it back. She shook her head and reached for another onion.

Abby held up a turquoise amulet hanging on a leather strap. "Lizzie, do we have enough for this?"

"I don't know, Abby. What do they want for it?"

One of the Indian women held up two fingers and pointed at the ribbon. Lizzie smiled and handed them over. Abby slipped the necklace over her head and raced off to show Sarah Johnson. Zeke walked up, proudly wearing a pair of tan buckskin pants, the fringe hanging down both sides of his legs. The tail of his flannel shirt hung loose over the top of the pants. Lizzie and Ida looked at each other and laughed. They loaded up their baskets with vegetables and headed back to camp.

Aiken patted his stomach after dinner that night. "I sure am glad I married me a practical woman," he said looking at Lizzie. "A lot of the women traded for silly trinkets, and here we are, stuffed to the gills on a filling stew."

"Amen to that," Luke added. He sat back, leaning on an elbow.

"And just what did the two of you get?" Ida asked, scraping the plates. "I saw you two looking everything over.

The two men looked sheepishly at each other. "I traded a shirt for a necklace for Lizzie," Aiken said. He pulled a beautiful turquoise and silver beaded chain from his pocket.

"And I traded a broken axle for this," Luke added. He pulled another necklace from his pocket and handed it to Ida.

"I sure am glad we married such practical men," Ida said, laughing.

"The dogs are gone," Zeke said, running up to them.

"I called for them and they didn't come." Abby joined him, tears welling up in her eyes.

"Where did you see them last?" Aiken sighed, and placed his hat back on his head.

"At the village," Zeke told him. "They followed me to the village and that's the last time I saw them."

"All right. Luke?" Luke nodded and followed Aiken into the deepening dusk as he walked back towards the village.

Lizzie handed the children a plate of stew. "Here, eat. They'll find them."

The men returned an hour later, leading a mule, with Buster trailing behind. Aiken handed him over to Abby. "I'm sorry, kids. The Indians had them. We couldn't find Boomer." He handed the reins of the mule to Zeke. "Got another mule though, to replace the one we lost."

He joined Lizzie back by the fire. "They had already eaten Boomer," he told Lizzie quietly. "We got them to give us that broken down mule in exchange for him." Lizzie looked up at him, her hand over her mouth. "We'll let the children believe that he just wandered off. The Indians thought they were wild dogs. They didn't see any reason to turn down easy food."

Lizzie blanched and set her plate down, suddenly losing her appetite. "Poor Boomer."

Ida clutched her stomach and rushed away from the fire, losing her dinner in the bushes. Luke held her shoulders as she vomited. She wiped her mouth with her apron and straightened. "What a waste of good vegetables," she said angrily. "I couldn't even keep them down."

"Did they tell you they ate him?" Lizzie asked. "Maybe it wasn't him."

Aiken shrugged. "Looked like a dog carcass on the spit. They don't speak English very well. I guess we could've been mistaken, but it's not likely." He turned to Luke. "That mule don't look like much, Luke. Hitch him to the wagon tomorrow and rotate him with the others as long as he lasts. That'll help keep the others healthy for the last set of mountains."

Chapter 21

Buster's excited barking interrupted their breakfast the next morning, and they all turned to see Boomer come limping into camp, trailing a frayed rope behind him. Abby squealed and dropped her plate, wrapping her arms around the dog's neck.

"Well, I'll be," Luke stated. "Guess we *were* mistaken after all."

Aiken ruffled the dog's fur. "You must have been saved for the next meal, huh boy?" A grin split his face. He put an arm around Lizzie's shoulders and gave her a quick squeeze. "I'm glad I was wrong," he said, looking at Abby's happy face.

It was still hot and dusty as they traveled that day, struggling up hills and down. The sun beat down upon their heads, and the women had taken to wearing their face rags and britches or bloomers again. Lizzie convinced Aiken to let the dogs ride in the wagon, and she rode up front with Ida, her leg beginning to mend. Abby was happy to run alongside the wagon with her friend Sarah.

In the early afternoon it started to rain, making their descent through the hills precarious as the wagons slid from side to side. One wagon came perilously close to the edge and Aiken called a halt to camp in the next hollow.

They camped next to a soda spring and the children had their fill of the bubbly water. The spring sprouted up about a foot and a half from a cleft in the rock. Abby took one of her sister's face rags and let the water suck it in and spit it back out. She and Sarah would try to catch it when it would shoot into the air, and they squealed with laughter. When Lizzie found out what they were using, she confiscated the rag and stuck it into her pocket.

Ben Johnson hurried over to their wagon while the women were preparing supper. "It's Alice, Ida. It's her time."

Lizzie and Ida looked at each other. "It's too early isn't it, Ida?"

Ida nodded. "Gather up your medicine chest, Lizzie, and

whatever clean rags you can find. I'll go on over and start tending to her." Lizzie limped off to gather up the needed supplies and joined Ida at the Johnson wagon about half an hour later. She could hear Alice's moans before she reached the wagon. Aiken stood next to Ben, his arm around the other man's shoulders. Aiken shook his head at Lizzie's worried glance.

"Alice?" Lizzie asked, crawling into the wagon. "How are you doing?"

The woman's face was red with the effort and sweat poured down her face. "The pains...started...this morning," she said, between breaths. "Slow...at first. They got...worse after...we stopped." She moaned again and laid back against the quilts Ida had rolled up behind her for support.

"She's hurting, Miss Lizzie," Ida whispered. "I think the baby is turned around. It hasn't dropped into position yet."

Lizzie looked up at her in horror. "What can we do?"

"Nothing. There's nothing we can do but wait it out and hope the baby turns." Ida picked up a rag from the pan sitting next to her and gently mopped Alice's face with it. Ida and Lizzie tended to Alice for several hours through the night while the men smoked and talked around the fire. Ben often cast a worried look toward the wagon when one of Alice's shrill screams rent the afternoon.

The women took turns wiping the sweat from Alice's brow with water cooled rags and washing down her arms and neck. Lizzie's hands were sore from Alice squeezing them, grinding her knuckles together. The heat under the canvas wagon cover was sweltering and soon Lizzie's and Ida's dresses were plastered to their bodies. Alice had become too exhausted to do much more than moan and lie still.

"Ida, look." Lizzie drew attention to where blood was pooling under Alice's body. "That's an awful lot of blood, isn't it?"

Ida held a lantern closer to Alice and noticed the shallow breathing and pallid complexion. "We're going to lose her, Lizzie, and probably the baby, too." Ida patted Alice's cheeks, attempting to revive her. "Miss Alice? Miss Alice we've got to get this baby out, you hear me?"

Alice moaned.

"I know you're hurting, Miss Alice, but if you want to save your child you're going to have to push. Come on, Miss Alice. Lizzie, get behind her and push her up into a sitting position. I'm going to try and turn this baby. I'm sorry, Miss Alice, but this is going to hurt." Ida reached up into the woman's womb, attempting to turn the baby around. "Push, now. Push!" she ordered.

Alice screamed shrilly from the pain, and Ben poked his head into the wagon to check on his wife's progress. Ida looked up. "Out, Mr. Johnson," she ordered, sharply. The three women continued to labor, Lizzie helping Alice to push while Ida encouraged them and tried to staunch the flow of blood from between the woman's legs.

Suddenly, Alice gave a final push and collapsed back with a shudder. Ida held a tiny baby girl in her hands. She felt around in the baby's mouth then gave it a smart whack on its tiny bottom. A small wail, no bigger than what a kitten might make, issued from the baby's mouth—but it was alive. Ida wrapped it in a small square of fabric and laid it on its mother's chest. "It's a girl, Miss Alice. A beautiful, baby girl."

Alice gave a weak smile and reached for the baby. Her arm fell limply to her side, and she shuddered again before growing still. "Alice!" Lizzie gently shook her. "Wake up, Alice," she implored. "See your new baby."

More blood gushed from beneath the unconscious woman. Ida shoved the baby quickly into Lizzie's hands and wadded up bedding to shove between Alice's legs. Within seconds, the clean bedding was soaked. Lizzie fell to her knees beside Alice. The woman weakly reached again toward the baby...and stopped breathing, her eyes staring without seeing at the infant Lizzie held.

"No," Lizzie whispered, her eyes wide in her face. She shook her head. "No, Ida. It can't be."

A lone tear slid down Ida's face. "She's gone, Lizzie. There's nothing we can do. I couldn't stop the bleeding." She cleaned her hands on her apron and tossed it down. "We'll try to keep the baby alive. Give her to me. I'll have to tell Mr. Johnson."

Lizzie handed the baby over to Ida, stunned. Tears coursed their way down her face. She nodded. "I'll tend to Alice."

Ida climbed slowly from the wagon and turned to face the Johnson family. She walked up to Ben and placed his child in his arms. "She's fine, Mr. Johnson. Small and beautiful."

"And my wife?" He peered over her shoulder.

Ida shook her head. "I'm sorry, sir. The baby was turned wrong. We did all we could." Ida took the baby back as the man's shoulders began to shake. He tilted his head back and howled. The grief for his wife was overwhelming. He turned and ran for the wagon.

Aiken drew Ben's children to him as Luke went to stand next to his wife. He drew Ida and the child into his arms as Ida allowed the sobs she had been holding in to rack her body. He held her tightly until she calmed. They could hear Ben Johnson's cries coming from the wagon and Lizzie's calm words trying to soothe him. Eventually, Lizzie emerged from the wagon and left him alone with his grief.

Lizzie approached Ida and took the baby from her. "Let me give her to him. Maybe it'll help," she said. She held the baby close to her bosom and headed back to Mr. Johnson.

The next morning, Ben approached their fire with the baby in one arm and leading a cow with the other. He handed the baby to Lizzie and turned, leaving the cow. "I want you to have her," he said quietly. "I can't care for her without Alice, and she would have wanted it this way."

"But, Mr. Johnson…"

He shook his head. "I named her Alice, after my wife." He softly touched the baby's cheek. "She needs a woman to care for her. She's so tiny. I'll have my hands full enough with the other ones."

Lizzie straightened her back and placed a hand over Ben's. "I consider it an honor to care for Alice's daughter," she told him. Ben placed a tender kiss on the baby's soft head. Then he turned and walked away, without looking back.

"Oh, William." Lizzie began to cry. Aiken wrapped his arms around her and the baby.

"Elizabeth? Can you do this?"

"I don't know, William. With Ida's help, I guess I can. I don't know much about babies." She looked at the cow. "I hope that cow holds up until we reach Oregon." The baby began to squirm and cry from being pressed between their bodies and Lizzie smiled. She brushed her lips tenderly across the baby's forehead and touched the downy soft hair on top of its head. "Little Alice," she whispered. "I won't let you forget your mother, I promise." She squatted down so Abby and Zeke could see her closer, smiling at her husband over their heads.

The baby began crying in earnest then, drawing Ida over to them. Lizzie looked up at them helplessly. "What are we going to feed her, Ida?" Lizzie wanted to know. "I don't have any bottles."

Ida stood and thought for a minute then turned to rummage in the wagon. She emerged with a glove and tossed it into the pot of boiling water. She let it boil for several minutes then used a stick to fish it out with. She poked a couple of holes in one of the fingers with a needle. "Luke," she called. "Do you know how to milk a cow?" He nodded and, taking up a bucket, headed over to where they had tied the cow. "We'll have to boil the milk. Then let it cool," Ida instructed Lizzie. "Let her suck on your finger until then."

"She's so small, Ida. Will she live?"

"She's only a month early. She's got a real good chance. Probably hasn't had a thing to eat since she was born, though. We can do it," she told Lizzie, with determination. "With God's help, we'll pull this little girl through." She smoothed her apron over her slightly protruding belly. "I'd have plenty of milk, if my own was here."

Aiken took the baby from Lizzie and dipped his kerchief in his cup of water. He held it to the baby's lips and smiled as she sucked on it. "This ought to hold her until the milk is done," he said proudly. "I use to help my momma with my younger brothers."

Alice Johnson's funeral was held later that afternoon. A slight rain had begun as the men lowered the simple wooden casket that Luke had hurriedly built into the freshly dug hole. Lizzie looked up into the grey skies. *How fitting*, she thought. *Grey skies for the funeral of a dear friend.*

Ben Johnson and his children stood huddled together on the opposite side of the gaping hole. One of the older sons had his arm around Sarah who was silently crying, her small shoulders shaking.

Lizzie held little Alice tighter against her bosom, shielding her from the rain. Ida had sewn together a sling made from some scrap flannel for Lizzie to wear around her neck, making it easier to carry the infant. Aiken read a short passage from Lizzie's Bible and led the mourners in a short prayer...and that was that. The end of a mother and a wife's life. One life given for another. Lizzie sniffed and wiped away a tear, watching as Ben and his children dropped handfuls of the damp earth on top of the casket. The thuds seemed abnormally loud in the still air.

Chapter 22

They reached the fork the next day that split off with one road heading to California and the other to Oregon. Ten wagons took the turn to California, one of them the widow who had lost her husband to cholera, and those that were Oregon bound stopped and watched them leave.

Aiken tried to dissuade the ones leaving, mentioning that they had no one with them that was qualified to lead them across the desert. Those headed to California were determined as they had heard the way was shorter, and they were tired of the hardships they had already encountered. It seemed as if Alice's death was the final straw for some of them. They wanted to settle as soon as possible, preferring the trek across the desert to the more strenuous climbing of the mountains. Aiken told them there was more water and grass on the road to Oregon, but they shook their heads and drove off.

Aiken put his arm around Lizzie's shoulders. "Well...that's that then. I tried to give them back some of their money, seeing as how they had paid me to lead them to Oregon. Some took it back and some didn't. God be with them." He gave Lizzie a quick squeeze then helped her back onto the wagon seat. "Let's go, folks!" He mounted his horse and waved them forward.

Lizzie looked across the horizon at the mountains looming before them. She sighed and looked at Ida. "William said these mountains are small compared to what's coming." She glanced down at the mules. "The mules are worn out, Ida, and I think one is going lame. Maybe we should have turned off to California, too."

"Your husband already has land in Oregon, Lizzie. God has promised to see us through. Those of us who don't make it, well, we weren't meant to." She flicked the reins, urging the mules to pick up the pace. "I prefer the mountains to the scorching desert anytime. I'm not nad've enough to think that we won't have our spells without water, but it won't be as long as those poor souls."

"I think William is disheartened with them leaving. He took his responsibility toward them seriously."

"Nothing he can do about it. You can't waste energy worrying about something that's out of your control."

Lizzie sighed and shifted the sling which carried Alice. "You're right, Ida. I guess I'm just feeling a little tired myself."

Ida smiled. "Well, you *are* a new momma."

Lizzie laughed softly. "I am at that."

They camped on the shore of a small creek named after the Shoshone Indians. Lizzie tried catching up on the washing, but the water was too hard with alkali deposits to get rid of much of the dinginess. She sighed and stretched her back, glancing over at the basket where she had placed Alice. The baby was sleeping. Lizzie looked around her. They were hidden from the wagons by a small rise, but by standing on her toes she was able to locate Abby helping Ida with their supper. She lay down on the grass next to the basket, hoping to catch a nap herself.

She jumped awake as a shadow fell across her face. She sat up quickly, brushing the hair from her eyes. Edward Newton stood over her, frowning down at the baby. He noticed Lizzie had awoken and turned.

"Another surprise, Elizabeth." He looked down at her, his eyes cold and stern on her face. "It can't be yours. Not unless you were expecting when you started this journey and managed to hide the fact." He smoothed his moustache. "I was hoping to catch you with your pretty little sister, but—babies fetch a good price out here, too." He pulled a small derringer from his vest pocket. "Get up."

"Mr. Newton, I—"

"Now, Elizabeth," he interrupted her. "They'll be calling you to dinner soon, and I'd rather not be found. I'm afraid your husband might feel the need to call me out, and then things could get ugly." He waved the gun in the direction of the bushes. "Get the basket and let's go. You first."

Lizzie picked up the basket and looked over in the direction of the wagons. She was inclined to yell for help, but the presence of the gun swayed her. She knew Edward Newton would have no qualms about pulling the trigger, and she didn't want to risk the baby's life. She sighed heavily and hoisted the basket onto her hip. Newton noticed the improvement of her limp with satisfaction.

"I'm glad to see your limp won't be permanent."

"I'd like to put the basket down and carry the baby, if you don't mind." She stopped.

He poked the gun into her back. "Not yet." His horse, along with another, was waiting just a short ways down the creek. He stood off to the side, his gun aimed at her while she tied the sling around her neck and placed Alice in it. The baby began to cry upon being woken up. "Shut it up, Elizabeth, unless you'd like to leave it here. I'm sure the wolves won't mind."

Lizzie looked up at him, startled by his crudeness and tried to shush the baby. Newton waved the gun again in her direction. "On the horse, my dear."

Her healing leg threatened to buckle under her weight as she lifted herself into the saddle. She thought longingly of the crutch she had left back by the creek. Alice's cries began to increase in volume, and Lizzie patted her back, trying to shush her. Newton mounted his horse and grabbed the reins to Lizzie's. He dug his spurs into the flank of his horse and led them off at a gallop.

After an hour of hard riding and the baby's screeches reverberating in their ears, Newton called a halt. He jumped from his horse and stood before Lizzie. "I warned you, Elizabeth. Give me the child."

Lizzie shook her head and held Alice tight to her. "What did you expect, Mr. Newton? You took us with no way for me to feed her. You know that she isn't mine. I have no milk for her. Let me down and I'll try to pacify her with some water."

He shook his head. "I don't think so, Elizabeth. Hand her to me."

"No!"

"Elizabeth…" he warned. He glanced behind them and noticed the dust cloud hovering on the horizon. He swore loudly and rushed back to his horse. Lizzie followed his gaze and smiled. As Newton hurried them on again, she let her face rag fall to the ground. Newton drove them unmercifully into the evening, Alice's wails finally subsiding from exhaustion.

"Mr. Newton," Lizzie called. "I can't continue to go on at this pace."

"You have no choice in the matter, my dear."

"You don't want to arrive with damaged merchandise, do you? If we don't stop to rest, I am going to fall off this horse."

Newton swore again and stopped, looking around them. A small valley was off to their right, the creek they had left winding through it. Stiff rock faces were on their left. "Give me the child's blanket," he ordered.

"She'll be cold."

"Give me something of hers…or yours. I don't care which." He held out his hand. Lizzie untied her bonnet and gave it to him. "Now give me the child."

"No."

"I will give her back to you, Elizabeth. I'm just using her to ensure that you don't leave." He motioned with his fingers for her to hand Alice to him. Lizzie handed over the baby reluctantly and watched as Newton rode a ways up the trail in front of them and dropped Lizzie's bonnet. He returned, handed Alice back to her, and led them off in the direction of the creek.

He watched as Lizzie tried coaxing water down the baby. He studied the dirty blond hair that hung down her back and the stained dress she wore beneath an even more stained apron. He scowled and walked back to his horse. He pulled a wrapped package from his saddle bag. He tossed it to Lizzie. "Wash up in the creek and put this on."

"What?"

"Strip down, wash up, and put this on." Newton stood towering over her. "Elizabeth, I advise you to do what I tell you at all times." He nodded toward the baby. "I have a wonderful bargaining chip, you see." He folded his arms across his chest.

"Turn around."

"I don't think so. Don't be modest around me. You'll be used to being ogled before long."

Lizzie took a deep breath, squared her shoulders, and strode into the icy waters of the creek. She immersed herself under the water as best she could and removed her soiled clothes. She used the sand from the creek bottom to scrub her body and scalp. "Hand me the dress, Mr. Newton," she called.

"It's silk, my dear. It's not something that holds up well to water." He leaned against a tree and lit a cigar. He watched as she strode defiantly towards him. Her undergarments covered her some, but not well enough. They clung to her curves, and Lizzie gave thanks that it was too dark for him to see clearly. She held out her hand for the dress and slipped it over her head.

She grimaced. The dress was a blood red silk. The bodice was cut indecently low, sheer lace trimming the edges. "Readying me for my new job already, Mr. Newton? It's a little inappropriate for out here, don't you think? I'm cold."

He tossed her a black lace shawl. "You're as lovely as I imagined you would be. Once you got out of those peasant clothes." He silently studied the pale skin showing above the bodice of the gown. He reached out and ran his fingers through her wet hair. "Pity you cut it. But it'll grow back." He let his hand fall. "Grab the child, and let's go."

Lizzie took her time tying Alice back around her neck, purposely leaving behind her old clothing as a clue. She prayed that her husband would see through Newton's trick of leading them in the opposite direction and would find them. She adjusted the sling that held the baby and remounted her horse. Newton once again headed off at a fast pace. She felt her head fall forward as exhaustion threatened to overtake her and she almost slid from her horse. Newton noticed and swore again. He led them up the side of a mountain, having them take refuge behind some large rocks.

"We'll camp here," he told her reluctantly. "No fire though—and keep that kid quiet." Lizzie slid gratefully from her horse, her aching leg buckling beneath her. Newton grabbed her arm before she collapsed to the ground and dragged her over beneath a low hanging bush. He shoved her roughly beneath it and went to tether the horses. He ducked as a bullet whistled past him, striking the dirt by his feet.

"Newton!" Aiken yelled from a rock face above them. "Let Lizzie and the baby go and I won't have to kill you."

Newton dove for cover, pulling out his own pistol from its holster. "You'll have to come and get her," he shouted back. "I definitely have the advantage here, Aiken. Keep shooting and a ricochet could kill her, or the child." Pebbles rained down on them and Newton fired in the direction they came from. He peered through the gloom of the night, trying to make out a human shape amongst the shadows. Lizzie scurried farther into the bushes, clasping the crying Alice tightly to her.

Another bullet whizzed past them from the opposite direction and Newton whirled around. He fired again. Several minutes passed as they listened to the silence. Then Alice began to cry in earnest. "Shut her up!" Newton screamed. He yelped and dove again as another bullet came close to where he was hiding.

Lizzie scrambled out from her hiding place and began crawling in the direction she had heard Aiken's voice. Newton cursed and started after her. A bullet kicked up the dirt in front of him, sending him back into hiding. He tried sneaking around the back of their campsite, all the while keeping Lizzie in his eyesight.

She tucked the dress up into the waistband of her bloomers, giving her more freedom of movement and, wincing against the rocks cutting into her knees, crawled faster. She looked up in alarm as Newton stepped out, blocking her path. He leveled his pistol at her and she threw herself flat on the ground as another shot rang out. She watched as Newton looked down at the spreading stain across his purple vest. His eyes widened in shock and stared down at her, a drop of blood in the corner of his mouth. He fell forward and lay still. She stared down at him for a second and then whirled around.

Lizzie ran to where the shot was fired from. Aiken slid down the rock face and reached for her. She ran full tilt into him, causing him to lose his balance. He wrapped his arms around her as they fell. She began to cry and cover his face with kisses, unmindful of the crying infant between them.

"I knew you would come, William. I knew it."

He returned her kisses. "I thought I had lost you, Lizzie." He held her back so he could look into her face. "I thought I had lost you." He pulled her tightly to his chest again before helping her to her feet. "Let's go back."

"What about him?" she nodded towards the fallen Newton.

"He's dead. I don't think we need to worry about him anymore." He looked down at the dress she was wearing. "Now—that's becoming," he said sarcastically.

"William, really."

"I think we'll save it for when we're home alone, though." He wrapped the shawl tighter around her and tucked the ends into the bodice of her dress. "Not something you want company seeing you in."

She smiled up at him. "I'd rather burn it than wear it again. Even for you."

"Well, that can be arranged, too." He mounted his horse and held his hand down to her, pulling her up in front of him. "Luke is stationed just over there. Let's get him and head back."

Luke waited patiently at the head of the trail, his face lit up with a smile when he saw them. "You sure do get into some trouble, Mrs. Aiken," he joked. "I don't reckon Mr. Aiken will ever be bored, married to you."

Aiken laughed. "Don't reckon I will, Luke. Don't reckon I will." He kicked the horse's flanks, and they galloped back the way they had come, Lizzie's arm wrapped tightly around her husband's waist.

Chapter 23

Aiken led them nine miles the next day and Lizzie found herself next to Ida on the wagon seat, looking rather dubiously at the rough wooden bridge across yet another creek. She was taking her turn at driving while Ida watched Alice. She turned to make sure that Abby was situated securely in the back of the wagon and flicked the reins to start the mules across the bridge. Halfway across, the mules balked. She sighed heavily and handed the reins to Ida. She had taken to wearing her britches again since the weather had heated up considerably. She was able to climb effortlessly down from the wagon.

"Come on, you guys," she implored the mules, catching hold of the harness. "Good thing we're next to last in this train. You balk every time we have to cross a bridge." She tugged roughly at them. "I'm going to shoot you when we get to Oregon," she threatened. "I don't want to have to do this every time we cross water." The lead mule twitched an ear forward as she spoke and still refused to move. She looked behind them to where the Johnson wagon was waiting to cross.

"Get the switch and swat him," the oldest Johnson boy yelled. "Show them who's boss!"

Lizzie shook her head and planted her hands on her hips. "Abby, toss me down one of those carrots that we have left." Lizzie held the carrot temptingly under the mule's nose. The lead mule wrinkled his nose at the carrot and took a step forward. "It's going to work, Ida," she yelled triumphantly. As soon as her attention was diverted, the mule snatched the carrot from her hand, ate it, and refused to move farther.

A shot rang out from the Johnson wagon, startling the mules into a dash across the bridge. Lizzie, who was still standing in their path, was knocked backwards and over the split railing of the bridge. She screamed in surprise as she tumbled over and hit the icy water below. She flailed her arms around before she managed to get her feet planted under her and stood to find out that the water only came to her chest. Joshua Johnson stood on the bridge looking down at her.

"Gee, I'm sorry, Lizzie. I was only trying to help. Are you all right?" His young face was creased with worry.

Lizzie glared up at him. "What were you thinking, Joshua Johnson? You could have killed me!"

"I said I was sorry. You were holding everyone up. I thought the shot would startle them into moving, and it did. Do you want me to come down and help you out of there?"

"No, I do not." She retied her sodden bonnet on her head. "I can walk out of here myself." She heard laughter and looked over to see her husband and Luke standing on the bank of the creek, bent over, hats in hand, laughing. Her bonnet hung down in her face, partially obscuring her view, and her hair was plastered down her back. She angrily shoved the bonnet out of her face and glared at the two laughing men.

"You look like a drowned cat," Aiken told her.

"It's not funny, William. Please, don't bust a rib laughing." She strode past him, not looking in his direction.

His eyes widened as he saw how the britches she wore outlined her legs, not leaving her feminine shape to anyone's imagination. What the britches outlined on her bottom half, the cotton blouse she wore on top did the same. He saw the Johnson boys watching her, their mouths agape. He realized belatedly that his wife was just as good as naked in the young boys' eyes. He whipped his shirt quickly from off his back and wrapped it around her.

"Is it still funny?" she asked, scolding. "Now that the whole train has seen me? Who's laughing now?" She held the shirt around her and strode angrily to the wagon. Aiken watched her go, her back ramrod straight, and burst into laughter again.

He turned to Luke. "You're right, my friend. Life will not be boring with this one. Calamity follows her wherever she goes. Calamity. Well, looks like I've found my pet name for her."

"Don't you *dare* call me that, William Aiken," Lizzie yelled from the back of the wagon.

They traveled on another eight miles before stopping to camp at the top of a small mountain. A large spring of water ran out from under the snowy mountain range ahead of them. Ida and Abby headed down to fill their water barrels.

"It's cold!" Abby exclaimed. "But, it's so hot out here."

"The water comes down from that mountain," Ida pointed. "Probably keeps it cold all year." She looked up in fear as two men walked into the clearing. She stood up, shoving Abby behind her.

"Well, if we ain't got ourselves a pretty little quadroon here," one of the men said. They both wore stained buckskins, their faces hidden with heavy dark beards. "Where's your people, woman?"

"My *people* are over there," she told him warily, keeping her body between them and Abby. She eyed the guns they carried, warily.

"The train master? Where do you suppose I could find him?"

"Next to last wagon." She watched as the men headed off in the direction she had pointed out to them. Then she looked down at Abby. "You've got to warn Luke to stay out of sight, Abby. Do you understand? They're looking for him." The little girl nodded. "It's very important that you find him before those men do. He's with the stock—over there." She gave the girl a shove and picked up their water buckets. She watched Abby run, then praying quickly, followed the bounty hunters to the wagon.

Aiken and Lizzie had pulled up a couple of stumps around the fire and he was watching as she fed Alice. He tilted his hat back from his face as he looked up at the two men standing there. "Evening, gentlemen. What can I do for you?"

"We're looking for a runaway slave. Got reason to believe he's hitched up with one of these here wagon trains heading to California or Oregon."

"He's not here." Aiken stood. "I'm afraid you've wasted your time. The only colored person around here is my wife's servant." He saw Ida walking towards them. "But I guess you've already met her."

The man spat on the ground. "Yep. The one we're looking for is a big buck. Standing six feet tall. A blacksmith by trade. There's a reward out for his return. A good reward."

"I've told you he's not here. Maybe you should check with the half of the train that turned to California." Aiken folded his arms across his chest.

"Already did." The man spat again. "They said they split off from you and that you had a big black feller traveling with you. That he had hitched himself up with a little colored woman." The man lifted his rifle slightly.

Aiken narrowed his eyes at the sight. "I—"

"He's gone," Ida interrupted them. "He did travel with us for a while, sir, but then he up and left."

They transferred their attention to her. She set the water buckets down and straightened, allowing the fabric to stretch across her growing belly. "Got me with child and headed on."

"Well, then, we'll just have to take you in trade." The man grinned at his partner, revealing tobacco stained teeth.

"She's not for sale," Lizzie spoke up. "She's been freed for a long time. Would you like to see the papers?"

"Can't read no how." He continued to watch Ida. "You know what they do to runaways, don't you girl?" She nodded mutely. "Well, then—I guess we'll be on our way. Probably meet up with you folks again at Fort Boise." He spat at Aiken's feet.

Ida's legs gave way as the men left and she crumbled to the ground. She put her hands to her face, breathing hard. Lizzie rushed to her side and put her arms around her.

"It's best that Luke stay gone for a while," Aiken told them.

Lizzie lifted her face to him. "How long?"

He shrugged. "Until we're sure those men have moved on. Where is he?"

Ida spoke from underneath her hands. "I sent Abby to warn him. He'll know what to do. He's made it safely this far." She looked up expectantly as Abby and Zeke approached them.

"He took off as soon as Abby told him what you said," Zeke told them. "Said he'll stay gone until it's dark and then he will sneak in for supplies. Those men are still here though, Aiken. They've been talking to some of the other wagons."

Ida looked up at him in alarm. Aiken reassured her. "I'll talk to everyone. Make sure they back up the story you've told. Everyone here values Luke. He's helped all of us in one way or another on this trip. It'll be fine." He patted her shoulder. "Zeke, stay here with the women. If those men come back, send Abby after me." Zeke nodded.

It was past midnight when Luke poked his head into Lizzie and Aiken's wagon. "Aiken," he whispered.

"Luke?" Aiken sat up, being careful not to awaken Lizzie or Abby.

"Yeah, it's me. I'm leaving now." Luke stepped back to allow Aiken to jump down. "I'll catch up with you before you cross those mountains. If I don't, watch out for Ida, will you? Don't wait for me. If something happens and I don't catch up, take care of her and the baby?"

"Sure." Aiken pulled him close for a quick hug. "You be careful, Luke. Take my rifle with you."

Luke shook his head. "I'm a dead man if I get caught with a weapon. I'll make do with my knife. It'll be easier to toss away if I need to." Luke slung the supplies he had wrapped in an old blanket, over his shoulder.

"Be careful, friend." Luke nodded, and Aiken watched as he disappeared into the shadows. "We'll see you again."

Chapter 24

They descended the mountain the next morning straight into what Lizzie could only describe as hell. They traveled through dust, sand, and sagebrush. They traveled over hard baked ground in scorching temperatures. The far off mountain range shimmered before them, beckoning to them. Teasing them.

Ida kept mostly to herself, her depression over Luke enveloping her and spreading to the others. Lizzie struggled to care for Alice while keeping the wagon going. To add to their misery, the gnats and mosquitoes were the worse they had ever been, buzzing around the travelers' heads with their constant biting. Many times over the next few days, Lizzie found herself at the point of tears and snapping at Abby and Zeke whenever they were misfortunate enough to cross her path.

Three days later they reached the banks of the Snake River and looked down at it in despair. Several waterfalls cascaded down into the wide and swift river with plenty of grass and shade on its opposite banks. There was no way for them to cross it. They continued on through the dust, glancing back often at the cooling image of the river. They traveled each day from dawn until dusk, with nothing before them but a sandy desert covered with wild sage brush and dried up with the heat.

Lizzie turned the care of Alice over to Abby and Ida, focusing her attention on just moving them forward each day. Aiken rode up and down the wagon train, doing his best to encourage and drive everyone forward. Even his own optimism sagged by the end of each day. By the end of the week, they reached a spot in the Snake River that Aiken felt was safe enough for them to cross.

He ordered everyone to raise their wagon beds a foot in order to ford the river. Without Luke there to help, this took most of the day. When they were finished, Aiken spurred the group on. They camped a mile from the river by several small pools of water. Aiken warned the men to keep the stock and children close to the wagons. The pools were full of poison water.

"How will Luke make it through by himself?" Ida asked. "A week without grass or shade and very little water. What's he going to hunt? At least we had our water barrels. He has nothing but what he could carry on his back." Her shoulders slumped.

Lizzie rose and put her arms around the stricken woman. "He'll be okay, Ida. Luke is smart and strong. He can make much better time alone than we can."

"We've another week of scarce water ahead of us," Aiken told them. "And we'll be traveling through Digger Indian country. If we're lucky, we'll hit a small bit of water in a couple of days, but our journey through there has to be quick."

"Are the Indians dangerous?" Zeke asked.

"They can be. They're mostly thieves, though they have been known to kill." Aiken stood up. "I'll be driving the wagon through for the next few days, Lizzie. I don't want you women alone back here."

"Can't we move up front?" Abby scooted closer to her sister. "We've been in the back the whole trip."

"I'm sorry, Abby. We stay in the order we've been driving. Lots were drawn. People get upset if you bump them out of their spot."

Abby pouted. "I'm tired of eating dust. It's even worse if I ride with the Johnsons, and the sand is so thick I can't hardly walk in it. I've got holes in the bottom of my shoes, and my moccasins are starting to wear through too."

Aiken patted her on the head. "Another month and we'll be in our own place, putting up a new house." He looked over at Ida. "And Luke will have caught up with us."

"The supplies are getting low, William. I hadn't planned on feeding this many extra people." Lizzie took off her bonnet, trying to catch a breeze.

"We'll hit Fort Boise in a little over a week. We can make it until then."

"Money is getting low, too."

Aiken slapped his hat against his leg, losing his patience. "Dang it, Lizzie! I've got money. Plenty of it, and I'm doing the best I can." He looked around at them. "I've never met such a group of whiners. I get it from the others all day. I don't expect to get it around my own fire!" He spun on his heel and left, heading to the Johnsons' wagon.

Lizzie's eyes swelled with tears. She looked helplessly at the others. "I didn't mean to accuse him."

"We know that, Lizzie," Ida reassured her. "The heat gets to Mr. Aiken, same as everyone else." She handed Alice to Lizzie. "Here's one person that won't complain. She's been fed, changed, and now she's ready for love from her momma."

Lizzie smiled at her gratefully. "Thank you, Ida." Lizzie hugged the baby close to her.

The others got up and went to bed, leaving Lizzie and the baby waiting at the fire. Lizzie could see her husband sitting with Ben Johnson, and sighed. She would wait up for him and apologize. She needed to be supportive, not complaining.

She dozed off and was awakened by her husband's hand on her shoulder. She placed her own hand over his and tilted her head up to face him. "I'm sorry, William. I never meant to accuse you or to complain. I know how hard you work."

He bent down to kiss her. "I know that, Calamity. I'm sorry I lost my temper. Still love me?"

She wrinkled her nose at him. "Only if you don't call me by that name." He laughed and led her to a bed under the wagon. It was too hot to sleep inside.

They began climbing a very steep mountain the next day. Halfway up, Ida yelled, and Aiken pulled up on the reins, halting the mule team. Their ascent was so steep that the women were losing supplies out the back of the wagon. Lizzie and Ida had chosen to walk rather than ride and were busy picking up their belongings from the road and tossing them back in the wagon. They would toss things back in, and others would roll out.

Aiken began to set the brake on the wagon and noticed that the mules were losing the battle against the steepness of the road. "I can't stop here!" He yelled back. "Yah!"

He set his whip against the mules' back, prodding them onward. Soon Abby, Lizzie, and Ida's arms were overflowing. They reached the top, tossed their things back in the wagon, and collapsed on the ground.

"Just a minute, William," Lizzie begged in between breaths. "Just a quick breath before we start back down."

"I can't stop here, Lizzie. Ben's trying to come up right behind me. You women fall back, and we'll wait for you at the bottom."

They moved to sit on the side of the road when Abby looked up at the mountain ridge and pointed. "Indians, Lizzie." They could make out the shapes of several Indian braves against the skyline.

Lizzie and Ida followed her finger, glanced at each other, and decided against staying there to rest. The women had chosen to wear their britches that day to make the heat more bearable and were able to set off at a quick pace to catch up with the wagons, Lizzie holding Alice tight against her to keep her from bouncing around. Lizzie pointed out the Indians to Aiken when they caught up with him.

He pushed her down next to the wagon wheel and retrieved his rifle from the wagon seat. The others had been alerted by this time and the other men gathered around Aiken. "What do you think they want, Aiken?" one of them asked.

Aiken shook his head. "I don't know. They just seem to be watching us."

"Maybe we should shoot. Scare them off."

"Or it might just make them mad." Aiken thought for a minute. "I know everyone's tired, but let's keep moving. Get away from this mountain. We're sitting ducks up here."

They camped several miles farther on in a small valley, and Aiken had them pull their wagons into a tight circle. With only ten wagons out of the thirty left, it was a small circle. "No one sleeps outside tonight," he told them all. "The men will take watch in shifts and in pairs. Yell out if you see or hear anything. Zeke and I'll take the first watch."

The Indians arrived just as the sun was making its appearance over the top of the mountain. Aiken awoke to whoops, screams, and gunfire. Grabbing his rife, he leaped from the wagon.

"William?"

"Stay in the wagon, Lizzie." He tossed his rifle to Zeke and reached for his pistol.

"But—"

"Stay in the wagon!"

"But I can shoot, William!"

"Then shoot from the wagon!" He grabbed Zeke and pulled him along with him. "They're going after the stock."

"God, help us," Ida said, falling to her knees. She pulled Abby down beside her and grabbed the baby. They took cover behind some boxes. Lizzie took up her pistol and took aim out the back of the wagon.

Pandemonium reigned outside. Men ran, ducked, shot—and were shot at. The Indians rode by so fast Lizzie couldn't get a head count and found it hard to find a target. The dust kicked up by the horses hung heavy in the air and Lizzie peered through it, blinking often to keep it from getting in her eyes.

She spotted Aiken and Zeke taking cover behind some boulders. Zeke would load one rifle, hand it to Aiken, and reload the one that Aiken had tossed down. Aiken shot as quickly as Zeke handed him a newly loaded rifle.

The Indians rode hanging off of one side of their horses, using their horses as shields. This made it difficult for the white men to get an unobstructed view in order to shoot. Occasionally, one of the men from the wagon train would stand to draw the Indians out from behind their horses.

Arrows zipped past them, causing the women to stay low in the wagons. The side of Lizzie's wagon was riddled with arrows sticking out from it. She yanked Abby back as the little girl went to reach out and pull one from the wood.

"Get back, you little fool," Lizzie hissed. She took aim with her pistol and saw, with satisfaction, her bullet take one of the Indians in the leg, causing him to fall from his horse. Her glory was short lived.

Lizzie watched in shock as Aiken took an arrow in the shoulder and fell back. Zeke took up the rifle and aimed carefully, taking down the Indian who had fired the shot. Lizzie jumped from the wagon and rushed to her husband's side. He was just getting to his knees when she reached him.

"I told you to stay in the wagon."

"You're shot, William. I can help you."

He shoved her down behind the boulder and crouched down next to her. She reached for the arrow in his shoulder, and he shoved her hand away. "Not now." He took aim with his good hand, using his pistol, and brought down another brave.

Lizzie sat up and peered over the boulder, aiming her pistol at the screaming Indians. She fired and winged one, but not bad enough to cause him to fall from his mount. The battle lasted only a matter of minutes, leaving five Indians dead, several wounded, and Aiken and one other white man wounded. The remaining Indians rode off, leaving behind their dead and the travelers' stock.

Lizzie helped Aiken over to the shelter of the wagon and assisted him in sitting propped against the wagon wheel. Zeke wanted to retrieve the fallen Indians' horses and Aiken stopped him. "Leave the horses, Zeke. They'll be back for them when they collect their dead. We don't want them following us to get their horses back."

He paled and groaned as Lizzie grasped the arrow and quickly pulled it from his shoulder. She cleaned and wrapped the wound, winding a strip from one of her petticoats tightly around it. He struggled to his feet. "Zeke, check on the others. We can't stay here. We've got to be leaving."

The boy nodded and raced off to do his bidding. Quickly, the wagons headed back out into the dust of the desert with Lizzie driving again. They camped in the welcome shade of a small canyon when night fell. A light rain began to fall, washing the dirt from their faces. Lizzie stood next to the wagon, face turned to the sky, eyes closed, letting the rain wash away the traces of the trail.

Aiken walked up and wrapped his unbandaged arm around her. "You did good today, Lizzie."

She smiled up at him. "It was me who thought I had lost *you*, today."

"The tables do have a way of turning when you least expect it, don't they?"

She murmured and shifted so she was standing with her back touching his chest. "How's your arm?"

"Sore."

"Why did they attack us? We didn't provoke them."

He shrugged. "Maybe they just wanted the stock. Maybe they were angry because we were traveling across their land. I don't know. The more the white men cut across on their way west, the more the Indians feel infringed upon." He stepped back. "Come on in the wagon, Lizzie. Don't stay out here in the rain."

She nodded and followed him inside.

Chapter 25

They trekked on through more heat and dirt, occasionally crossing small creeks. At one point they stopped and drove their stock a mile and a half to fresh water, taking them down a steep precipice. After watering the animals, they had to whip them to spur them back up to where the wagons were waiting.

The fatigue began to show on man and animal alike. Zeke's young shoulders slumped under the burden he carried without Luke, now not only caring for the mules, but also Aiken's horse and the milk cow. Lizzie and Ida were run ragged caring for Abby and Alice along with the Johnsons' youngest. Lizzie watched in dismay as their supplies continued to dwindle.

"Ida," she spoke up one morning, "we're going to have to ask Ben Johnson to start contributing supplies to the care of his children. We're getting dangerously low, and Fort Boise is still days ahead." She put the lid back on the flour barrel. "I know we have the cow, but even it isn't giving much more milk than what Alice needs. We're totally out of meat now. We have some beans left, flour, no honey, very little sugar, and only a couple more of the pickles."

Aiken walked up with his rifle. "You go talk to Ben, Lizzie. I'm going to see what I can hunt up out here in this scraggly sage brush."

"With one arm, William?"

"I can shoot just fine with one arm. Besides, I'm taking Zeke. Go on and talk to Ben. We'll camp here tonight. The stock can't go any farther after that drive to the water." He kissed her forehead. "I'll be back soon."

While Aiken and Zeke headed off into the desert to hunt what they could find, Lizzie left Alice with Ida and set off to talk to Ben. He was whittling next to his wagon, a small pile of shavings building up at his feet. She stood silently before him for a minute, waiting for him to acknowledge her. He didn't, so she spoke first.

"Who's been doing your cooking for you, Mr. Johnson?" she asked, coming right to the point.

"We get by." He continued to whittle.

"Well…I have a proposition for you. We're getting low on supplies, Mr. Johnson, what with feeding Sarah and often one or more of your sons. If you would be willing to pool your supplies with ours, Ida and I could do the cooking for all us."

He stopped whittling and looked up. "Take what you need. It sounds like a fair trade to me. The boys are hungry—I know that. I'm afraid I'm not much of a cook, and they stay too busy to worry about cooking."

She nodded. "Well, then—thank you." She turned to walk away.

"Mrs. Aiken," he stopped her. "I'm thinking about courting the widow Martin, what with her and her boys being all alone and all."

Lizzie turned back to him. "But it's so soon, Ben. You're still in mourning for Alice."

"My kids need a mother. Her boys need a father."

"Have you prayed about it?" Lizzie thought about the quiet, plain woman who had been married to the bigoted Mr. Martin.

"Alice did the praying for us. Mrs. Martin is a good woman, Lizzie. She'll make a good wife and mother. I'll treat her better than Mr. Martin did." He set down his knife and stick. "Do you think she would allow it?" He looked at her with sad eyes.

Lizzie smiled. "I'm sure she'd be proud to have you court her, Ben."

"What do you think Alice would want?"

"Alice would want her children cared for and for you to be happy."

He nodded. "Don't know if I'll ever be happy again, Mrs. Aiken." He brushed the dust from his clothes. "Well, then. Guess I'll clean myself up and go talk to the widow. I'll send my boys over with the supplies."

"Would it be possible to leave them in your wagon? Our wagon is so small. There's not much room with all of us as it is. We'll come get what we need each day."

He nodded and walked away, his shoulders rounded by his sadness. Lizzie watched him go, her smile fading. She missed her friend, but she was able to see the logic in Ben's plan. He had to do what was right for him and his family. What was left of it. "Wait, Mr. Johnson," she stopped him, a scary thought crossing her mind. "Will you be taking little Alice back. If the widow marries you?"

He shook his head. "No, Lizzie. She's yours. You're her momma now. The only one she knows. I think my Alice would have wanted that." He continued on without turning in her direction.

Aiken and Zeke returned late that afternoon with a couple of scrawny rabbits. Zeke handed them to his sister. "I shot these, Lizzie!" he told her, excited. "I know they're not much, but maybe you can make a stew with them."

"They're great, Zeke." She took the rabbits from him. "There's no vegetables left, but we'll cook these on a spit." She smiled at Aiken over Zeke's head. "You men will have to skin them, though. I haven't the slightest idea how."

Later that night, on a quilt beneath the wagon, Lizzie told her husband of her conversation with Ben. Aiken lay with his good arm folded behind his head and Lizzie's head pillowed on his chest. "Out here, Lizzie, men do what they have to. It'll be a good match for everyone involved. It makes good sense."

"He said we could keep Alice."

"Did he, now? Well, that's great, honey. I know how attached you've gotten to her."

"Hmmm. But do you think it's right, William? I mean Ben is her father, and if he's getting remarried..."

He unfolded his arm and placed it around her. "Ben lost part of his heart when Alice died. That baby is just a reminder of his pain."

"But—"

"I'm not saying it's right. Just that, that is the way it is. Out here on the trail, and out West, people do what they have to, to survive. Lizzie, you'll find yourself doing all sorts of things out here that you never would have imagined."

"I guess. I'm worried about Ida, too. She's not herself since Luke left. She's very depressed. Won't eat much, and she's got to think of her own baby."

Aiken smiled down at her. "I think she'll be feeling a lot better in a day or two."

Lizzie sat up. "What do you know, William?"

"I spoke to Luke today, while Zeke and I were out hunting. He's never far from this wagon train. Only reason we didn't see him during the Indian fight was because he didn't have a gun. He said he would be here to help us over the mountains, and he will."

She moved to get up. "I've got to tell Ida."

He pulled her back down to him, drawing her close for a kiss. "Tell her in the morning."

They crossed the Snake River the next day on a ferry, paying four dollars a wagon, which set Lizzie off on one of her rampages again. She cut off her flow of words a short way from the river and held her rag over her nose. The stench was unbearable on this side of the river. Dead cattle, mules, and horses lay everywhere. Buzzards rose slowly from their meal as the wagons passed by, settling back down almost before they had passed. Aiken called a halt for lunch a short ways on.

"We'll eat here," he told them. "We've got to rest the animals. Lizzie, I'm afraid we lost another mule. He just dropped dead once we crossed the river. One of Ben's oxen died, too. Who knows how many more of these beasts will die before we're through?"

"I can't eat with this smell," Ida told him. "I'm going to lose my breakfast as it is."

Aiken tilted his hat back, a slow grin spreading across his sunburned face. "Oh, I don't know, Ida. Looks like the scenery might be improving, and we left the smell a mile back." He pointed behind them.

"Luke!" she shouted, hurrying down from the wagon seat. Luke walked towards them, tired, and skinnier than when he had left. "Luke!" She gathered up her skirt, her britches no longer fitting over her stomach, and ran. Tears streamed down her face as she threw herself into his arms. "Oh, Luke!"

He picked her up in his strong arms and carried her back to the others. "I'm back, honey, and I'm staying."

She stepped back and looked at him, long and hard. "What about the bounty hunters, Luke? Did you forget about them?"

He shook his head. "No, I didn't. I'll hide out when people come close. You all need me. Especially, now." He patted her stomach. "Not leaving my wife and child again. Not ever. I've gotten too use to having you by my side. The nights have been mighty lonesome."

Five miles into the next day, the travelers stopped. They stood and stared at a nightmare of a bridge which crossed over a creek that was aptly named Bridge Creek. A natural stone bridge arced over the creek, only wide enough for one person at a time to cross over. Fifteen feet below them, water tumbled and roared over the rocks. Around them were more rocks, towering around them on all sides. In parts of the bridge, the water poured over it, crashing into the water below them.

Lizzie looked up at her husband in terror. "Isn't there another way, William?"

"Nope. This is it, if you want to get to the other side." Up and down the creek the murmurings of the others from the wagons, echoed around them.

"How do we get the wagons across...or the stock?" She looked across the creek. "Is that an island?" In the center of the wide creek was a solid rock, large enough to hold a number of people, and more of the roaring creek was on the other side of it.

"Listen up!" Aiken raised his voice to carry over the water. "The wagons must be taken apart and carried across to the island. Then the bottoms are put together, held into place with ropes and chains, and you cross over the island on the other side on that wagon bed, like a bridge, leading across your stock one at a time. If we had an abundance of stock, we'd lead them down the creek and lower them with ropes and pulleys. Be glad we don't have to do that. We'll camp on the other side and put the wagons back together. Anything you don't want to carry across gets left behind here."

He looked around at their shocked faces. "It's hard work, folks. I won't deny that, but we've done more dangerous crossings. This is my third trip across this bridge, and no one has ever been lost. We'll cross over in the order we've been traveling, everyone pulling together. We'll all be across that bridge by nightfall."

The men worked in teams, dismantling each wagon one at a time and carrying it over, then leading over the stock and reassembling the wagon before heading on to the next one.

Lizzie walked carefully over the wet rock bridge with Alice tied firmly across her chest. She then left the baby in the care of the other women and set off to start moving over supplies. Ida took Abby firmly by the hand and instructed her to hold on to the back of her skirt as they walked over.

On the way back, her arms full of supplies, Lizzie's feet slipped on the wet rocks. She couldn't see where to put her foot for the next step. She froze in the middle of the bridge, legs shaking, and tried to calm her breathing. She could feel as the water ran across the tops of her feet, falling over the bridge. She looked down at the water rushing beneath her. The roar of the water drowned out the sound around her until she heard people begin to yell behind her for her to move on. *I'm scared*, she thought. *I can't do this*. Her heart pounded loud enough that she thought for sure the others could hear it above the roaring of the water. She breathed a huge sigh of relief when Aiken walked up behind her and placed his hands on her shoulders.

"Come on, sweetheart. I'm right behind you." He pushed her slowly before him until they reached the other side. Lizzie collapsed on the wet ground of the island. "You stay here. Zeke, Luke, and I will carry the rest."

"Thank you," she whispered. It was easier to walk across the suspended wagon bed and Lizzie directed her efforts on moving things from the island to the far creek bank.

She watched fearfully as the men struggled across the bridge, carrying across heavy lumber, axles, and wagon wheels. She prayed fervently that no one would slip and fall to the rocks below. She watched as one of the Johnson boys slipped, almost losing his footing. His slipping caused his brother to drop his end of Lizzie's extra axle, and it crashed to the rocks below. Luke shot out his hand

and steadied the boy before he fell, too. Lizzie saw his lips moving as he calmed the boy, but she couldn't make out the words. *Well*, she thought, *I hope the axle we're using now doesn't break.*

She watched as Zeke pulled and tugged on one of the mule's reins, trying to get it to cross the rock bridge. It balked and brayed, tugging hard against him. He just knew that if he could get one to cross, the others would follow. "Come on, boy," he encouraged. "Help me out here." His feet slipped out from under him, landing him hard on his backside. Then the mule decided to cross, dragging Zeke with him. He tried to get his feet back under him, but there wasn't room on that narrow rock. He felt the mule's legs kick him several times as he was dragged along.

Once on the other side, he got to his feet, doubled up his fist, and landed a hard knock on the mule's nose. "I've had it with you!" he yelled. "You sit and holler—then you go on and bang me up. I ought to shoot you where you stand and serve you for dinner. I would, too, if we didn't need you to pull the wagon." He turned and stared stormily at the others who were laughing. Abby pointed to the bridge. Sure enough, in a single file were the other mules crossing the rock bridge.

"Stop laughing! I'm all bruised up, Lizzie. My legs hurt, and I think I scraped up my back."

She struggled to control her laughter. "I'm sorry, Zeke. I'll look at them for you, if you want. Your bumps and bruises, I mean."

"I'll do it myself." He stormed off, leaving the mule standing there.

Lizzie wiped the tears from her eyes. "We shouldn't have laughed. It sure was funny though. I thought at first he was going to go over the bridge. Then when the mule started moving, and Zeke started yelling, well…I couldn't help it."

"Stress sometimes leads to laughter," Ida told her. "Beats the alternative though, doesn't it?" They stood back and watched as Luke led the mules, one at a time, from the island to the other side of the creek.

Night had settled by the time everything and everyone was over, and they commenced working on putting the wagons back together. Everyone moved slowly after the stress of the day. Even the children and animals were quieter.

Aiken hadn't complained once that long day, but Lizzie could see the strain and pain from his wounded shoulder, etched across his face. She coaxed him to sit while she put on a pot of water to boil for coffee. "You've got to rest that arm, William. It'll never heal at this rate."

He nodded wearily. "It'll heal. There wasn't any help for it today, though. Every man was needed. God, I am tired." He laid his head back against the wagon and closed his eyes. "Forget the coffee, Lizzie. I'm going to sleep." He patted the ground next to him. "Come sit with me." She curled up next to him in the crook of his arm, and soon he was out.

Lizzie lay there, content by his side and listened to the sounds of the water cascading over the rocks. She said a silent prayer of thanksgiving for their safe passage over the bridge, remembering her fear at her own crossing and at Zeke being dragged across. Again, she wondered whether their father had had any idea of what this trip would entail.

Aiken pulled her tighter against him as he slept and she smiled. No matter what befell them, she was still blessed. God had given her a loving husband and family.

Chapter 26

They were back to traveling in the heat and the dust. The only water to be found was not fit for drinking for the people or the animals. Lizzie and Ida went back to taking turns driving the wagon. Lizzie ordered and nagged her husband until he reluctantly relinquished the reins and relented to rest his wounded shoulder. She absolutely refused to let him ride his horse or drive the wagon. He took over the care of Alice and sat in the back of the wagon playing games with Abby.

Ida beamed with happiness with the return of her husband. Her eyes were often searching for him throughout the day. Her pleasure on seeing him close by gave her a happiness that was contagious.

The first night after Rock Bridge they spent camped on a high, round, sand hill which seemed home to a hundred rattlesnakes. An exaggeration, Aiken told Lizzie, but she was fearful of walking very far from the wagon. Aiken told Zeke to take the broom and sweep around him in large arcs as he walked. This was to scare away any snakes he might come in contact with. Lizzie watched from the back of the wagon, expecting Zeke to be bitten at any moment.

Aiken laughed. "It's not as bad as you think, Lizzie. The snakes are more afraid of you than you are of them."

"Right." She wasn't convinced.

"Two snakes do not a hundred make," he told her, smiling.

"Two snakes at once is a lot, William! You can't make me think otherwise. I am not leaving this wagon."

"Not even to use the necessary?" He teased.

"Not even then. I'll hold it."

"You ought to be more worried about the Indians. We're sitting up here on this hill in plain sight, probably outlined by the moon."

"Indians, William?" His ploy worked. Momentarily, she was distracted from the snakes. She looked out over the desert below them. "Then why did we camp here?"

"We had to get the animals away from the poison water down there." He shrugged. "It seemed the lesser of the two evils."

She sat down next to him, smoothing back her sleeping sister's hair. "How much longer through the desert, William?"

"We won't reach the high mountains for another few weeks." Seeing her dismayed look, he quickly added. "But we'll hit the hot springs in a couple of days and Ft. Boise a few days after that." He beckoned for her to sit next to him. "You can have a hot bath at the springs, Lizzie, and hot water to wash laundry."

She snuggled up close to him. "Hmm, sounds heavenly."

Heavenly wasn't the word she used to describe it once they arrived. The water bubbled up out of the earth, boiling hot. The steam rising into the already hot air made the air humid and heavy to breathe. Ida filled the coffee pot directly out of the stream and set it on a rock.

"Coffee's done," she announced.

Luke looked up at her from where he sat pulling on his boots. He frowned and looked from her to the coffee pot. He shrugged and reached for his mug.

Lizzie stared down at the boiling stream of water. Tentatively, she stuck in her toe. "Ouch! I can't bathe in that. I'll scald myself."

"I feel like I'm in hell," Ida added. "The air is hot, the sun is hot, and the water is hot. All we need now are flames and a wicked man with a pitchfork."

"You've felt like that a lot on this trail," Luke pointed out. Ida glared at him.

Aiken laughed. "Luke and I will walk you women down the creek a ways. The water will be a little cooler."

Lizzie glanced dubiously at him before going and gathering up their dirty laundry. The men led them quite a ways from the camp, as far down the creek as they deemed safe. The women and Abby, along with Sarah Johnson, stripped down to their undergarments and waded in.

"It's still hot," Lizzie observed, "but at least it's bearable."

"It's too hot to feel refreshing on such a hot day," Ida told her. The women washed themselves quickly before dunking in the laundry. The steam and heat from the water kept their wet garments from cooling, and they worked up a sweat, even standing in the water.

Lizzie shoved her damp hair out of her eyes. "Maybe I should have prayed for a tepid bath. It's going to be hard to sleep tonight with all this damp heat."

"At least we'll be clean," Abby piped up. "It's been a long time since I've felt clean. When we get to Oregon, I'm going to take a bath every day."

Lizzie's and Ida's eyes met over the little girl's head. "Sure you will, Abby," Lizzie told her, smiling. "Sure you will."

When they had finished bathing and washing the clothes, Aiken ordered everyone to fill all their empty containers with water to cool down by morning. They were going to be traveling without access to fresh water for a couple of days. They filled everything they had that would hold water, no matter how small the amount. They needed water not only for themselves but for their animals.

By the time they again camped by fresh water, more of the wagons had lost some of their stock. Aiken called an early stop that day, allowing the stock to rest. The next day, he led them to a spot next to the Boise River. Wild currants were growing along the creek banks in red, yellow, and black. The women exclaimed happily over this new sweet treat, greedily picking all that their containers would hold, while the children picked and ate all they could get away with. There was plenty of grass for the weary stock and Aiken gave them all an extra day to rest.

Lizzie grew excited at the prospect of soon reaching Fort Boise and restocking their dwindling supplies. She was severely disappointed when they crossed the river and arrived. The fort was small. Fort Boise consisted of three fairly new buildings owned by the Hudson Bay Company. They could see a few company officials, some Frenchmen, and a lot of half-naked Indians. A small ferry sat next to a dock.

Lizzie sighed heavily as she stopped the wagon on the bank of the river. Aiken jumped down and approached one of the company officials. They conversed together for a few minutes, and he returned.

"They do carry a small supply of foodstuffs, and the Indians are friendly and willing to trade," he told them. "The cost for the ferry is three dollars a wagon. You can swim your own stock across, or pay the Indians to do it." He looked around the group of wagons. "We'll stay here tonight and cross over in the morning. As tired as all you folks are, my advice for you would be to pay the Indians to take your stock across."

He held up a hand to help Lizzie and Ida down. "There's a French man and his Indian wife over there with fresh salmon to sell. Would taste mighty good for dinner, don't you think?"

"Salmon!" Lizzie's eyes lit up with pleasure. She turned back to Ida. "Maybe they've got fresh vegetables, too. Do we have enough money?"

"We've got plenty, Lizzie," Aiken told her. "You get what you want. Buy as much dry foods as you can. Make sure it's enough to last several more months. We won't have time to get a garden in before winter hits. We'll be relying on what I can hunt. I'm going to tell Luke to hold back. We don't know if those bounty hunters have been through here."

She nodded, mentally making a list in her head. "Abby, run and get your brother. He'll have to help us carry. Ida, let's go buy some fish before it's gone. Then we'll do up a quick inventory." She picked up the baby and placed her in the sling around her shoulders. "Maybe they'll have some smoked salmon we can buy. That way it'll keep for a few days."

They were able to purchase the salmon and a few vegetables, and to Lizzie's delight, the Indians also had some of the salmon dried and packaged like jerky. Several loose chickens pecked the ground around their feet and they were also able to purchase some eggs, along with the flour, sugar, and beans.

Abby came running up as they were cooking the fish, a kitten held tightly in her arms. "Can I keep it, Lizzie? Please?"

Lizzie stood up, hands on her hips. "What about the dogs, Abby?

They won't like you getting a kitten."

"They'll get use to her. Please. She can keep the mice away when we get settled. She won't eat much. Alice doesn't use *all* the milk from the cow. The kitten can have some of mine." Abby's big blue eyes pleaded with Lizzie.

"What did you give for her?"

Abby looked at the ground and mumbled.

"What? I didn't hear you."

"My black shoes."

"Your shoes! Why Abigail Springer, I could—"

"I don't need them out here," she argued. "I wear my moccasins all the time anyway. That's what the girl wanted, so I let her have them."

"Fine," Lizzie relented, "but that cat is your responsibility."

"Thanks, Lizzie!" Abby shot her a grateful smile and ran off to show Sarah her new friend. Lizzie looked around to find the dogs, relieved to see them slumbering under the wagon. She looked at Ida and laughed.

"That girl is always picking up strays. Use to drive my mother crazy." Lizzie sighed again. "I miss her…my mother. Nothing used to frazzle her. She would have been calm and collected this entire trip. Not like me, crying, whining, and fearful."

"You're doing great, Lizzie," Ida told her. "A girl right from the city, thrust into the wilderness, and yet you keep going. Your momma would be proud."

"Did you realize that you haven't called me Miss Lizzie in weeks?"

Ida's eyes widened. "Is that all right?"

"It's more than all right, Ida. You're my friend. My equal." Lizzie smiled and turned as she heard her husband's voice. He was accompanied by Zeke and they were each carrying cages with chickens. Aiken's face was split wide with a grin. "Chickens, my love. Three hens and a rooster."

"William. However did you get them?"

"I bought them. It's nice to know that money is still valuable way out here." He set the cage down. "They'll get you started when we reach Oregon, and hopefully, give us some fresh eggs now."

She looked up at him. "A milk cow and now chickens. Why, William, we're positively rich."

He kissed her tenderly. "Yes, we are. In more ways than one."

Chapter 27

They traveled through yet more days of endless dust and dead cattle with little water to be found. The two dogs had begun to lag and Abby put them in the back of the wagon with her to prevent them from being left behind. They barked incessantly at the small kitten, setting everyone's nerves on edge.

"Stop the dogs barking, Abby," Lizzie ordered, "or I *will* leave them behind."

"I can't help it! The kitten is hiding behind the sacks of flour and Boomer and Buster know it's there. They won't stop barking."

"Then muzzle them. If they don't stop, they'll have to walk."

"They can't walk. They're too tired. Boomer's feet were bleeding yesterday," Abby argued and closed the canvas covering on the wagon. Within seconds, she had opened it again, as it caused the heat inside the wagon to escalate.

Lizzie sighed in aggravation. Aiken had taken to riding his horse again, leaving her and Ida to once again drive the team. Each day they seemed to travel a shorter distance in order to spare the animals for the trip over the mountains.

The days were hot, and the nights were growing cooler. Lizzie sighed again and looked around them. She wrinkled her nose at the odor of decaying animals. It seemed they had been smelling the odor for so long that it had permeated into everything they owned. Buzzards fed on the carcasses, not even bothering to fly away as the wagons passed.

Aiken called a short break in the early afternoon to rest the teams. Abby left the dogs sleeping in the wagon and told Lizzie she was taking the kitten to play in the Johnson wagon. Lizzie absently waved a hand in her direction and began boiling milk for the baby. After an hour, they set off again, not stopping until nightfall.

Ida set to cooking their dinner while Lizzie walked back to the Johnson wagon to fetch Abby.

"Ben, would you bring Abby with you when you come to dinner? It should be ready shortly."

Ben poked his head out of the back of his wagon. "Abby's not here, Lizzie. Sarah was sleeping when she came by and Abby said she was going to walk awhile and catch back up with you."

Lizzie's eyes grew larger as she peered down the trail behind them. "She never came back, Ben." Her voice trembled. "I'd better go find William." She took off running towards the front of the wagon train. Her husband was helping Luke repair a loose wagon wheel when she found him.

"Abby's gone, William. She went to the Johnson wagon when we stopped to rest. Ben said she didn't stay—and now I can't find her."

Aiken wiped his hands on a rag and put his arm around his wife. "Don't fret, Lizzie. We'll find her. Luke, you ready for another hunting trip? I swear these Springer women are something else."

"Right behind you." The two men took off on a couple of horses, leaving Lizzie staring down the trail after them. Zeke came up and stood beside her.

"Where are they going, Lizzie?"

"To find Abby. We left her behind when we stopped to rest."

"Left her behind?" His voice cracked as he raised it. "How could you do something like that?"

"I didn't do it on purpose, Zeke! She said she was going to see Sarah. She took that darn kitten of hers with her." Lizzie wiped away a tear. "I don't need you scolding me, Ezekiel Springer."

They ate supper that evening in silence, waiting for the men to return with Abby. Lizzie looked repeatedly down the trail. She couldn't see because of the dark, but she kept looking anyway. She ate a few bites of the food Ida prepared, and then set her plate aside. She got up and walked away from the fire to where she could see into the night better. She stood there and waited—and prayed.

Several hours later, Aiken and Luke returned with a very dirty Abby. Her head had fallen forward in sleep as she sat in front of Aiken. He carefully handed her down to Luke before walking over to Lizzie.

"She's all right. Another wagon train picked her up."

"Picked her up? William…" She checked her sister over for injuries. She could see the tear tracks left in the dirt on Abby's cheeks.

He handed the reins of the two horses to Zeke. "It seems she wandered off to pick wildflowers. Do you remember seeing that tiny creek close to where we stopped? Anyway, when she found out that Sarah was sleeping, she wandered off. Said she tried yelling to us when we pulled out, but we didn't hear her. Another wagon found her crying on the side of the trail, holding on to that kitten. They figured they would try to catch up to us in a day or two."

Lizzie dipped the corner of her apron in water and washed Abby's face. "Thank God she's all right. I was so worried, William."

"I'm fine," Abby murmured. "I'm just tired." Abby tightened her arms around Luke's neck.

"Don't you ever wander off again, Abigail. Do you understand me?"

"I won't."

"Let me put her in the wagon," Luke told them. "I think she's learned her lesson today."

Lizzie shivered. "It's getting colder, William. How much farther until we reach the mountains?"

"We're climbing into the foothills of some of them now. The bad ones are still several weeks away." He put his arms around her and pulled her close, sharing his body heat. "After those mountains, we'll be almost home."

"Home." She leaned into him. "That sounds wonderful."

"What river is this?" Lizzie asked Aiken the next morning, as he rode beside the wagon. "We've crossed it several times already today."

"It's named the Burnt River, if you want to call it a river. We'll be crossing it a few more times today. It's pretty winding. It's good for the wagon wheels, though. It swells the wood so they fit tighter to the rims. And it's water for the stock. We'll stop early tonight so you women can catch up on your laundry."

"Laundry," Ida said sarcastically. "We'll stop so *we* can do laundry and they can rest is more like it. Seems we measure how far we've gone by when was the last time we got to stop and do laundry."

"I'm glad for any chance to stop," Lizzie answered, "even if it is to do laundry. I'm really beginning to hate this wagon."

"Don't hate it too much. You'll still be living in it until your cabin is built."

"Don't remind me. Now what?" The mules had stopped. The two women jumped down to lead them on, only to see that one of the mules had fallen to its knees. The poor animal continued to drop until it was lying dead. The women looked at each other. "What do we do now?"

Luke came up behind them. "Unhitch the dead one and pull with three."

"What do we do with the dead mule?" Ida wanted to know.

"Leave it."

"In the middle of the road?" Lizzie was shocked.

"Do you expect us to move it?" Luke smiled at her. "It's pretty heavy."

Aiken joined them. "Well now, we're in a tight spot."

"William, can we pull the wagon with only three mules?"

"Sure. You're not loaded down. Only the person driving will be able to ride though. You've got to keep the load light."

Aiken and Luke unhitched the dead mule and rigged the front harness for one mule. The two weakest mules were left in the back. They traveled a few more miles before reaching a small branch off the river and stopped to camp.

Abby was inconsolable when she found out about the dead mule. "He pulled us all this way just to die and be left for the buzzards. It's not right, Lizzie!"

She wrapped her arms around her sister. "I know it's sad, Abby. But really, there wasn't anything we could do. One minute he was alive—the next he dropped dead. He was just worn out, that's all."

"Well, I hope *I* don't drop dead out here. You all will leave me lying on the road, too."

Lizzie laughed. "Don't be silly. Go wash your face and get some rest. William said we'll have to walk more now. You'll need your strength tomorrow."

Abby pulled away. "I'll ride with the Johnsons. They still have all four of their oxen and one more besides." She stalked away, leaving Lizzie smiling in amusement.

Two more days and they were camping beside small pools of water that needed to be strained before they could use it. Lizzie and Ida looked down in disgust at the film and insects floating on top of the pools of water. "That's hardly fit for the beasts," Ida declared, "much less for us."

"It's all there is," Lizzie told her. "We'll strain it through some muslin and then boil it. I'm not using it unless it's been boiled."

Several more days of dust and no water, then more water that was bad. Back and forth the days went. The Johnsons lost one of their oxen to the trail and now had only the four hitched to their wagon. Others in the wagon train were also still losing stock. The trail was wearing on them all. Lizzie carefully set water out each night for the caged chickens and milk cow, sometimes giving them water before taking any for herself.

A day later, the wagon sat at the top of a steep hill. Before them, a mile down, lay the prettiest valley the travelers had seen in a long time. A small band of Indians camped in the valley next to a spring of fresh water. Lizzie looked down the steep rocky hill before them and gripped the reins tighter. Ida had the baby tied across her chest and was walking beside the wagon. With a flick of her wrists, the mules started the descent.

Young Cayuse Indian braves rode their painted ponies around the wagons, whooping and hollering. The travelers were frightened at first until they noticed the smiles on the young Indians' faces. The Indians also had two trading posts set up in the valley and Lizzie looked forward to purchasing more fresh food.

After commanding Abby to stay close to her, and watching Zeke run off with a couple of the younger Indians, Lizzie and Ida headed off to the trading posts, leaving their men to care for the animals.

Lizzie purchased more salmon and was elated to find that the Indians had honey. She walked along the counter of the store, fingering the beaded clothing and blankets.

"Do you want that, Lizzie?" She looked up into her husband's eyes. "It's beautiful." She rubbed her hand across the bleached doeskin of the blanket. An intricate beaded design was punched into the leather.

"It's used to make clothing," he told her.

"I'd hang it on the wall of our cabin. It would be a shame to cut it up."

"Then it's yours." Aiken wrangled with the Indian man for several minutes, finally agreeing to trade some bright colored shirts he had brought along in one of his saddle bags. "I won't have much opportunity to wear these anyway," he told Lizzie.

She smiled at him. "I'll make you more."

Zeke approached their supper fire later that evening, leading a painted pony by a beaded bridle. Lizzie frowned. "Where did you get that?"

"I won it," Zeke stated proudly. "Fair and square."

"Playing poker?"

"Yep." He ran his hand down the horse's muzzle. "Isn't he beautiful?" he asked proudly. "I've got my own pony now. No more walking or mule riding for me."

Aiken spoke up from where he was lying by the fire, his head propped up on his elbow. "I hope you won it fair, Zeke. Do the Indians understand that you'll be taking it with you when you leave?"

"One of them speaks *some* English." Zeke looked around the fire at their faces. "Do you think there'll be a problem?"

Aiken shook his head. "Probably not. These Indians don't look destitute. They do a fine business off the wagon trains passing through here. I doubt you'll be able to train that pony to saddle though."

"Sure I will. I'm going to start training him the first chance I get." Zeke laid his face against the pony's neck. "I'm tired of walking now that our extra mules are dead."

199

"Poor baby," Lizzie said with sarcasm in her voice. "*We* walk every day."

"What next?" Ida said. "Abby traded for a kitten, Zeke gambled for a horse, and Lizzie had Aiken trade for a length of leather for Lizzie to hang on a wall."

Luke laughed softly. "I repaired some things today in exchange for some brightly woven blankets. Quite a few of them in fact. They'll look mighty pretty in our new home. There was a lot of things that needed fixing. I sold Aiken here a couple of blankets, and Ben Johnson bought one to give to the widow. I actually made us some good money today.

"I've been thinking, Ida," he told her, "that once we reach Oregon I may set up a blacksmith shop and maybe even hire myself out for handy work. I'm not too partial to farming anymore. I've had my fill of that. You can have your small garden and I'll support us in other ways."

Ida reached up and cupped his cheek. "I am a lucky woman," she whispered. "We'll be well taken care of. I think your being a blacksmith is a wonderful idea."

Chapter 28

They began their ascent of the Blue Mountains the next morning. Everyone was extremely happy to be leaving behind the dust and sagebrush. Thick pine timber covered the mountains and the children ran alongside the wagons, their laughter echoing through the woods. Lizzie and Ida sat bundled in their coats on the wagon seat, drinking in the splendor of the timber covered mountain.

"Can't say much for the ease of driving over this road," Ida commented, "but the scenery almost makes up for it."

Lizzie nodded in agreement as the wagon jolted across more rocks and holes. "By the time we reach Oregon, every bone in my body will be dislocated."

"Enjoy it, ladies," Aiken stated, riding up alongside them. "A couple more days, and it'll be warm weather and dust again."

Lizzie wrinkled her nose at him. "Go on and spoil our dreaming."
Aiken laughed and spurred his horse ahead.

The next day they woke to frozen water buckets and more bad roads. By nightfall they had begun to despair of finding water for the stock when they came across another band of Cayuse Indians. They led the men down the side of the mountain where they showed them the location of a small stream. The wagons camped among the timber while the men took the stock down to the water. Aiken returned with some potatoes he had bought from the Indians and handed them to Ida to cook with their supper.

"We've got a four mile descent tomorrow, Lizzie. Then we'll be in a valley where feed for the stock will be scarce," Aiken told her over supper. "There's water, but it's few and far between. I sure am glad that no one in this train has an excess of stock. We'd lose a lot of them over the next week or so, and folks are starting to run out of extra stock to lose. Once we're down in the valley, we'll be traveling in the early morning and evening. It'll be too hot during the main part of the day, so we'll rest then."

She sighed and handed him a cup of hot coffee. "This trip does seem never ending, William."

He smiled up at her. "Less than a month, Lizzie. Less than a month and we'll be home." He watched as Ben Johnson walked by. "Looks like the widow Martin will be part of Johnson's family by then. He visits her every evening."

"Yes, he does seem to eat supper at her fire more often than not." She drew a quilt tighter around her shoulders. "Another woman living close by will be welcome, especially with Ida's baby coming. I guess I need to make more of an effort to befriend the widow. She's just so quiet."

"There's time. She'll be welcome for the company when she sets up her own home." He set down his cup. "I'm going to head over and see how Zeke is doing with that Indian pony. He said he was going to try and start its training tonight."

"I'll come with you." She left Alice with Abby and Ida watching over her, and hitching the quilt up over her arms to prevent it from trailing on the ground, followed her husband to the temporary corral the men had set up.

Luke had a blindfold on the pony while Zeke stood next to it, whispering in its ear. The pony's ear twitched at his voice, and it stomped its foot. Luke motioned for Zeke to climb on the pony's back. Then, he quickly whipped off the blindfold. A second later, Zeke was flat on his back in the pine needles.

"Do it again, Zeke," Aiken yelled to him from the sidelines. "Show him that you're his boss. Be consistent. He's got to get used to the weight on his back. Use the saddle." Aiken walked up to them as he barked instructions.

He showed Zeke how to hold the saddle under the horse's nose, letting him get use to its smell. The pony snorted at the unfamiliar smell and drew back. Aiken laid the saddle on the ground under the horse's nose and stepped back, giving it room.

After several minutes, the horse no longer shied away from the strange object and Aiken instructed Zeke to slowly place it on the pony's back. Eventually the horse stood still long enough for the saddle to be cinched and Zeke got prepared to mount the pony again. "Hold tight to the pommel, Zeke. If he can't throw you, he'll eventually give up. A lot of the training is just who can last the longest." Aiken stood back as Luke let go of the reins. Zeke once again found himself looking up into the tree tops from his position on the ground. "Again," Aiken ordered.

"My backside hurts, Aiken," Zeke complained. "This pony doesn't want to be trained. You were right."

"No, I was wrong. He is trainable. Get back on him, Zeke." Aiken helped him up. "Be persistent. Talk to him. Tell him what you're going to do. Get him used to your voice."

"He doesn't understand what I'm saying!"

"You'd be surprised what that horse will understand."

Zeke huffed and went back to the pony. He looked forlornly over to where his sister stood watching. She nodded and smiled her encouragement. Aiken took over the holding of the reins from Luke. He kept his hold of the reins once Zeke was mounted, preventing the pony from rearing up completely. It became a test of wills between them and the pony. When the pony's struggles lessened, Aiken let go of the reins. The pony took off in a gallop around the perimeter of the corral, a white faced Zeke holding on tight.

"Grab the reins, Zeke! You lead him!" Aiken ran alongside them. "Get him used to the bit in his mouth."

It was a tired, but triumphant Zeke that went to sleep that night. His pony was still skittish, but he was able to be ridden. Zeke lay in bed that evening trying to think of the perfect name for his horse.

"It's Spirit," he announced at breakfast the next morning. "My pony's name is Spirit."

Aiken clapped him on the shoulder. "That's a fine name, Zeke. It fits him. That Indian pony will fare the hot weather better than any of the other stock. He's used to it."

Day after day of stopping during the hottest part of the day and traveling in the morning and evening became their routine.

Occasionally, they would find water fit for drinking and washing, and rest the stock the entire day. Then it was move on through more heat and dust.

Aiken's prediction was true. The heat seemed to have little effect on Spirit and as the days went by, the pony began to welcome Zeke's presence, even allowing Zeke to give Abby and Sarah an occasional ride. The rest of the stock plodded along, their heads down, following the ones in front of them.

The clouds opened up on them one day, unleashing a storm that kept the travelers huddled in their wagons for two days while the rain poured from the sky. There was no dry wood for fire and they had to make do with cold provisions. The wind was so strong at times that they could hear their pots and pans come loose from the wagon and go bouncing across the ground.

Aiken braved the rain and wind twice to get milk for the baby and to care for the chickens. Lizzie fretted over the fact that she couldn't boil the milk and prayed that Alice wouldn't get sick from it. Whatever the baby wouldn't drink, she gave to Ida and Abby.

The morning the rains stopped, they emerged into the cold, damp air and began their search for their missing pots and pans. Lizzie and Ida found them wedged between rocks and hung up in bushes.

A couple of hours later, they drove on into a rock hollow that had them in fear of smashing up their wagons. The rock walls were so close that Lizzie could reach out and touch them as she drove by. She was grateful when they passed out of the oppressive shadow of that hollow.

Aiken led them on until they arrived in a small valley not far from the Columbia River. Here, there were several Indians camped and they were able to purchase more salmon for their supper.

The next morning they came to another river with swift running water and rapids. A ferry sat waiting by the bank. Lizzie watched in apprehension as the wagons before her drove onto the ferry and the ferrymen pulled them over by a rope tied to the opposite bank.

The water ran too swiftly for the stock to be swum across and they had to give up more of their precious funds to pay for the stock to be ferried over. One of the ferrymen offered to buy Zeke's pony and argued with the boy when he refused to sell. Lizzie breathed a sigh of relief when they were across and once again on their way.

When they came within sight of Mount Hood, St. Helens, and Jefferson, they camped in a valley near a French trading post. Many Indians also lived around this trading post, and the travelers were bombarded by the noise. Lizzie ordered Abby to tie up the dogs who were continually barking at the Indians milling around their wagon. Ida was startled as one of the Indians peered into the back of the wagon where she sat feeding the baby.

"Shoo!" she ordered him, waving a hand in his direction. "Go on now, git!" The Indian withdrew his head and went to peer into one of the other wagons. Lizzie, whose hair had begun to grow after she had cut it before, found herself trying to avoid the grasping hands of the curious Indians. She made a point to keep Abby close to her side.

They spent a sleepless night as the Indians drank whiskey and kept up a continuous racket through the night firing off pistols, and laughing. Luke, having had enough of the curiosity directed his way because of his dark skin, kept out of sight in the Aikens' wagon as much as possible. It seemed that few of the Indians had seen a man of his size with dark skin before.

Aiken had them move out the next morning before breakfast, leading them up the side of a steep mountain and stopping to camp on the bank of the Deschutes where there was water and feed for the stock. The mountains loomed over them, and they camped for several days to build up their strength and the strength of their animals.

Chapter 29

Lizzie stood at the foot of the Cascade Mountains, holding her tattered britches in one hand and a skirt in the other. Around her shoulders, she had draped a thick quilt against the chill of the morning. She had stopped wearing the britches lately, as they had become so full of holes to be almost indecent, yet she knew that traveling over the mountains in a skirt was going to be hazardous.

Aiken walked up and planted a soft kiss on the back of her neck. "What are you looking at?"

"The mountain. I can't decide whether I should wear these disgusting britches again or just throw them in the fire and be done with them."

"Let me help by telling you what to expect." He wrapped his arms around her waist. "You'll be walking and I'll be driving the wagon over these mountains. They are so steep that the wagons are going to be sliding all over the place, especially with the recent rains. The women and children will be climbing over fallen trees and boulders and tracking through the dense bushes. No one will be allowed in the wagons except the drivers."

She nodded. "The britches it is. I'll spend what time I have today trying to patch them up the best I can."

The wagon train entered the road through the mountains early the next morning during a slight drizzle of rain. The forest crowded in close on both sides of the wagons. Pine trees, fir, cedar, and redwood grew up and over the road, forming a dense canopy that almost shut out the weak light of the sun.

Lizzie stood still and craned her neck to see way up into the top branches. She grew dizzy and focused her attention back to the trail in front of her. If it could be called a trail. She was thankful for the fact that she had opted for the britches for herself and Abby as they climbed over rotting logs, slipping on the wet leaves under their feet.

She grimaced as she slipped and plunged her hand into a rotting log full of grubs and leaves.

The wagons bounced and slammed over holes as they slowly drove past. By the end of the first day, the others in the wagon train were once again going through their belongings, weeding out the things they could do without.

Lizzie now considered it a blessing that they had lost their extra axle. They had little weight and she wasn't concerned about lightening their load. Pots and books, furniture and tools began to join the piles of belongings from previous trains. Lizzie eyed a beautiful mirror with an ornately carved frame. She sighed and walked on past it. The rain continued to fall as they stopped in a small clearing for the night.

Aiken ordered all the stock to be tied up so they couldn't get to the laurel bushes growing abundantly around the clearing. The laurel was poison and would kill them if they ate it. He eyed the sky nervously, praying against a thunderstorm while they were in the mountains. He and Luke walked up and down the train checking the conditions of everyone's wagons. Luke volunteered to check the feet of the pack animals, prying out stones and checking for abrasions. The rain continued.

Lizzie had Abby watched over the baby as she and Ida struggled to prepare a meal in the slow falling rain. Lizzie shivered under the sodden woolen coat she wore. "This fire will never stay lit in this rain," she complained. "What do we have in the way of cold food?"

"Some hard biscuits and jerky," Ida answered. "That's about it. I was hoping to save that for lunch tomorrow."

Lizzie retrieved the cook stove from the back of the wagon and set it next to the fire. "We'll have to use some of our precious oil. The men have to at least have some hot coffee after working in this rain."

"And we'll need something hot in us before walking again in the morning, especially if it's still raining." Ida helped her set up the stove against the wagon, hunching over it to provide some protection against the weather. "I'll do this, Lizzie. Go on and milk the cow."

By bedtime, the rain had ceased, and they crawled gratefully into the back of the wagons, pulling the quilts over them. The cold nights made it necessary for them all to crowd in, sharing their warmth. Modesty had no place on the trail in the mountains.

The next morning, the wagons set out again, this time through thick mud and loose rock. The wagon teams fought their way through the mud to reach the top of the mountain, often sliding back two feet for every one that they gained.

The women and children found it harder going also as they crawled through the mud and climbed over the slippery rocks and fallen trees. The low hanging branches would often dump loads of water on the head and shoulders of anyone who crawled too close.

Most of the wagon train made it over the top before disaster struck. The previous wagons had loosened the rock and mud significantly and the later wagons were having a tougher time of it.

Lizzie looked up, startled, as she heard someone scream, and she clutched Alice tighter to her chest as she saw a wagon, a couple of yards ahead of their own, start sliding back down the steep hill. It started slowly at first and seemed to pick up speed the longer it slid. Luke shouted and took off running for the wagon, leaving Zeke behind with the extra stock. As other men, already to the top of the mountain or down the other side, saw what Luke was doing, they followed suit. There was nowhere to turn the wagons around on the close road and Aiken shouted back for Ben to start backing his team down the mountain as he tried to do the same with theirs.

Luke and another man held tight to the reins of the team leading the sliding wagon, their planted feet leaving deep furrows in the mud as the wagon continued to slide. The driver jumped from the wagon seat and hurried to help the other men try to hold the team. The mules brayed in alarm, their legs sliding out from beneath them.

The women and children watched in horror as the men lost the fight and the wagon pulled from their hands, sliding in the women's direction, dragging the struggling mules with it. Lizzie and the others scrambled to get out of the way as the wagon crashed into the trees close to them. She looked down the mountain to see that Aiken and Ben had just about reached the bottom.

The mules continued to struggle, trying to get their feet planted firmly beneath them but their struggles only succeeded in pulling the wagon free of the trees and allowing it to continue its muddy descent down the mountain.

Luke ran forward, knife in his hand, and fought to cut the mules free. One of the other men took up a knife of his own and went to help him. They sawed furiously through the reins, often losing their own footing in the thick slippery mud. They gave up after freeing the third mule and Luke yelled out a heads up as the wagon, and the fourth mule, careened down the mountain side. Aiken and Ben tugged fiercely on their own teams, pulling them out of the path of the runaway wagon.

Lizzie cringed as the wagon and mule struck the side of the rock face, bouncing and sliding over the trail into a small canyon below. Abby covered her ears against the screams of the dying mule. The rest of the wagon train stood and watched as the wagon slid down until it finally came to rest at the bottom. The wagon crashed against the rocks, coming free of the injured mule. The mule struggled to get to its feet, before falling in a heap against the shattered wagon.

The family who owned the wagon stood in shock, seeing their belongings scattered down the side of the mountain. The woman hid her face in her husband's shirt, moaning over the loss of their possessions.

"We'll climb down and help you salvage what we can," Aiken told them quietly. "Let's get the other wagons safely down and camp set up. Then Luke and I will help. Let's be thankful that no human lives were lost."

The owner of the wagon walked over to shake Luke's hand. "We would have lost a lot more if not for your quick thinking," he told him. "We're grateful to you." Luke nodded as the man took his family down the mountain to the designated campsite.

Lizzie looked up at her husband. "I was so afraid that wagon was going to hit you," she told him, tears welling up in her eyes.

He drew her close. "I thought for a minute it was," he admitted. "God has definitely been watching over us on this trip."

It was late by the time their husbands returned from salvaging what they could. Lizzie and Ida kept their coffee and supper hot over the fire. The women looked up as the two weary men returned to the wagon.

"Were you able to save much?" Lizzie asked.

"Most of their personal belongings," her husband answered. "Nothing of the wagon could be saved. Nothing at all. It was only good for firewood, and we had to kill the mule to put it out of its misery. Two of its legs were broken and it was pretty scraped up." He sipped the hot coffee gratefully.

"How will they make it from here? With no wagon—"

"They'll pack what they can on their remaining mules and on their backs. Some of the others have a little extra room in their wagons. They'll make it. We're almost there. These mountains are the last of the bad traveling. We'll be out of them in another day or two, depending on the weather. We'll stay here through tomorrow and let the road dry up some more. The bad thing is there's no food for the stock here."

"There's no water either that's not standing in mud holes," Luke added. "We'd best be good and sure the roads are sturdy when we set out because if these beasts smell even a hint of water, they're going to take off. A stampede might be worse than the sliding."

Aiken nodded. "There's water a day away from here. Tomorrow, you and Zeke, and anyone else that is free, go ahead and follow this road down. Take the extra stock to the water. We'll catch up with you there when the road is safe to travel."

Chapter 30

Two days later the train caught up with those driving the extra stock and stopped to camp beside a spring branch with plenty of swamp grass for the animals to feed on. The women took advantage of the rest to wash the mud out of their clothes. Lizzie fingered the fabric of her britches. "I'm burning these when we settle," she stated emphatically. "They're getting positively indecent."

Ida laughed and patted her stomach. "If this belly doesn't stop growing, I'll have nothing to wear. I've let out my skirts as far as they'll go."

Lizzie dropped her laundry next to the spring and laughed. "You'll be wearing Luke's shirt and britches before too long." She stooped and leaned back on her haunches, looking around her. The spring opened up a path through the dense trees, allowing the sun to filter through. She closed her eyes and let the sun warm her upturned face. "It really is beautiful country up here," she told Ida.

"Yes, it is." Ida sat down and leaned against a tree. "I'm grateful that Luke has decided to homestead some of William's land. You're one of the best friends I could ever have, Lizzie. I'm glad we're going to be close."

Lizzie reached over and took her hand. "Me too, Ida. Me too."

Zeke ran up to them, crashing through the underbrush. "Aiken says we're going to be crossing over the Devil's Backbone tomorrow, Lizzie. A group of three steep, small mountains, and the day after that we'll be home. Home, Lizzie! In two days!"

The two women gripped each other's hand tighter. "Praise God," Lizzie exclaimed, slumping back. "There is an end to this." She looked around her again. "But, I think I'll miss it, too. We've seen so many different scenes and experienced such an adventure. Yes, I think I may miss it."

"There's a lot more adventure just waiting for you," Ida told her. "If you've never built a home from the ground up before, you're in for one heck of an adventure. There's a garden to plant and food to hunt, skin, and smoke. The nearest town will probably be days away. You being a city girl and all…yes, I'd say you've got one heck of an adventure waiting for you."

Sure enough, before noon the next day they proceeded up the first mountain of the Devil's Backbone. Lizzie and the others wore their face rags against the stench of more dead cattle, oxen, and mules. Lizzie felt sad for the animals who had died so close to the end.

She moved the sling around and tied Alice to her back since she was growing and able to hold up her head now. This gave Lizzie the freedom of her hands as she fought her way through the thick underbrush. She was surprised to see that the group of walkers had beaten the wagons to the top of the mountain. She looked down the road towards the wagons.

One of the wagons had lost a wheel as it jolted over the rough road. It had stopped halfway up, and the men were struggling to hold it while Luke repaired the wheel the best he could. The road was so full of loose rocks and holes that Lizzie wondered that anyone had dared to call it a road in the first place.

The sun barely broke through the overhanging branches in a few areas, and she shivered against the cold of the day. Ida joined her as she watched the working men.

"Guess this will put off our arriving for a day," she said sadly.

Lizzie nodded. "We've been lucky, Ida," she said thoughtfully. "We've not lost a single member of our family. Actually, we've grown by two. Our food has lasted, with some left to help us through the winter. We've still got three mules," and she added with a smile, "and gained Zeke's painted pony. We've made friends that will last us a lifetime." She looked over to where Ben stood next to the widow. "And others have found new family." She thought of the baby on her back. "I even had my first child."

Ida laughed. "The easy way."

Lizzie thought for a moment. "I don't think it was the easy way.

I wish Alice was alive to see the end of the trail. She was so reluctant to go in the first place."

They watched with relief as Luke attached the repaired wheel and the wagons began to head forward again, the teams struggling to pull against the mountain. Lizzie looked around to locate her younger sister, and locating her, turned to head down and up the next mountain.

Halfway through the Devil's Backbone they pitched camp and headed out early again the following morning. They halted for a short time at a small farm, and Aiken called out a welcome as they pulled up.

A short wiry man emerged from the tiny log cabin, a smile splitting his bearded face. "William Aiken!" he greeted. He held out his hand as Aiken jumped down. "Been wondering when you were going to return home."

"I got myself a wife and family, too, while I was gone." Aiken motioned them forward. "This is my wife, Lizzie, her sister, Abby, and brother, Zeke. This is our adopted daughter, Alice, and our very good friends, Luke and Ida." The man smiled at each as they were introduced.

"All these wagons homesteading around you?"

"A couple of them. How's the farm, Rupert?"

"Doing good, Aiken. I got in that field of turnips and potatoes planted for you, and that upper meadow of yours is waist high with feed. I didn't have much time to start cutting timber for a cabin like you asked. All you'll have is that little shack, at first. I had to get in my own crops."

Aiken slapped him good naturedly on the shoulder. "That's fine, Rupert. I've lots of help with me. I appreciate what you were able to get done. I thought we were going to have to do without the garden this winter."

Lizzie looked up questioningly at her husband as they walked back to the wagon. "William, why would that man plant crops for you? Who is he?"

"Well, that's my uncle, Rupert, Lizzie. He...works for me. He came up with me on my first trip from the east. He's the only family I've still got, alive anyway. I wanted to surprise you." He turned to her. "We're just about at the beginning of our land, Elizabeth. I've a fairly good spread at the bottom of these mountains, in the prettiest valley you'll ever lay eyes on. I've got a small herd of cattle started, and someday I want to purchase horses to breed and sell. You married a soon to be well-to-do man, Elizabeth Aiken. You'll want for nothing as long as I'm alive."

Lizzie was overjoyed that God was providing enough food for them through the winter. With the animals and dried salmon they still had left, along with the produce from their garden, they would be all right. She smiled to herself and cast a prayer of thanksgiving heavenward.

Around supper time, Aiken called a short halt to the wagons and taking Lizzie by the hand, led her through some trees to the edge of a bluff. Spread out before them was the greenest valley Lizzie had ever seen. Wildflowers dotted the landscape and a clear stream of water meandered its way through the meadow. Tall cedars and pine grew alongside the stream and grew thick around the edges of the meadow. She looked up into the sky as a hawk flew past their heads.

A tear coursed its way down her cheek as she turned to her husband. "This is the most beautiful place I've ever seen."

He wiped away her tear and took her small hand in his. "Only the best for you, Lizzie. We've the beginnings of a grand life down there." He pointed. "Down there, a little ways back from the creek, is where I want to put our cabin. You can see where the garden has begun, and way over there is the fields planted with feed. We've got chickens and a milk cow," he chuckled. "That female mule of yours is with foal. It's a rare thing for a mule to get pregnant, Lizzie. Did you know that? Maybe I should turn to mule raising, instead of horses."

She squeezed his hand. "Or people raising."

He glanced quickly at her. "Lizzie?"

A slow smile crept across her face. "We'll be adding another one to our family, come the early spring." She laughed out loud as he swung her up in his arms.

He set her back on her feet, and head thrown back, arms held wide, yelled out, "Thank you, God!" His voice boomed out over the meadow. Lizzie watched as a doe and her fawn were startled and bounded away. Aiken turned back to Lizzie and drew her slowly toward him, lowering his face to kiss her.

Printed in the United States
26700LVS00003B/209

9 781413 747751